Also by Mary McBride

My Hero

Still Mr. & Mrs.

MS. SIMON SAYS

SAYS

~

MARY McBRIDE

WARNER

FOREVER

NEW YORK   BOSTON

Copyright © 2004 by Mary Vogt Myers
Excerpt from *Say It Again Sam* © 2004 by Mary Vogt Myers

Cover design by Diane Luger
Cover illustration by Mike Racz
Book design by Giorgetta Bell McRee

WARNER BOOKS

Time Warner Book Group
1271 Avenue of the Americas
New York, NY 10020
Visit our Web site at www.twbookmark.com

Printed in the United States of America

First Paperback Printing: March 2004

10 9 8 7 6 5 4 3 2 1

For Kasey Michaels and Leslie LaFoy

"Wit is the only wall
Between us and the dark."

—Mark Van Doren

MS. SIMON
SAYS

CHAPTER ONE

⁓

The first letter bomb exploded in the mailroom of the Hartford *Courier* at 8:06 A.M. The second bomb blew up at the Buffalo *Daily Express* at 8:18 A.M. By the time the third one went off ten minutes later at the Allentown *Scribe*, CNN was reporting a terrifying trend.

In Chicago, in her bedroom, a barely awake Shelby Simon grabbed the remote and turned up the volume of her TV several notches.

"*. . . no reports of injuries as yet, Diane, but authorities here in Hartford are confirming that at least one person was taken to a local hospital. At this point, what we do know is that all three newspapers are part of the Helm-Harris Syndicate, whose flagship paper is the Chicago* Daily Mirror."

"Uh-oh." At the mention of her employer, Shelby clicked the volume up again and continued to stare at the screen.

The camera came back to the anchor desk, where the perfectly coiffed and glossy-mouthed Diane Delgado said, "We're receiving a report that there's been another incident . . ." She paused, frowning as she concentrated on a piece of paper just handed to her from offscreen. "Apparently there's been a fourth letter bomb incident in the offices of the Columbus *Citizen*, another paper in the Helm-Harris Syndicate, if I'm not mistaken." The attractive blonde blinked into the camera and managed a thin imitation of a smile. "We'll be back with more details right after this break."

Shelby turned the volume down, reached for the phone beside her bed, and punched in the number of the Chicago *Daily Mirror*. What was she doing, anyway, watching breaking news on television, when she could get it faster and firsthand from the wires at her very own office?

"Come on. Somebody answer," she muttered after the fourth ring, just before the automatic system kicked in.

"You have reached the offices of the Chicago Daily Mirror. *We are unable to take your call right now . . ."*

While she listened to the smooth and efficient voice on the tape, Shelby glanced at the time on the TV screen. It was after eight. The auto answer at the paper should've been deactivated by now. They only used the system after regular business hours. By this time of the morning, at least half the staff would already be at work. She'd be there herself right now if the battery in her alarm clock hadn't croaked sometime during the previous night.

"Please leave a message after the tone."

"Shit."

It was the only message Shelby could think of just then.

She showered and dressed in record time, choosing slacks over one of her usual tailored suits, donning sneakers rather than heels in order to get downtown fast. In the background, CNN was reporting on a fifth incident—or was it a sixth?—and lining up their terrorism experts just in case.

"Have there been any threats against the Helm-Harris papers?" the blond anchor asked her correspondent in the field.

"Not that I'm aware of, Diane. If you'll recall, there was a walkout by the printers union last year, but that concluded in successful negotiations. Their contract won't be up for another three years. We're waiting right now for a briefing from postal inspectors here in Hartford."

"Thank you, Eric. We'll keep an eye on the monitor and get back to you as soon as that briefing begins. Now let's go to Susan Carey in Buffalo. Susan?"

Shelby clicked off the TV, grabbed her handbag, and hustled toward the front door of her apartment. The instant she closed the door behind her, though, she knew she'd made a terrible mistake because her neighbor's door immediately opened and Mo Pachinski, part-time mobster and full-time sexist pig, stepped into the hallway, blocking Shelby's passage.

What did the guy do? Wait with his hand on the knob and his eye on the peephole every morning? He'd been driving her nuts for months, ever since he moved in, accosting her in the hall this way, until she'd learned to outfox him by closing her door soundlessly and ducking past Apartment 12C. But this morning she'd been off her game, befuddled by oversleeping and then distracted by the news.

"Hiya, Doll."

Mo was wearing a gorilla-sized electric blue warm-up suit, its velour jacket unzipped a few calculated inches in order to display the gold chains nestled in the dark forest of his chest hair. As always, Old Spice radiated from his muscle-bound body like a toxic cloud, fairly knocking Shelby off her feet.

"Runnin' a little late this morning, huh, Doll?"

"As a matter of fact, I am."

She tried to sound rushed rather than impatient, polite rather than pissed, not wanting to offend him because she suspected, if he wasn't exactly *in* the Mob, he was at least connected to it. She'd asked him once what he did for a living, and his answer was a rather vague and smirky *I consult.*

Mobbed up or not, Mo had problems with the women in his life. There seemed to be a *lot* of women in his life, so the man had a *lot* of problems. And because Shelby was an advice columnist, Mo was constantly asking her for just that—advice. Should he send roses? Was four dozen too much? Or not enough? Red ones or pink? What about diamonds? What about your lesser jewels? What did Shelby think?

In the beginning, Shelby considered him a challenge. Now he was just a pest, especially this morning when the newspapers in which her column appeared seemed to be exploding all across the country.

"Could we talk later, Mo?"

"Yeah. Yeah, sure. Okay." He shrugged and stepped

aside just enough to let her pass through his aura of aftershave. "Later's okay," he grumbled. "When exactly?"

"Oh . . ." Shelby called over her shoulder as she sprinted for the elevator. "Just later."

"Like tonight?"

"Well . . ." She smiled sweetly, hit the DOWN button, and said, "We'll see," as the elevator doors slid closed.

Shelby jumped on the bus headed south on State Street, and wasn't at all surprised when the driver, a man she'd never seen before in her life, greeted her.

"Hey, Ms. Simon. How's it goin'?"

After all, how surprising was it that he recognized her when her face was plastered on both sides of his vehicle on five-foot-long banners that proclaimed "Ms. Simon Says . . . Read the *Daily Mirror*!"

Her picture had been running alongside her column for years, so she wasn't exactly unknown, but this latest ad campaign had suddenly vaulted Ms. Shelby Simon from minor, ho-hum celebrity to a kind of local stardom. People used to stop her in the street with "Oh, you look so familiar." Now it was "Hey, Ms. Simon. How's it goin'?" and "Yo, Shelby." She still wasn't sure exactly how she felt about the notoriety. What had been a real kick at first was now beginning to cloy, and even to annoy.

She hadn't become an advice columnist in order to be famous. In fact, she hadn't wanted to be one at all. It had never occurred to her. Well, whoever grew up wanting to be an advice columnist, for heaven's sake? Kids dreamed of being astronauts, great athletes, rock stars, and Pulitzer

Prize–winning investigative journalists. Which was what Shelby had every intention of being after she graduated from the journalism school at Northwestern.

Unfortunately, the day she interviewed at the *Daily Mirror* just happened to be the same day that the venerable and much beloved and hugely syndicated Dear Gabby passed away. Hal Stabler was the managing editor at the time, and he'd already asked better than half his staff who'd like to take over the paper's advice column, and had been met with everything from grim silence to polite demurrals to outright guffaws. The poor man had been desperate.

"Want to give it a whirl?" he'd asked his interviewee.

"Sure. Why not?" Shelby had replied.

The rest, as they say, was history. And now, twelve years later, that history included a certain high visibility she wasn't entirely comfortable with.

Still, she had a lot more to worry about this morning than her dubious fame. What in the world was going on with these letter bombs at the Helm-Harris papers? Was it the unions or some disgruntled ex-employee? Or could it really be some sort of terrorist attack as they had speculated on TV? How many people had been injured? Oh, God.

She jumped off the bus at Wacker Drive, then trotted the two blocks to the *Daily Mirror*, her anxiety increasing with every step, not to mention her blood pressure, as she saw the fire trucks and ambulances and squad cars in front of the building, and—God Almighty!—a big black box of a truck prominently labeled "Bomb Squad Disposal Unit."

A little moan of relief broke from her lips when she

spotted Derek McKay sitting on one of the huge cement flowerpots that decorated the courtyard of the *Daily Mirror*. Since it was October, the pots were brimming with chrysanthemums in shades of yellow and bronze, and the darker hues were a perfect complement to Derek's bushy auburn mustache and chronically tousled hair.

"Welcome to pandemonium," he said as she approached. "You're late this morning."

"I overslept." Shelby perched beside him. "What's going on?"

If anybody knew, it would be Derek, ace investigative reporter, winner of numerous awards, not the least of which was a Pulitzer. He and Shelby had had a pretty torrid affair right after she started working at the paper. It was, she later learned, sort of an initiation rite. Derek had affairs with all the bright young things who crossed the *Daily Mirror*'s threshold. Amazingly, they all forgave him. At least Shelby had.

Before he could answer her, she pointed to the tall paper cup in his hand. "I'd kill for a sip of coffee," she said.

"Be my guest."

He handed her the warm cup and Shelby took a gulp of the frothy brew, then promptly choked.

"Jesus, Derek," she sputtered. "What's in that?"

He grinned and pulled a tiny silver flask from the pocket of his corduroy jacket. "Greetings from Jamaica, mon."

"Rum? At this hour of the morning?"

"Hell, Shelby. It's almost nine."

She shook her head, handing the cup back to him.

"Thanks anyway. So tell me what's going on. Another letter bomb?"

"Probably. They're searching the building now."

"This is horrible." A little shiver coursed down her spine. "Any idea who might be behind it?"

Derek shook his head. "Nope. But they've got a pretty good idea who the target is."

"Oh, yeah? Who?"

He looked at her then with such warmth that for a split second Shelby felt a twinge of longing for their ancient affair. She reminded herself that it had happened scores of lovers ago. His. Not hers. "So who's the target?" she asked again.

"You," he said. "Every letter bomb was addressed to you."

Half an hour later—after the bomb sniffing dogs had successfully located the lethal letter and the bomb techs had sealed it in a metal canister and driven it away—and after the police and the postal inspectors had asked her a few preliminary questions—Shelby answered the summons to her boss's office, which was a glass-walled cubicle in the center of the Metro floor, usually referred to as the Sweat Box.

Her entire staff was already assembled there. And her entire staff—all three of them—were looking distinctly distraught.

Sandy Hovis, her loyal secretary and personal spell checker since day one of the column, was there. The only word that Sandy couldn't spell was diarrhea, which didn't matter all that much since Ms. Simon rarely said it. Sandy was sitting on the edge of a chair directly across from the managing editor's desk. She had obviously been crying and was clutching a wad of Kleenex as big as a softball and getting tissue lint all over her black wool skirt. Poor thing.

Still single as she approached the big Five O, Sandy was the sole support of an older brother with cerebral palsy. From the beginning, Shelby had made sure, with each new contract she'd signed, that her secretary received a handsome raise in the bargain.

In spite of her robust coloring, her plus size figure, and her ability to spell every word in the English language but one, Sandy had always been a bit fragile emotionally, always teetering on the brink of tears, but the past few years, as things had grown more and more unsettled in the world, the woman had become a certifiable nervous wreck. Shelby had been hounding her lately about signing up for a yoga class that apparently worked miracles with its students. Now didn't seem like a good time to hound her further, so she merely placed a reassuring hand on her secretary's shoulder.

"It's awful," Sandy said with a wet sniff and a linty flourish of her tissues. "Just awful. I'm so upset."

"It'll be okay," Shelby murmured. Well, it would, wouldn't it?

She gazed across the office, offering what she hoped was a buoyant smile to the other members of her staff.

Jeff Kerr, a thirty-something neo-beatnik and researcher par excellence, sat glumly on a leather couch, chewing on a cuticle, while next to him, Kellie Carter, the pretty young intern from Northwestern, sat staring straight ahead as she twisted the hell out of a long red skein of hair. The two of them reminded Shelby of Gilligan and Ginger under extreme duress.

She was just about to offer a word of encouragement to the troops when Hal Stabler blasted through the door and announced, "We're shutting down your column, Shelby. As of right now."

"You can't do that," she gasped. Could he?

"It's already done," Hal growled, angling his too-many-donuts-and-Danishes backside into the leather swivel chair behind his desk.

"But . . ."

He held up a hand in warning. "This is not negotiable, Shelby. I mean it. I've just been upstairs with Brian and Bob. This is their decision."

Brian and Bob, though the names may have sounded like a folksinging duo from the sixties, were actually Brian Helm and Bob Harris. The Helm and The Harris of the Syndicate. The Wunderkind of Newspaper Publishing. The Powers that be. Alpha and Omega. And in this case, apparently, the final word.

Canceled.

Oh, God.

Suddenly her knees felt a little wobbly so she sagged into the chair next to Sandy's. "This is horrible."

"You got that right," Hal said. He was a man who always looked harried and hassled, as if he bore the burdens of the entire planet on his beefy shoulders, but right now he looked particularly oppressed. Leaning back in his chair to a chorus of leather and metallic creaks, he said, "Frankly, it sucks. Still, it could suck worse. Brian and Bob think it *will* be worse if we keep running your column. So it's canceled. Temporarily, at least. Now, here's the deal . . ."

He went on to describe what amounted to a fairly generous offer of continued employment for her staff. "They can use you down in the Lifestyle department, Sandy. Talk to Jean Prewett. She'll get you settled in."

"Thank you, Mr. Stabler." Sandy's tears of anxiety turned to those of gratitude. "God bless you."

"Yeah. Yeah. You can stop crying now, all right? Jesus." Hal glowered and swiveled his chair toward the couch. "Jeff, *Weekend* magazine is planning some special editions and they can use an extra researcher. You'll want to check in with Joe Detweiler as soon as possible."

"Cool."

Now that Gilligan was all smiles, Hal directed his gaze at the winsome Ginger. More likely than not, he'd be sending her back to Northwestern on the very next train. "You'll be assigned to Derek McKay for the remainder of your internship, Kellie," he said. "Or until such time as the column resumes."

Kellie's reply was a rather breathless "Oh, thank you, Uncle Hal."

Shelby tried not to look too surprised or to blink uncontrollably. Uncle Hal? *Uncle* Hal? She'd had no idea that Kellie Carter was the managing editor's niece. Actually, she had no idea how the young woman had been selected for an internship. Like all the sweet young things who'd preceded her, they just showed up, semester after semester, year after year. Most of them considered the internship a way to goof off for a semester. Kellie, however, was enthusiastic, energetic, eager to please. The girl arrived early and stayed late. More often than not, she knew what Shelby wanted or needed—coffee, tuna on rye, a particular phone number—even before she knew it herself. Shelby had never had such a wonderful temporary assistant, and had even been considering Kellie for a full-time job after her graduation next year.

She glanced at Sandy to see if she, too, was surprised by the news. If she was, the surprise was diluted by her tears. Then Shelby reminded herself that she'd just been the recipient of six, seven, maybe eight or more letter bombs, so what difference did it make whether nepotism was running rampant at the *Daily Mirror* or not. Who cared?

Hal went on to suggest, in his inimitable way, that everyone calm the fuck down and go about their new assignments now. While Sandy and Jeff and Kellie all stood and prepared to leave, Shelby stood up, too, until Hal said rather grimly, "Shelby, sit the fuck down."

"Oh." She sat back down.

"Don't worry," Sandy whispered to her. "It'll all be fine."

"Take it easy, Shel," Jeff said.

"I'm so sorry, Shelby," Kellie said with tears in her eyes and a warm hand on Shelby's shoulder as she passed behind her chair. "This is awful. Poor you."

And that was exactly how she felt just then. Poor Shelby. Poor old canceled Shelby. Ms. Simon says *That's all for now, folks.*

She watched her colleagues through the glass wall of Hal's office as they drifted away in three different directions. Sandy went toward the elevator. Jeff disappeared into the stairwell. Kellie sauntered across the floor and perched on the corner of Derek McKay's desk. Derek glanced up at the young redhead with a wolfish grin, as if he'd been expecting her.

Well, what do you know! Kellie was quite obviously and quite happily the latest initiate in the Fresh Young Thing Club. How had Shelby missed that, she wondered. She usually didn't miss much. Maybe, considering the nepotism, Derek was being more discreet than usual. He better watch his lecherous step, too. She would absolutely kill him if he did anything to ruin the best internship in the history of the *Daily Mirror*.

Did Uncle Hal know? Shelby shifted her gaze to her boss, who was just then barking a few of his favorite four-letter words into the phone.

He covered the mouthpiece with his hand. "I'll be right with you," he told her. "Sit tight."

Shelby sat tight. What choice did she have? Outside Hal's office, at the various Metro desks, people were already writing articles about the events of the morning. Until now, she really hadn't had time to think about those events. And even now she didn't want to contemplate the letter bombs that had suddenly blown up her column, her career, and quite possibly her whole life.

Who hated her that much? Who wanted her maimed or dead? How could this be happening? The postal inspectors had asked her if she'd received any threats, and Shelby had told them in all honesty that there hadn't been any. Oh, there had been the usual snotty letters and E-mails from people who disagreed with her advice, along with the usual off-the-wall rants that had nothing to do with anything Ms. Simon had ever said.

Once there was an unpleasant incident when Shelby had gotten a pie in her face from a woman whose boyfriend had moved out based on Ms. Simon's advice. But, by and large, there had never been anything that threatened more than a fierce determination to never read her column again. At least, not to her knowledge.

Of course, it wasn't like the old days when she'd personally read every piece of mail that came in. The success of Ms. Simon Says and its syndication in scores of papers meant a huge increase in the volume of her mail, and Shelby couldn't read everything anymore. Between her speaking engagements and her media appearances, there just wasn't time. Sandy and whatever intern was on staff did the initial reading these days, and then passed the most interesting correspondence along to Shelby for a reply. The letters she didn't see were answered with a form letter and whatever helpful printed matter that pertained to the particular writer's problem.

She still felt guilty about that. It was better in the old days when she read everything and answered everything. But such was the price of success.

Some success, she thought bleakly. Unless she could talk Hal or Brian and Bob out of their decision, she was temporarily out of a job. On the bright side, maybe they'd give her a desk out in Metro, where she could put her old journalism skills to good use. That was what she'd dreamed of, after all, a dozen years ago when she'd been a fresh young thing herself.

While she perused the activity outside Hal's office, Shelby saw a man leaning against Hal's secretary's desk. Her gaze strayed past him, and then jerked back to scrutinize him more closely.

He wore dirty blue-and-white Reeboks, jeans that were ripped at both knees, and a plaid flannel shirt that looked just this side of the rag bag. Over the faded shirt was a dark blue down vest, patched here and there with . . . Was that duct tape? Good God.

The guy's shaggy brown hair was long enough to curl over the collar of his shirt, and when he reached up to rake his fingers through his hair, Shelby could see that his forehead was deeply furrowed, as if a permanent headache were etched across his brow. It suddenly occurred to her that he was actually good-looking in an unkempt and dangerous sort of way.

That was when she noticed that his mouth turned down in an expression somewhere between disgust and anger, probably not so different from the way her letter bomber might look.

Did Security know this guy was up here? Who the hell was he? Just as Shelby began to feel panic begin to claw at the back of her throat, the guy looked directly into Hal's office, right at her. As if he knew just who she was. As if . . .

"Shelby, did you hear what I just said?"

"What?"

She turned to find Hal glaring at her across his desk, obviously finished with his phone call.

"I'm talking to you," he bellowed. "Now will you please pay attention and listen the fuck up."

Shelby blinked, trying her best to concentrate on his words at the same time that she tried to keep an eye on the probable felon just outside Hal's glass door.

"Brian and Bob have talked to the police, and they're advising that certain precautions ought to be taken," Hal said.

"Precautions?" Shelby echoed.

"To keep you safe," he said. "Just in case this letter bomber tries anything else."

She swallowed hard. Her palms were sweating now. It wasn't so easy to breathe. "Anything else?"

"They want to relocate you."

"Relocate?" She was starting to sound like a damn parrot, she thought, but her mind didn't seem to be generating anything but fear at the moment.

"Just in case this guy knows where you live, Shelby. Brian and Bob want to get you out of town ASAP. So they've . . ."

"Out of town?" Polly want a cracker?

". . . used their contacts at the Chicago PD, who're supposed to be sending somebody to make sure that you get away okay. Safely. You know."

No, she didn't know. Not much of anything just then. Except that she didn't want to leave town. Except that the angry looking guy was still there, lurking no more than fifteen or twenty feet from her.

"Let me check on that with Doris," Hal said, picking up his phone again and punching in his secretary's extension.

On the other side of the glass, Doris picked up her own phone and nodded as she said something into the receiver. The woman seemed completely oblivious to the criminal loitering around her desk. Or maybe she was wisely ignoring him, maintaining the appearance of calm while she waited for Security.

"That was quick," Hal said on his end of the phone. "What's his name? Okay. Well, great. Thanks, Doris. Yeah, go ahead and send him in."

Send who in? Shelby wondered. Then she watched in

horror as the felon, the perp, the possible letter bomber and probable serial killer in the duct-taped vest levered off the edge of Doris's desk and walked the short distance to Hal's glass door.

And then opened it!

Hal immediately rose from his chair, hopefully to defend her, to throw his bulk between Shelby and certain death, but instead he said quite cheerfully, "Come on in. Glad to see you."

Shelby decided it was a conspiracy. Her life—all thirty-four glorious and too few years of it—flashed before her eyes, then came to an abrupt halt when Hal announced, "Ms. Shelby Simon, meet Lieutenant Mick Callahan."

CHAPTER TWO

~

Mick Callahan wished he were anywhere in the world but where he was at the moment. Anywhere. Stretched out in the middle of the Dan Ryan Expressway. Parachuting into Afghanistan. At the North Pole in his BVDs. Hell.

Still, it probably wasn't much worse being here at the *Daily Mirror* than half an hour ago when he'd walked into his captain's office, after being summoned on his pager.

Captain Rita Bruzzi hadn't even said "Good morning." She'd looked up from the open file on her desk and said, "How are those anger management classes going, Lieutenant?"

There wasn't much sense lying since she was looking at his damned personnel jacket. "I'm having a hard time fitting them into my schedule," he said.

"Right." She sighed deep within her ample, Wagnerian chest and closed the file, then clasped her hands on top of it almost as if she were praying. "Headquarters has a special assignment for you. Starting today."

"Yeah, but I . . ."

Those prayerful hands flew up in a gesture demanding silence. "Maybe you didn't hear me, Callahan. I said *Headquarters* has a special assignment for you. Now sit your rogue ass down in that chair"—she stabbed a finger across her desktop—"and keep your legendary anger managed and your mouth shut while I tell you what you're going to do. *Capisce?*"

Rogue ass? He almost laughed. Then he was tempted to say, "Rita, you're beautiful when you're mad," because she truly was, but the captain was wearing her service revolver, so Mick kept his mouth shut and lowered himself into the designated chair.

She briefed him on the letter bombs, the tight relationship—as in I'll scratch your back if you'll scratch mine—between city government and the Helm-Harris Syndicate, and the reason why he was going to comply with this order. Namely because he'd find himself behind a desk for the next six months if he didn't.

"I've got a lot going down on the street right now," he said.

"It'll all still be here when you get back."

Hell. How could he argue with that?

But that didn't mean he had to be happy about baby-sitting some idiot columnist who'd obviously offended some whack job. And now that he noticed, the idiot columnist didn't look all that happy about it either.

Ms. Simon was even better-looking than her picture. Of course, most of the ones he saw on buses in the Eleventh District had a blacked-out front tooth or a mustache, and instead of saying "Read the *Daily Mirror*" Ms. Simon usually said "Fuck you."

Not unlike her expression at the moment.

Stabler, on the other hand, seemed delighted to see him, no doubt because Ms. Shelby Simon would soon be Mick's problem instead of his.

"Well," the newspaperman said, "what happens now?"

"The sooner we leave the building, the better," Mick answered. He turned to his assignee. "Anything you need to get before we go? You probably won't be back here for a while."

He reached out to take her arm, but she pulled away and turned to her boss, hissing. "Isn't this just a little excessive, Hal, for heaven's sake?"

"I don't think you appreciate the kind of danger you're in, Shelby," he said. "And what's more, I don't think I should have to point out the risk you pose to your colleagues by your very presence. Isn't that right, Lieutenant?"

"That's right." Mick reached out for her arm again, this time grasping it with more authority than before. "Let's go, Ms. Simon."

Five minutes later, in her corner office on the eighth floor, Shelby opened the center drawer of her desk, glared at the contents, then slammed it closed. She repeated the process with the three drawers on the left and the three on the right.

Her office was a mess after the bomb people and their dogs had searched it. Several file drawers gaped open. The trash basket had been overturned, and the usual foot-high stack of incoming mail on her credenza was nowhere in sight.

"If there's nothing here you need, let's get going," the formerly nefarious guy said. He was leaning in her doorway, no doubt anticipating an escape attempt on her part.

She'd whisked past him through Hal's glass door, then ignored him in the elevator and pretended he didn't exist as he followed her along the corridor that led to her office. And she ignored him now, which probably wasn't fair since this mess wasn't his fault, but she needed a target for her anger, dammit, and Lieutenant Mick Callahan just happened to be the nearest one.

It wasn't anger so much as fear that she felt, Shelby acknowledged. But on second thought, she wasn't really afraid. There just hadn't been time to comprehend the situation or to consider these letter bombs as a personal threat. They still felt more like breaking news, something happening someplace else—in Buffalo and Hartford—happening to someone else, certainly not to her. And the only really scary person she'd seen all morning had turned out to be her very own bodyguard, compliments of the Chicago PD.

She felt off balance, at odds with reality. Maybe her column had been canceled for her own good, but Shelby felt as if she'd been fired. Out of sheer frustration, she slammed her desk drawer again. Harder.

"Hey, I don't like this any more than you do, lady. Okay?" the lieutenant said from the doorway. "Just get whatever you need and let's go."

"I don't know what I need. I can't think," she replied, sounding childish now and almost as helpless as she felt.

"Handbag?" he suggested. "Laptop?" He shoved off

the door frame and sauntered toward her desk. "Date-book?"

She stared at him a second. Son of a gun. Those were the exact items she needed. "What do you do?" she asked him. "A mind-reading act in a nightclub in your off-duty hours?"

He smiled for the very first time. All the worry lines in his face disappeared, and that hard, almost cruel mouth gave way to a brief but exquisite grin. "Something like that," he said. "Is this your laptop?" He pointed to the black leather case on her desktop.

"That's it."

"Okay."

He hiked the strap up his arm and settled it over his shoulder while Shelby gathered up her handbag and planner.

"Where's your car?" he asked.

"I don't have one. I take the bus or the El."

"Well, that's one less thing to worry about. Come on. I'm parked down in front."

Indeed he was. His ancient dark green, fastback Mustang was parked directly in front of the *Daily Mirror* building in a No Parking zone with a young patrolman standing guard nearby.

"Hey, Lieutenant," the kid cop said with a wave of his hand. "You ever want to get rid of this mean green machine, just give me a call, okay?"

"Will do," Callahan said as he opened the passenger door, then promptly swore under his breath and began pitching junk from the front seat into the back.

Coffee cups and lids. Big Mac boxes. Water bottles. A paperback book. A pair of jeans.

Shelby stood behind him, clucking her tongue at the incredible mess and doing her best not to ogle his very nice backside where a small frayed hole near the bottom of a pocket revealed that the lieutenant was wearing purple briefs.

"I wasn't expecting company," he muttered over his shoulder.

"Yeah, I can tell. I wasn't expecting to *be* company."

He was down to seat leather now, picking up loose change and paper clips, plastic spoons and a few AA batteries.

"There." He straightened up and gestured for Shelby to get in.

But she didn't.

"Wait a minute," she said. "Wait just a minute." Suddenly she wasn't quite so sure she wanted to go along with this bodyguard thing. How many years had she been advising her readers to be cautious about strangers, particularly those in uniform.

She didn't know this Mick Callahan from Adam. What's more, if he was a cop, why didn't he dress like one instead of looking like some ratty homeless guy? And what about those purple briefs? They certainly weren't Chicago PD standard issue. She lifted her chin in defiance and demanded, "Do you have a badge or something? Some ID? I mean, how do I know who you really are?"

He rolled his eyes—which she just happened to notice were a stunning hazel, a bit more green than brown—and then jammed his hand into his pocket, producing a metal shield clipped to a small black leather case.

"There." He held it in front of her face, but far too close for her to properly focus on. "Satisfied?"

"Not quite." She rummaged in her handbag for her drugstore reading glasses, snapped them open, jammed them on her face, and then grabbed the badge. It looked real enough, so she handed it back. But she wasn't done yet. "What about something with your picture on it?"

"Jesus, lady." He ripped his fingers through his already rumpled hair. "Will you get in the goddamned car instead of standing out here like a target?"

"Oh." Once more, she seemed to have forgotten that she was supposed to be afraid.

"Yeah," he muttered. "Oh. Just get in, will you, and then I'll show you my whole frigging family album, if you want."

"That won't be necessary." She angled into the now clean passenger seat and had barely tucked her right leg inside the vehicle when he slammed the door.

Callahan stalked around the front of the car, slid behind the steering wheel, and jabbed the key in the ignition. The Mustang roared to life, vibrating like a small jet. "We'll stop by your place for a suitcase or whatever," he said. "Where's home?"

"The Canfield Towers on North State."

"I should have guessed." He rolled his eyes again.

Shelby glared at him. "What's that supposed to mean?"

"Nothing." He took the emergency brake off, wrenched the gearshift into first, and pulled away from the curb.

Steaming at his remark, Shelby crossed her arms and stared straight ahead. How rude was that? So she lived in a luxurious high-rise. So what? She didn't have to apologize for that. She was proud of it. Ms. Simon worked damned hard for every single cent she made, and if she chose to spend an outrageous sum for rent, well then, by God she had every right to do just that.

"Where do you live, Callahan?" She snorted, not too attractively, as she turned her glare on him. "In a refrigerator box under the Green Line?"

He smiled again. This time, though, it was less of a grin that blazed across his face, and more like an involuntary, sideways twitch of his lips.

"Something like that," he said.

Shifting around, Shelby perused the clutter in the backseat. He probably lived here, she thought. In his car. It smelled like burgers and fries and dirty socks. She wondered what kind of policeman he was, and she was just about to ask when he reached across to the glove compartment, grabbed a cell phone, and thumbed in a number.

"It's Callahan," he told whoever answered. "Put me through to the captain." After a moment he said, "I've got her."

Shelby assumed he meant her.

"We're headed to her residence at the Canfield Towers. Yeah. Nope. I'll let you know." He clicked off, then stashed the phone in a side pocket of his down vest.

"You'll let them know what?" she asked.

"Where you decide to relocate."

"Oh, God." She'd forgotten about that. It seemed as if he were just escorting her safely home. "I don't see why I can't just hang out in my apartment. It's plenty safe. There's a man on the door twenty-four/seven. I can order in groceries."

"Forget it," he said.

"I will not. Nobody asked me about this, you know. Just because my employers think it's a good idea doesn't mean—"

"Is that your building up there on the left?"

Shelby looked ahead, where the newly constructed luxury high-rise towered over the block. She'd been one of the first residents there and she loved her spacious one bedroom/one bath on the twelfth floor, even as she aspired to the three-bedroom penthouse on the thirtieth and thirty-first floors. Someday. If the column continued to be popular . . . If her speaking engagements increased . . . If she survived this current mess . . .

A few minutes later, Callahan pulled up at the curb in front. "I'm assuming you don't have a pass for the garage, right?"

"Right. No car. No pass."

He killed the engine and got out.

"You can't park here," Shelby said when he opened her door.

"Yes, I can," he said. "Come on."

From close behind him, she heard Dave the Doorman's voice. "Hey, buddy, you can't park there. Oh, hello, Ms. Simon." He peered through the window on the passenger side. "I'm afraid your friend can't . . ."

Callahan swore, dug his badge out of his back pocket, and flashed it at Dave, who mumbled something that sounded like an apology.

"We won't be here long," Callahan told him.

"Yessir."

After Shelby got out of the low-slung car, the doorman, still obviously suspicious of a man in ripped jeans and a duct-taped vest, badge or no badge, leaned close and whispered to her, "Is everything okay, Ms. Simon?"

"Everything's fine, Dave. Thanks."

The man looked at her as if to say, *Well, okay. If you say so,* then he loped ahead of them to open the door to the lobby.

Once inside the marble and sleek chrome entry, Shelby pulled her keys from her purse and headed for the little room off the main foyer where the mailboxes were located.

"Whoa. Wait a minute. Hold on." Mick Callahan caught her arm. "What the hell are you doing?"

"I'm going to check my mail."

"You're going to . . . !" He still had her by the arm, and now he was shaking his head and sort of growling. "What are you? Stupid? Deaf? Suicidal?"

"Excuse me?" she shrieked.

He gave her a look of undisguised disgust, then called across the lobby to Dave, who'd returned to the relative peace and quiet of his desk. "Have the police been here yet this morning?"

Dave shook his head and called back. "No, they haven't. I'm positive. I've been on duty here since seven, so I would've seen any sort of police activity."

The lieutenant pulled out his cell phone, stabbed at it, asked for his captain again, and then inquired about "the bomb guys" just as the big black box of a truck pulled up outside the building, right behind the Mustang. "Never mind. They're here," Callahan said, then hung up abruptly.

He turned to Shelby. "Look. I'm sorry I yelled," he yelled.

She might've laughed if she hadn't been so pissed at him, and at herself, as well, for almost opening a mailbox that could conceivably blow off her hand. Or more. Little wonder he'd accused her of stupidity. "So, what happens now?" she asked.

"The bomb guys will check out the mail room here, and then make a sweep of your apartment. It won't take too long, assuming they don't find anything." He pointed to a little grouping of chairs on the far side of the lobby. "Why don't you just sit and relax for a minute?"

She looked in the direction of the expensive cream leather club chairs and for a moment she felt so exhausted that she could hardly keep standing. In a matter of a few hours, her entire world seemed to have changed beyond all recognition. She must've swayed or something, because she immediately felt a steadying hand on her back and heard Callahan say, "Come on. Let's get you in a chair."

Shelby sat, trying to concentrate on the copy of today's *Daily Mirror* that someone had left on the table beside her chair. The headlines read like old news to her since they didn't include this morning's series of letter bomb incidents. Those would be all over tomorrow's edition.

She turned to the inside pages and read her own column—twice—with a critical eye, trying to figure out if her words were in any way inflammatory or if they could offend anyone to the point that they'd want to blow her up.

There certainly wasn't anything offensive in this column. She'd written it just a few days ago, advising Over the Hill in Oklahoma to move heaven and earth in order to pursue her dream of a college education despite the fact that Over the Hill considered herself too old at the age of forty-two. In her encouraging reply, Shelby had included phone numbers and Web sites to assist the woman in her quest for tuition money. Also, in a rare personal note, Shelby wrote that her very own mother had started a business—a very successful one—at the ripe old age of fifty-something.

She smiled weakly, wondering if maybe the mysterious letter bomber was her mother, taking issue with her daughter for using her as an example of an old dog capable of learning new tricks. Nah. Her mother was enormously proud of her midlife success and didn't hesitate to tell anyone about it, sometimes at great length.

This would probably be her last column for a while, Shelby thought. She wondered if her readers would miss her advice. What if they got out of the habit of reading her, or while she was on hold, what if they got used to reading "Ask Alice" instead? Now there was a depressing thought. Alice, despite the matronly picture that accompanied the popular column, was really Alvin Wexler, a sixty-year-old curmudgeon whose "advice" was really just an excuse to parade his numerous alleged degrees in the social sciences. Ms. Simon wrote rings around him, in Shelby's opinion anyway.

Just then she heard the elevator doors whooshing open, and out stepped her neighbor, Mo Pachinski. He'd traded his electric blue velour outfit for a gray sharkskin suit that was almost iridescent, complemented by a dark purple shirt and matching tie. After he exited the elevator, Mo scanned the lobby as if he half expected somebody with a submachine gun to be lurking behind one of the potted ficus trees. Then he spotted Shelby, smiled the way a piranha might smile at the sight of human flesh, and—after shooting his purple French cuffs—sauntered toward her.

But Mick Callahan got to her first. He practically sprinted across the marble floor to insert himself between Shelby and the oncoming Mo, who looked startled for a second, then grinned.

"How's it hangin', Lieutenant?" Mo asked. He shot his cuffs again. It must've been a nervous tic, or else some involuntary reaction to a sudden rush of testosterone.

Callahan, whose plaid flannel cuffs were rolled halfway up his rangy forearms and therefore unshootable, merely shifted his shoulders in a macho, John Wayne kind of way. "What's up, Morris? When'd you get out?"

"Christmas last year. Hey, I'd've sent you a card if I thought you cared."

"Yeah. Yeah."

The smirk on the mobster's face seemed to soften just a bit then when he said, "I heard about your wife, Callahan. My condolences."

Mick Callahan's face, however, hardened to granite as he responded with a terse "Thanks."

A wife? Condolences? What was that all about? Shelby was wondering just as Mo turned to her and asked, "You know this guy, Doll?"

"Sort of," she said.

"Hey, Lieutenant," someone called from across the lobby. "We're ready to go up to the residence now."

"Let's go," Callahan said to Shelby. "Take it easy, Morris."

"What's the deal here?" Mo asked, looking from

Shelby to the lieutenant and back. "What's going on? You got some kinda problem I oughta know about, Doll?"

She didn't know how to answer, so it was a good thing that her stick-like-glue bodyguard intervened with, "Nah. No problem. Ms. Simon asked the CPD to check the locks in her apartment. Just one of the little civic services we provide when we're not hassling you and your associates."

"Ha ha," Mo said as his mouth resumed its standard smirk. "You oughta do stand-up, Callahan." He straightened his tie. "See ya, Doll," he said to Shelby, then strode to the door.

"How do you know that guy?" the lieutenant growled, his gaze still trained on the sharkskin suit now exiting the building.

"I don't really *know* him. He lives across the hall. How do *you* know him?"

"I helped put him in jail five years ago. He's bad news. I'd avoid him if I were you."

"I try," she said with a sigh, and then she gasped. "Oh, my God. You don't think it's Mo who's threatening me, do you?"

He shook his head. "Guys like Morris Pachinski don't make threats. If he wanted you dead, you'd already be that way."

Shelby didn't exactly find that a comforting thought. She wanted to ask him about his wife, but when she stood up, Callahan practically rushed her toward the elevator.

They rode up to the twelfth floor with two men in thickly padded jumpsuits and a black Lab that seemed to really enjoy his job. He licked Shelby's hand and gazed up at her as if to say, *Some fun, huh?* When she patted his sleek black head, one of the bomb technicians said, "Please don't distract him, ma'am."

As they walked down the hall toward her apartment, Callahan held out his hand. "Keys," he said.

"Right."

Shelby rummaged through her purse. She had so many doodads on her key chain—a flashlight, a whistle, a mini Etch-A-Sketch—that her keys tended to settle rather quickly to the bottom of her bag. The entourage of bomb guys, bomb dog, and bodyguard stood in front of her door, waiting with that sort of masculine patience that wasn't really patience at all, but a controlled kind of menace.

She laughed nervously. "I know they're in here." And then her fingers touched metal, and she plucked the heavy key chain from the depths of her bag. No sooner were they out than Callahan grabbed them from her and tossed them to the bomb guy closest to the door.

"It's the gold one with the little dab of red nail polish," Shelby said as she was frantically trying to recall whether or not she'd made her bed this morning, and if there were dirty dishes in the sink, and what was hung up to dry over the shower door. She wasn't the neatest person in the world, but she usually had time to clean up before company came.

The officer stuck the key in the lock and pushed open the door. Shelby stepped forward, only to be yanked back.

"We'll wait out here while they check it out," Callahan said.

"Right." She'd forgotten again that she was in danger, but surely she'd have noticed any kind of explosive device in her very own apartment. What was in yesterday's mail? Had she opened everything? Or was there a lethal envelope lurking under this week's copies of *The New Yorker* and *Ladies' Home Journal*?

Callahan was leaning against the wall, gazing down as if studying the pattern of the carpet.

"I guess there's a lot of hurry-up-and-wait in your business," she said, lowering herself to the floor.

"Enough," he said.

"How long have you been a cop?"

"A long time."

Hearing the plaintive note in his voice, Shelby looked up. The lieutenant wasn't staring at the carpet anymore, but rather gazing down the corridor toward the huge plate-glass window that displayed a big rectangle of bright Chicago skyline. He didn't seem to be focused on anything in particular. In fact, his gaze seemed to travel beyond anything actually visible beyond the glass. His forehead was furrowed. His mouth bore down at the corners. A muscle twitched in his cheek. He looked so incredibly sad. Just lost. Lost and so terribly, terribly alone.

If he'd been a child on a street corner, Shelby would've stopped in her tracks to kneel down and take him in her arms, to whisper, "There. There. Everything will be all right."

But he wasn't a child, of course. Far from it. And she hadn't a clue about the origin of Mick Callahan's sudden desolate visage, although she wondered if it might have something to do with Mo's condolences, expressed earlier in the lobby. As someone who made her living giving advice, Shelby wasn't used to holding her tongue when she encountered obvious sadness or visible depression. A soft and sincere "How can I help?" from Ms. Simon would usually elicit a lengthy tale of woe, and no matter the problem, she was almost always able to make the person feel better, even if only for a while.

But, along with the sadness, there was also something forbidding in Callahan's expression. Something cold. Something that warned, *Leave me the hell alone.*

She was debating whether or not to do just that when one of the bomb techs stepped out into the hallway.

"We're done in here, Lieutenant. It's clean."

Thank God, Shelby thought. That meant she'd probably made her bed.

"Okay. Thanks, guys," Callahan said, his expression back to its normal severity. "After you," he said to Shelby, gesturing toward her door.

It was odd, stepping into her own living room and seeing everything just a bit different from the way she'd left it a few hours before. The chairs and sofa weren't properly centered around the fireplace. Lamps and picture frames looked out of kilter on tabletops. A quick glance into the little kitchen revealed cabinet doors and drawers not quite closed.

She put her handbag and laptop down on a table and immediately began to make adjustments to the decor, re-aligning a lampshade, sliding a small Waterford crystal vase from one side of an end table to the other, tossing a velvet throw pillow from a chair into a bare corner of the sofa.

"We haven't got time for that," Callahan said, scowling at his watch. "Pack a bag and let's go. I'd like to be out of here in ten or fifteen minutes, tops."

With her knee, Shelby shoved the sofa a few inches to the right. "Where are we going?" she asked.

He shrugged and said, "That's entirely up to you, Ms. Simon."

"Oh."

Oh, brother.

Ms. Simon didn't have a clue.

CHAPTER THREE

◡

Mick looked at his watch for the thousandth time while he mentally inventoried his patience only to find it rapidly waning, then decided to give Shelby Simon another five minutes to pack. Assuming that's what she was doing in the other room. It sounded to him like she was just slamming doors and drawers, rattling hangers, dropping things, and swearing creatively.

He gazed around her living room, wondering what sort of woman paid what must be a small fortune in rent and then chose to furnish the place in a single boring color. Beige. Or maybe sand was a better description of the carpet and drapes and walls. The chairs and the sofa where he sat were a similar neutral shade. The tables were chrome and glass, and the lamps were made of various metals, mostly copper. With the exception of a few brightly colored tapestry pillows, the place looked like the frigging Sahara.

Her bathroom was beige, as well, including the fixtures and the thick terry towels. The only color in there came from an assortment of perfume bottles on the beige marble vanity. Strange. The outfit she was wearing today—black slacks and a white top and a black hand-bag—was colorless, too, unless he counted the blue swoosh on each of her shoes or the red highlights in her long, shiny hair.

Still, this Simon woman didn't strike him as colorless or neutral in any way. But what did he know? In his thirty-eight years, he'd really only known one woman well and then it turned out he hadn't known her nearly as well as he imagined.

"Well, I'm packed," she announced from the bedroom doorway. "More or less."

Mick suspected it was more rather than less.

~

While the lieutenant rearranged the crappola in the trunk of his car to make room for her two big suitcases, Shelby tried once more to contact her parents in Michigan to tell them she would be visiting them for a while. It seemed the logical, the sensible thing to do. Plus she'd been so busy that she hadn't seen her mother and father for over a year, so she'd managed to convince herself that this exile from work at least had an upside.

Actually, now that she'd had a little time to think about it, Shelby was almost looking forward to spending some time at the old place on Heart Lake where she'd spent every long, lovely summer of her life until she was nine-teen or twenty. The huge old Victorian house had been in her family since it was built in the 1880s by her great-great-grandfather, Orvis Shelby, Sr.

Judging from his portrait, which still hung over the

fireplace in the parlor, old Orvis bore a strong resemblance to Teddy Roosevelt with his ample paunch, rugged mustache, and rimless glasses. He'd been a lumber baron on a minor scale in Michigan's Lower Peninsula, but successful enough to put together a pretty hefty fortune. His heirs, however, weren't quite so enterprising, and by the time the fortune had passed through the hands of Orvis Jr. and Orvis the Third, all that was left for Shelby's mother to inherit was the Heart Lake property.

It would be gorgeous up there now, with October turning all the trees to paint-box colors and the lake to beautiful shades of gunmetal and pewter.

She shifted around to look out the back window of the car. The lieutenant had just slammed the trunk lid, and was standing there looking typically pissed at the world in general and probably at her and her suitcases in particular, just as a red, white, and blue mail truck pulled up behind him.

Callahan walked to the driver's open door and said something to him that Shelby couldn't hear. Shelby recognized the mailman. It was Joe, a tall, skinny guy in his late twenties or early thirties, who'd told her once that he always read her column and had even written to her a couple of times. It was on her advice, in fact, that Joe had decided to attend his first AA meeting. She wondered how it was going for him, but now probably wasn't a good time to inquire.

Right now Joe was stepping out of his vehicle onto the sidewalk, looking none too pleased with whatever Callahan had just said to him. He responded with something as loud as it was incomprehensible, then shrugged, turned to the rear of his truck, and hauled out a large canvas container marked "Canfield Towers." That was how they delivered the tons of mail, mostly junk, to all three hundred or so residents of her building. The mailman would roll the big container into the mailroom off the lobby, then stand for at least an hour shoving the envelopes and flyers and small packages into the proper boxes.

Callahan, still looking crabby, slid into the driver's seat and closed the door.

"What was that all about?" Shelby asked.

"I wanted to make sure the post office people had put a hold on your mail," he growled.

"Did they?"

He shook his head. "I have no idea. Fucking idiot said I'd have to take that up with his supervisor. No wonder those people are always shooting each other." He dragged in what Shelby hoped was a calming breath, then stabbed his key into the ignition and asked her, "Where to?"

"My parents' place," she said, but then, suddenly unsure, she corrected herself. "Oh, well, maybe not. I don't know how this bodyguard deal is supposed to work. Their place is up in Michigan. It's about a five hour trip, so maybe that's too far. Maybe you're not even authorized to leave the state."

"Michigan," he grumbled.

"Well, if that's such a problem . . ."

"No," he said. "It's not a problem. It's as good a place as any, I guess." He started the car. "I just need to stop by my place first to pick up a few things."

"So you can leave town just like that?" She snapped her fingers.

"Yeah. Just like that."

"What about your family?" she asked. "What about your job?"

"No family. And right now you're my job." Then he added under his breath a distinctly snarky, "Such as it is."

His enthusiasm was pretty underwhelming, Shelby thought. Even a little insulting. More than a little. *Such as it is!* Hell. She hadn't asked for this, after all. It wasn't her idea. She wasn't going *anyplace* with *him*.

He hadn't put the car in gear yet, so she reached for the door handle. "You know, on second thought, I don't want to go to Michigan. I don't really want to go anywhere, Callahan. Especially with you. I'll be just fine right here."

She wrenched open the door and got her right foot out and onto the pavement, but the rest of her wasn't fast enough to escape Callahan's grasp.

"Let me go, dammit." The harder she tried to pull away, the more his grip tightened on her upper arm.

"Settle down," he yelled at her.

"I will not."

His voice dropped to a menacing level. "Get back in the car and close the goddamned door." Then he shouted again. "Please."

"No. Let me go, Callahan. I mean it." She felt like screaming bloody murder, and she almost did when she told him, "I'll have you arrested for kidnapping. Or police brutality. Or . . . Or . . ." Hell. She couldn't think of any other appropriate charges. "Or terrorism."

"Go ahead," he said, daring her and still not letting her go. "Be my guest."

"Hey, Ms. Simon?" It was Joe, calling to Shelby from

a distance of fifteen or twenty feet across the sidewalk. "Can I help you or anything?"

Heaven help her. In the two hours or so that Mick Callahan had been her protector, three different men—Dave the Doorman, Mo, and now Joe—had offered their assistance. She didn't need any help. She needed to get out of this stupid car, away from this maniac.

"No. That's okay," she shouted out the window. "Thanks anyway. I'm . . ."

Joe's rolling mail cart exploded with a horrific blast that sent black smoke and bright flames in every direction. His lanky body went pinwheeling backward down the sidewalk, bowling over half a dozen oncoming pedestrians, and flaming mail began raining down on the pavement.

Shelby might have screamed. She wasn't sure. But she was sure that she'd been forcefully yanked back into the seat and Callahan had lunged across her to close her door, then pulled away from the curb with a frightful, almost sickening screech. In less than a few seconds, the Mustang was gunning southbound on North State while its driver was barking instructions on his cell phone.

Through the rear window, she could see several people staggering through the smoke and burning bits of paper. Poor Joe! Oh, my God.

"We need to go back and help them," she said.

"Help's on the way. Do me a favor and scoot down in the seat, will you?"

"But I . . ."

"Just do it," he yelled.

Shelby slid down, and as she did she heard sirens screaming up the opposite side of the street. She tried to peek up through the windshield, but a firm hand on her head promptly shoved her back down . . .

. . . where she decided she'd stay. With her hands clenched and her eyes tightly closed. God. She really was in trouble, wasn't she?

⟶

It was a lot more than Mick had bargained for. Not more than he could handle, of course. But whoever was after Shelby Simon was after her in a big way, and there was no reason to believe the guy would limit himself to letter bombs and no way to know how close he'd come to his target. The fucker could be anywhere—holed up in an eight-by-ten cabin in Montana like the infamous Unabomber, or right here, right now, a mere three cars behind them in traffic. Until the investigators came up with some viable leads, Mick didn't have a clue who or what he was dealing with. Other than a woman who didn't seem to have sense enough to be afraid.

Well, maybe a little afraid. She was still hunkered down on the passenger side, her legs—all six miles of them—curled under the dash and her head cradled in her arms on the seat. With her eyes closed, she might even have been asleep. Now that he really looked at her, she appeared to be a lot more relaxed than he was. For a minute he'd been tempted to say something reassuring to her, like "It'll be okay." But he decided against it. A little healthy fear was probably a good thing in this case.

He pulled up in front of his apartment building on the near West Side—in actual distance only a matter of a few miles from the Canfield Towers, but light-years away in terms of style and status. In other words, the place was the pits, a three-story six-family brown brick box with a rotting roof, a broken concrete sidewalk, three boarded windows, and odors in the hallway thick enough to cut with a machete.

The place was ideal for working undercover, and Mick really hadn't minded that Home Sweet Home for the past two years was a one-bedroom rattrap on a bad street in a worse neighborhood. He actually liked it in a weird way because it sort of suited his prevailing moods. Still, it wasn't anyplace he wanted to show off. Not to a woman like Shelby Simon, anyway.

"We're here," he said. "You need to come inside with me. It's not safe here out on the street."

She lifted her head, blinked her whiskey-colored eyes a few times, and looked out the window, showing very little change in her expression. At least there was no outright distaste or disgust that Mick was able to discern while watching her take in his street, his building, his native habitat. She didn't say "Eeuuww" or "What a dump."

"Where's here?" she asked.

"My place. I've been working undercover so it's not exactly a palace or anything."

"No, I guess not," she said in a neutral sort of way.

"Yeah, well . . ."

He helped her and her six miles of stiff legs out of the car, then kept hold of her arm along the cracked and hazardous sidewalk to the front door of the building. As soon as he opened the door, they were greeted by a blast of rancid cooking oils and the underlying stench of urine and mold.

Home sweet home.

"Up here," he said, starting up the dilapidated stairs to the second floor.

"It's dark." She sounded a little tentative, nervously polite.

"Dark. Yeah. Well, that's probably a good thing." It meant she couldn't see the broken light fixture above them, the peeling hospital green paint, or the crud that coated the floor. One of these days, when he was done playing wigged-out doper, wanna-be gang banger, and all-around bad guy, he was going to go after the absentee landlord of this stinking hovel on behalf of Hattie Grimes and Lena Slotnik, the elderly tenants who lived here because they had no place else to go.

"Here we are," he said.

He unlocked the upper and then the lower deadbolts, and pushed in the door, sniffing to make sure the half dozen or so air fresheners were still on the job. Of course, those didn't always smell that great, either, because he always forgot what brand and scent to get, so typically there was an ongoing battle between citrus and pine and some god-awful garden fragrance. Pine, he decided while stepping over the threshold, was dominant today. Greetings from the cool north woods.

Shelby followed him in, and to her credit, didn't come out with an insincere "Oh, this is nice" or a sarcastic "Your cleaning lady must be on vacation." Her expression remained impassive, and after she'd looked around a couple of seconds, she merely asked, "How long have you lived here?"

"About two years." He shrugged. "Give or take a few weeks."

Actually, there was no give or take about it. Mick

knew the exact date he'd moved in here, three days after his wife's funeral. He'd cleared his clothes and books and firearms out of their town house on Rush Street, and left everything else—the expensive leather couch, the antique dining-room pieces, the brand-new Thomasville bedroom suite, the oriental rugs, the good lamps, everything—to be dealt with, divvied up, or destroyed by Julie's cousin, Nicole.

"Even the pictures?" Nicole had asked him. "All the albums of you and Julie?"

"Especially those."

"Aw, Mick."

Such were the last, sad words he heard Nicole say because he'd walked out then, for good, and hadn't spoken to her or anyone in his late wife's family since. Then he'd come here, to this dump, and spent the next two years furnishing it with selected Salvation Army pieces and curb-sale shit and the odd, discarded Dumpster find.

It was the pits. But at least it was colorful.

"Have a seat." He gestured toward his couch with its slipcover of dinner-plate-size sunflowers on a dark blue background, then preceded her across the room in order to gather up magazines and newspapers to make room for her. "I'll just throw some things together. It won't take long."

Mick, his arms stuffed with three days' worth of crumpled *Daily Mirrors*, assorted take-out menus, and the latest issue of *Playboy*, headed toward the bedroom, praying his guest wouldn't ask to use his about-as-clean-as-a-gas-station bathroom.

Shelby had heard the expression "shabby chic," but this was the first time she'd ever encountered it in real life. Well, actually the place was a lot shabbier than chic.

The sunflowery couch beneath her looked like Vincent van Gogh's worst nightmare. Across from the couch, the green plaid La-Z-Boy sat half reclined while it spewed stuffing from its back and seat cushion and both arms. In between the couch and the chair was a table of unknown construction and height, covered as it was with precarious towers of magazines and paperbacks, an open pretzel bag, a box of Ritz crackers, one giant Slurpy cup, and empty, mismatched coffee mugs—three to be exact. No—four. One was hiding under *Newsweek.*

Several crushed beer cans were relegated to a battered end table, along with an open jar of dry roasted peanuts and the remote for the TV. There was a dead philodendron, too. Shelby didn't think anyone could kill a philodendron.

The only spot of relative order in the room was a homemade bookcase, fashioned of cement blocks and two-by-fours, on the wall opposite the couch. Shelby got up to inspect the titles. The majority of Callahan's library was nonfiction, and most of those books were devoted to major conflicts, such as the American Revolution, the Civil War, both World Wars, and more. Although she found the collection really intriguing, it probably wasn't all that surprising. Given his occupation, it made sense that the man relaxed with guns and gore.

She heard his footsteps coming from the bedroom.

"While you're over there," he said, "hand me that Ulysses Grant biography, will you? The one on the bottom left."

She plucked the big, heavy book from the shelf and turned to hand it to him, surprised that he'd not only packed in such a short time but changed clothes as well. This current flannel shirt was a bit less washed-out than its predecessor, and these jeans, while faded, didn't appear to be ripped in any strategic places.

"Thanks." He took the book from her, shoved it in the gym bag he was carrying, then said, "I'm ready. Let's go."

"That was quick," Shelby said. She smiled up at him as she angled her head toward his bookcase. "I see you're a student of military history."

Callahan gave her such an odd, forbidding look that Shelby immediately regretted her impulsive comment about his reading preference. The expression on his face was similar to the one she'd witnessed earlier, in the hallway outside her apartment door. That cold, *leave me the hell alone* look. Clearly, the man had no intention of sharing anything of his personal life with her, even something as relatively insignificant as his books. She was just his job. *Such as it was.*

Before he could come up with some sort of snide reply, Shelby turned her back on him. "Well, let's hit the road," she said, walking to the door.

⌒

Mick secured his deadbolts, then trotted down the stairs in Ms. Shelby Simon's hot little wake. He could tell she was pissed—boy, was she pissed!—at his lack of a response to her comment about his books, and he couldn't really blame her. It was just that she'd caught him off guard with that "student of military history" phrase, which just happened to be the way Julie used to introduce him to her medical cronies.

It was never "This is my husband, the cop," or ". . . my husband, Lieutenant Mick Callahan of the Chicago PD," but always "This is my husband, who's in law enforcement and a student of military history."

The instant the Simon woman had said those same words, he'd felt the old and all-too-familiar tic of anger that he used to experience with Julie. When had his being a cop turned into an embarrassment for her? It had been good enough to put her through med school, hadn't it? When had she stopped loving him?

Why the hell was he thinking about her now? Jesus. Julie was usually banished to those wee, small, inebriated hours of the morning when no amount of liquor could drown the memories, good and bad alike.

Mick shook his head to clear it of the intrusive thoughts, and then swallowed hard to get rid of the sudden, unexpected tightness in his throat. He continued down the stairs, and by the time he got outside, Shelby Simon was standing in the middle of the sidewalk, flanked by his neighbors, Hattie Grimes and Lena Slotnik.

The two of them were like day and night—literally. Round little Hattie's skin was dark mahogany and she dressed in large, long, and darkly exotic dashikis that she ran up on her ancient Singer sewing machine. Long, tall Lena's skin, in contrast, was white as the snows of her native Vladivostok, and she always wore blue—dresses, slacks, whatever—along with some kind of sweater or wrap, even during the hottest days of summer.

They had met about a hundred years ago when they worked as lunch ladies in the cafeteria at Lawndale High. After retirement they'd apparently struck some sort of pact to serve and protect each other in their sunset years.

In his two years in residence here, Mick had never seen one without the other. Hattie and Lena were inseparable, joined at their mismatched hips, black and white Siamese twins who pulled their shopping carts to and from the market together every Monday and Thursday, who went to Mass at Saint Jerome's every day and played Bingo there every Tuesday night, and who seemed to consider their downstairs neighbor a soul-in-jeopardy, someone in desperate need of their prayers.

Hell. He probably was, but what he didn't need right now was for Hattie and Lena to delay his mission of getting Shelby Simon quickly and safely out of town.

"Ladies," he said, approaching the little triad on the sidewalk.

Hattie wrapped her fleshy arms around him. "Let me hug you, sweet boy. Let Hattie hug the daylights out of you."

"He looks tired forever," Lena said in her perpetually thick and dour accent. "He looks like he never sleeps. You will get sick, Mikhail, I warn you, and then where will you be? You'll see."

Mick rolled his eyes in Shelby's direction. "My mother hens," he said, somewhat sheepishly.

"I can tell."

Lena pointed to Shelby. "This is lady in picture on bus. Ms. Simon Says. No? Only without the mustache."

"No," Mick replied. "She just looks like the lady on the bus. This is my sister."

All three of them looked surprised, Shelby most of all. Her light brown eyes opened wide.

"Your sister!" all three of them exclaimed.

"Honey, you never said anything about a sister." Hattie stepped back, then stared from Mick to Shelby and back again. "She don't look nuthin' like you."

"Half sister," Mick corrected himself. Half ass was what he was thinking. All he was trying to do was maintain a low, even invisible profile for the woman he was protecting, so he'd said the first thing that came into his head. Stupid. But he was stuck with it now. "Different fathers."

Shelby was looking at him as if he'd just dropped fifty or sixty I.Q. points. He could only hope she'd instinctively know why he'd lied—for her own good—and that she wouldn't dispute it.

"So," Lena said to her, her pale Russian eyes growing slitty with suspicion, "you two have same mother, then."

"Um. Well. Yes," Shelby answered. "The same mother. Yes, we do. Good ol' Mama. Bless her heart."

With a deep sigh of brotherly relief, Mick grasped Shelby's arm and turned her in the direction of his car. "Come on, sis."

Hattie stopped them with an insistent "Hold on now. Wait a minute. Don't you be rushing her off that way. There's something I want to say to this sister of yours, Mick."

He halted. What? What now? "Okay. But we're in a hurry," he said, hoping to speed the woman up. Hattie tended to be pretty long-winded if given the slightest encouragement.

"What hurry?" Lena demanded.

"We're . . . uh . . . we're late for . . . uh . . ." Shit. His mind went blank all of a sudden. He probably *had* lost a dozen or so I.Q. points over the course of the past few hours.

"For a family reunion," Shelby said, coming to his rescue with a level voice and a totally straight face.

"Family is good," Lena said, nodding sagely.

Hattie, however, was not to be denied. "This won't take long," she said. She practically ripped Shelby's arm out of his and marched her up the sidewalk, near the building's front door, where she appeared to launch into a multigestured harangue. Mick couldn't hear what she was saying, nor could he even imagine what the woman felt so compelled to tell his "sister."

"Family," Lena murmured as she, too, watched the animated monologue taking place several yards away. "Family is good. Important. You have pretty sister."

Sometimes Lena sounded so much like Natasha, of Boris and Natasha fame, that it was all Mick could do not to laugh, but he limited himself to a smile while he looked at Shelby Simon. She was more than pretty. Aside from her shiny dark brown hair, and those long legs, and the suggestion of Victoria's Secret breasts beneath her tailored white shirt, there was the sparkle of intelligence in her whiskey brown eyes and a suggestion of confidence and inner strength in her posture. She was probably five feet six inches, give or take an inch, but she stood as tall as any WNBA player.

Not that her looks mattered, he reminded himself. Still, if he had to spend a significant length of time with an endangered female, it was nice that she was fairly easy on the eyes.

Hattie walked her back down the sidewalk and turned her over to him with a wave of her hand.

"I said my piece," she announced. "You children go on now and have yourselves a big ol' time at that reunion."

After several fleshy hugs from Hattie and a warm but stoic handshake from Lena, Mick finally got Shelby inside the Mustang.

"To Michigan," he said, pulling away from the curb.

"To Michigan," she echoed, not too enthusiastically.

He turned east, toward the Interstate. "Maybe you should give me a general idea of where. It's a pretty big state."

"Just head in the general direction of Grand Rapids for now."

"Right." That would take care of the next four hours or so. He wouldn't need to ask for more specific directions until close to sunset. He wouldn't need to talk at all. Only . . .

"So, what did Hattie have to say?" he asked. Not that he cared. He was simply curious.

"She said you drink too much, stay out too late, don't eat right, live in a pigsty, hang around with the wrong people, and don't go to church. In a nutshell, Callahan, she said you're on the fast track to hell in a handbasket."

"Sorry I asked."

"I'll bet. So? Is she right?"

"Well . . ."

He glanced toward his passenger, who had one shapely eyebrow raised and a funny—cute, actually— quirk to her mouth. Hell, if he had to be saddled with a woman at all, it was definitely better that she had a face that could stop traffic.

"Yeah," he said. "She's right."

"Uh-huh. That's what I thought."

He chuckled, which wasn't really like him. Usually he either yelled or growled. But the sound that had just come out of him was such a reasonable facsimile of genuine laughter that it startled him. "You're not going to start giving me advice, are you, Ms. Simon?"

"Who me?" she exclaimed. "I wouldn't dream of it, Callahan."

CHAPTER FOUR

~

Traffic wasn't too terrible, and Callahan had a lead foot and an aversion to staying in one lane for more than thirty seconds, so after about forty-five minutes the ancient Mustang had roared across the state line into Indiana. Shelby stared out the passenger window at the smokestacks of Gary while she contemplated her current, pitiful, sorry-ass plight.

How had this happened? From the moment she had opened her eyes this morning, her life had been spinning faster and faster out of control, and now here she was—jobless, homeless for all practical purposes, threatened, and speeding north in a smelly car with a maniac at the wheel.

The last thing the maniac had said to her, maybe ten minutes ago after he'd talked once more to his supervisor back in Chicago, was that the authorities wanted Shelby to make a list for them of possible enemies. Enemies! She didn't have any *enemies*, for heaven's sake. She barely had any *friends* these days, given her incredibly busy schedule. She hadn't had time for a luncheon get-together or a girls' night out in more months than she could remember. It seemed as if E-mail and cell phones had pretty well replaced any face-to-face contact with her pals lately.

"Enemies!" she muttered. "How about you, Callahan? Do you have enemies?"

"Plenty," he answered without elaboration and without taking his eyes off the road.

Well, no surprise there. His neighbor, Hattie Grimes, had painted a fairly vivid picture of Mick Callahan's lifestyle. Of course, the woman didn't know that he was a cop working undercover, but she seemed to have a fairly good handle on his comings and goings. "Late to bed and late to rise" in her words. "That boy's got one foot in perdition already, I'm telling you here and now, sister girl. You help him. You hear me?"

Help him! Ha! She apparently couldn't even help herself at the moment. As for her proclivity to tender advice, Callahan had already made it clear that he didn't want any.

Fine. Great. For once in her life, she'd keep her mouth shut. Anyway, she was the one who needed advice right now. Shelby tilted her head back against the seat, closed her eyes, and composed a letter to herself.

Dear Ms. Simon,
Help! Somebody's trying to kill me. I'll bet you think shit like this only happens in movies or in cheesy melodramas on TV. Ha! A lot you know. The thing is, though, it feels like it's happening to somebody else. The danger just doesn't feel real. And to make matters worse, there's this guy who's sup-

*posed to protect me, and instead of being grateful
and cooperative, I'm being a bitch, which really
isn't like me at all. I'm a nice person, dammit. None
of this makes sense.*

   Signed,
   Edgy in Indiana

Shelby sighed quietly. In twelve years of writing her
column, she didn't think she'd ever gotten a letter from
someone under duress of one kind or another who wasn't
scared out of his or her mind. Women wrote in all too frequently about husbands who'd threatened to kill them.
Sometimes it was children in mortal fear of a parent.
Once an elderly man sent her a long, shakily printed letter about his suspicion that his wife of fifty years was lac-
ing her meat loaf with ground glass.

In such instances, Ms. Simon's advice was usually a
variation on a single theme. Get help. Tell someone. Alert
your local police, your minister, your teacher, a neighbor,
somebody. Just get help. And get it now.

She opened one eye and took in her helper's profile.
He really was good-looking, despite his perpetually furrowed forehead and the sour slant of his mouth. His chin
was strong and his jaw pleasantly angular. He hadn't
shaved today, she noticed, but the stubble on his cheeks
and chin had a certain appeal in a *Miami Vice* kind of
way.

The hands that gripped the steering wheel were tan
and strong, with blunt fingers and surprisingly nice nails.
At least he didn't bite them as far as Shelby could tell.
His legs . . . Well, all she could see at the moment was the

suggestion of hard-muscled quads beneath their faded blue covering of denim. That was nice . . .

She closed her eyes again, reminding herself that Callahan's looks, good or bad or indifferent, weren't important. Was he good at his job? That's what mattered.

> *Dear Edgy,*
> *It'll be okay. Ms. Simon says so.*

It would, wouldn't it?

~

Mick's passenger had been asleep for almost two hours when they neared Grand Rapids. How could she sleep? he wondered. Either she had a lot of confidence in him or she'd taken a tranq at some point or she still didn't have the slightest comprehension of the danger she was in. Maybe all three.

Nah. He didn't get the impression that Ms. Shelby Simon had any confidence in him at all. Why would she, especially after good old Hattie's keen observations and dire predictions?

He did drink too much, keep unhealthy hours, and all the rest, including no doubt having one foot already planted in perdition, but Shelby Simon didn't necessarily know that. All she really knew about him was that he lived in a crappy apartment, drove a dark green beater, and wasn't the most cheerful guy she'd ever met. Oh, yeah. And then there was that "student of military history" thing.

Don't start thinking about that again, he warned himself. Then, for further distraction, and because he hadn't eaten all day, he took the next exit and quickly located a fast-food drive-thru.

His passenger stirred, stretched, and blinked.

"Hungry?" he asked her.

"Mm. Starving." She peered out the window. "Is this the place with the Double Whammy burger?"

"This is the place," he said.

"Well, if you'll order me a Double Whammy, fries, and a large diet cola, I'm going to go inside to the rest room."

While she spoke she was rummaging through her handbag. She came up with a twenty, and then handed it to Mick, saying, "My treat, Callahan."

His first instinct was to decline her offer. What? Did she think he couldn't afford a couple burgers? But then he decided he was being a macho jerk, so he took the bill and said, "Thanks. Keep your eyes open inside, okay?"

She laughed and her eyes widened in mock fear. "Ooh. You mean there might be a letter bomber lurking in the handicapped stall in the ladies' room?"

"I mean just be aware of your surroundings. That's all."

He watched her walk to the front door of the building as much to make sure that no one accosted her as to enjoy the way she moved. Her stride was smooth and long, and there was a beguiling sway to her backside. Not a come-and-get-it wiggle. Nothing overtly sexual. Just a pleasant, eye-appealing motion. She walked with just the right amount of confidence. Fearlessly. Probably too fearless for her own good, he thought.

Still, he'd been aware of the surrounding traffic when

they'd left Chicago, and he'd switched lanes often enough to ditch anybody who might be on their tail. He doubted that the guy was close. Letter bombers struck from afar. It was their M.O. At least that appeared to be this guy's opening gambit.

Or not. Right now speculation was only good for covering all the bases in order to keep her safe. Which he had no doubt that he'd do even though it wasn't his usual work. Five or six years ago he'd assisted a federal marshal while he baby-sat serial killer Joe Earl Moffett during his month-long trial. Mick had been bored out of his skull, hanging out in the courthouse day after day, forced to listen to Moffett's continual Bible quotes and sick jokes. Compared to that, baby-sitting Ms. Shelby Simon was going to be like a vacation at Club Med.

He drove ahead to the pickup window for their order, and then parked where he had an unblocked view of the restaurant's front door. The delicious fumes from the French fries wafted out of the bag, making his mouth water and his stomach growl, but he decided it would be rude to start eating without his companion, especially since she was the one who'd paid.

How much did a syndicated advice columnist make? he wondered. Plenty, judging from her place at the Canfield Towers. A hell of a lot more than a lieutenant with nearly seventeen years on the job, he was sure.

His fingers drummed on the steering wheel. Why couldn't women just take a piss and leave the bathroom? Over the years, he'd probably spent a total of two or three days waiting for Julie. "I'll be right back" translated to a guaranteed ten minutes, often fifteen or twenty if she did the whole makeup repair and hair brushing routine. He'd always groused at her, but in truth he hadn't minded all that much. It was nice, seeing his wife coming out of the john looking so pretty and pleased with herself, watching heads turn as she walked in his direction.

He caught himself smiling, and immediately adjusted his face to its normal, antisocial mein just as Shelby Simon came strolling out the restaurant door. End of day sunlight streaked her long hair with tones of red and gold. She waved when she spotted him, and started toward the car when all of a sudden two women rushed out the door behind her and raced in Shelby's direction.

Mick was out of the car already, his hand on the gun stashed in his waistband, when he realized the women were simply enthusiastic fans who wanted autographs. They were laughing and waving pens and copies of newspapers in the air. Then, while the famous Ms. Simon graciously smiled and schmoozed and signed her name, Mick breathed deeply to dilute the adrenaline that had flooded his system and to coax his heart back to a regular beat. He got back in the car and slammed the door.

Dammit. He kept forgetting what a celebrity this woman was with her face in scores of daily papers as well as slapped onto the sides of buses. That notoriety certainly didn't make his job any easier. If anybody bent on doing her harm wanted to locate Shelby Simon, it wouldn't exactly be like looking for a needle in a haystack.

Maybe he should convince her to wear some kind of disguise, at least until he had delivered her to the safety of her parents' place. He tried to picture her in thick black glasses with bushy eyebrows and a bulbous false nose. Or maybe a platinum blond wig and big wax lips. Even so, the woman still looked pretty good in his imagination.

Finally, after shaking hands with her happy little fan club and bidding them farewell, the famous Ms. Simon sauntered toward the car. "Oh, God. Those French fries smell so good," she exclaimed, barely in the seat before she plunged into one of the paper sacks and came up with a handful of greasy shoestring potatoes.

"Knock yourself out," he said.

She did. He'd have thought she hadn't eaten in a month the way she attacked her Double Whammy, wholly oblivious to the Secret Sauce that was running down her chin, and all the while making little orgasmic mews of pleasure so distracting that Mick could hardly swallow his own burger and fries. When her tongue peeked out to catch an errant crumb in the corner of her mouth, he felt the unsettling turn of his appetite away from food in the direction of more visceral pleasures.

He gulped three-fourths of his large soft drink to put out the sudden and unexpected flames, then finished his meal staring straight ahead out the windshield without a single sidelong glance at the woman in the passenger seat, tuning out her sensual little noises as best he could. When he was done, he pitched his empty cartons in the backseat and started the car.

"Next stop—your folks' place. What's the name of the nearest town?" he asked, easing out of the parking lot and back toward the highway.

"Shelbyville," she said, licking the last of the salt from her fingers.

"Excuse me?"

"Shelbyville. That's the name of the town nearest to Heart Lake."

"Shelbyville," he repeated, thinking he'd heard her wrong. "Like your name?"

"Yes," she said somewhat defensively. "Just like my name. What's wrong with that? The town was founded by my great-great-grandfather, Orvis Shelby."

"I didn't say there was anything wrong with it, did I?" He shook his head. "Hell, if a man wants to name a town for himself, more power to him. And if a family wants to recycle a dumb name, that's okay, too."

Now she was more than defensive. She was indignant. "My name's not dumb or recycled. It's tradition, Callahan. Who were you named for? Mickey Mouse?"

He laughed. Again. That made at least four or five times she'd managed to cut through his normal gloom in the space of a few hours. And that hadn't happened to him in a long, long time.

⁓

Shelby stared out the window, seemingly entranced by the beautiful autumn colors along the roadside while she was actually trying not to laugh out loud at the lieutenant's earlier remark. It *was* a dumb name. Despite her protest to Callahan, she'd hated her name when she was a kid and not only considered it dumb but embarrassing to boot, especially when the local kids at Heart Lake, who attended school in nearby Shelbyville, teased her.

For years she'd wished she'd been born second instead of first, and that her sister, Beth, had been graced with the family moniker. It was good she and Beth didn't have a brother. The poor guy probably would've been saddled with Orvis.

Still, she wasn't about to admit those feelings to Callahan. Damn him. Where did he get off, anyway, criticizing
her place of residence and then her name? The jerk.

The only good thing at the moment, as far as Shelby
could see, was that with every mile she was getting closer
to Heart Lake, the place she loved more than any other in
the world.

It wasn't the house itself that claimed her heart, although she knew and loved every square inch of the huge
old Victorian mansion. And it wasn't the lake itself with
its ever-changing water, which could be cold and gray in
the morning, but azure and warm by afternoon, or smooth
as glass only to turn wild with whitecaps in a sudden
wind. It wasn't the trees she climbed or the frogs and but-
terflies she chased or the thousands of marshmallows
she'd toasted over the years or her very first kiss under a
full moon on a long-ago Fourth of July, or . . .

It was all of that. And so much more.

Considering her love for the place, it seemed strange
that she hadn't been back there in this past year, after her
parents had sold their house in Evanston and moved per-
manently to Heart Lake following her father's retirement
from his law practice. She'd been horrendously busy this
past year, but that didn't seem like such a good excuse at
the moment. Even her sister Beth, who lived in California now, had been back to Heart Lake more recently than
Shelby had.

Poor Beth. Shelby may have been cursed with the family name, but her sister seemed to have been cursed with
bad luck from the cradle. She'd started out as a preemie
in an incubator. At age two she needed night braces on
her feet. Ten years later came the braces on her teeth. For

a while the poor kid was allergic to everything. The list went on and on. If life seemed a breeze to Shelby, it was more a battle waged daily for Beth.

Several years ago, when Beth was again between careers, it had been her dream to renovate the hundred-plus-year-old house from its rugs to its rafters, and then to turn the place into a bona fide as well as profitable Victorian bed and breakfast. Her parents didn't object. They were wild about the idea, and even subsidized the renovation. There was plenty of room, after all, for vacationing family as well as paying guests.

Bethie worked her ass off for the better part of a year—stripping, sanding, painting, staining, repairing old furnishings, acquiring new when the old stuff wouldn't do. She lived in a sea of turpentine, paint chips, fabric swatches, and plaster dust for month after month. Heart Lake froze over, melted, and froze over again. Then, finally, when she was done, the house looked so spectacular that her parents had promptly declared it their ideal retirement home. They'd recompensed their younger daughter handsomely for her efforts, but still . . .

In a righteous snit, Beth had run off to California with one of her painting subcontractors, yet another in a long string of bad choices in men. Undeterred, Mom and Dad had moved in, and as far as Shelby knew, they were loving every minute they spent in the big old Victorian hulk on the eastern shore of Heart Lake.

Given Callahan's proclivity for speed, even on fairly narrow two-lane state roads, they weren't all that far away from the lake right now. The rural landscape hadn't changed all that much during Shelby's thirty-four years. White frame farmhouses and double wides hunkered down amid the acreage of corn and sugar beets and fruit trees. Over there on the right, by the side of the road, was the dilapidated fruit stand where her mother would always stop on the way to the lake for tomatoes and cucumbers. Off in the distance she glimpsed the bulbous white water tower, which always was and probably always would be the tallest edifice in Shelbyville.

She was used to seeing everything colored a summer green rather than the vivid reds and yellows and golds that predominated in October. Even the occasional cows and pigs looked a little different. Maybe they were chilly. She imagined the house would look a little different, too, and quite spectacular nestled against its hillside of evergreens and birches that would seem less like trees now than glowing candles, their yellow flames flickering against a darkening sky.

Callahan reached out to turn on the headlights just then, making Shelby realize how late it really was. Since the clock on the dashboard registered a permanent twelve thirty-five, from an afternoon in 1980 no doubt, she squinted to check her watch. It was nearly six-thirty. Already? How could that be?

"Long day," the lieutenant said as if reading her mind.

She murmured her agreement. "Shelbyville's just down the road. The lake is only three or four miles beyond that. We're almost there."

"Great."

He sounded tired. Actually, he sounded like he was trying hard not to sound exhausted. It suddenly occurred to her that there was no way she could simply let Mick Callahan drop her off at the house and then send him on his way back to Chicago, a long and grueling five-hour trip. Even if he was a total jerk, Shelby didn't have it in her to be deliberately rude or cruel. And anyway, jerk or not, the guy had put himself in harm's way today on her behalf. She remembered the way he'd whisked her away from the explosion in front of her building, the way he'd sprung out of the car when her eager fans had accosted her not too long ago, and it hadn't escaped her attention that he'd spent an inordinate amount of time this afternoon consulting the rearview mirror just in case someone was following them. She was grateful to him for that. The least she could do was see that he got a good night's sleep before he went back to Chicago.

"Listen," she said. "Why don't you plan on staying at my folks' house tonight, Callahan. There's plenty of room."

He flashed her a quick, rather quizzical look, as if he were surprised by the offer, before he said, "Thanks. I'd appreciate that."

"Okay. Well, good. Then it's settled."

Except . . .

Oh, Lord. How was she going to explain him? There was no way she was going to tell her mother and father that he was a cop assigned to protect her because she was the target of a crazed letter bomber. In the first place, she didn't want to worry them, and in the second place—and in all honesty—she really, really didn't want to deal with their possible overreactions to her current plight.

Now she was almost glad she hadn't been able to reach them by phone earlier today, when she probably would've blurted out the truth. Her visit was going to be a surprise. That meant she had to come up with a legitimate reason why now, when her schedule was still jammed, she suddenly felt compelled to drop in at the old homestead. To drop in not alone, but with a gorgeous guy.

Knowing her parents, no matter how she explained her companion, whether it was a business associate, a reporter doing an extended interview of her, or merely a friend, they'd jump to the conclusion that he was her boyfriend. And the harder she insisted he wasn't, the more certain they would be that he was.

Strange. After her thirtieth birthday, it wasn't her own biological clock that had speeded up, but her parents'. They rarely missed an opportunity to inquire about her love life or to drop not-so-veiled hints about grandchildren. Her mother had even written a not very well disguised letter to Ms. Simon a year or so ago, pointing out the decrease in fertility in females over a certain age.

Okay. So she'd let them assume that Callahan was her boyfriend. That would work. Anything to keep them from worrying unnecessarily about this bomb deal.

"Do me a favor, will you, Callahan?"

"What's that?"

"I'd rather my folks didn't know about this letter bomb business," she said. "No point in getting them all upset. So let's not tell them you're a cop, okay?"

"Okay." There was a note of skepticism in his voice, a hint of reluctance, as if he clearly didn't relish subterfuge. "So if I'm not a cop, then what am I supposed to be?"

"Um. Well . . ." She closed her eyes a second and dragged in a breath. God. She hated this. Just hated it. "I was thinking about introducing you as my boyfriend."

"Your boyfriend!"

"Well, you don't have to sound all shocked and awed, for God's sake. It's not unthinkable, after all, that some-

body like me might find somebody like you attractive
or . . ."

He snorted. "Or that somebody like me might find
somebody like you the least bit fun to be around."

"I'm fun," she shot back.

"Oh, yeah? When?"

"Well, not right now. This isn't fun."

He rolled his eyes for about the seventeenth time
today. "You're telling me."

"Look. Will you just do it?" she shrieked, hating the
exasperated tone of her own voice. "Please."

"Yeah. Okay," he grumbled. "Whatever."

"Thank you." She pointed ahead. "Turn right at the
stop sign. The lake is just a mile or so down the road."

⌒

Well, maybe it was a mile or so to a crow, Mick soon
discovered. Once they turned off the blacktop, the final
half mile to the lake wound its way through a deep forest
of pines that looked damned near virgin timber to his un-
trained eyes. Hey, if Shelby Simon had to hide out for a
while, the forest primeval was probably the perfect
choice.

She was sitting forward in the passenger seat, her nose
practically pressed to the windshield, unable to disguise
her excitement over this homecoming.

"Turn here," she said, pointing right.

He swung the Mustang into a pebbled drive that
crunched under his tires, then finally pulled up in front of
some sort of fancy detached garage. Well, it seemed

fancy until his gaze encountered the house not too far away up a sloping lawn.

"Whoa," he murmured. "That's some house."

"It is, isn't it?" she responded, already halfway out of the car. "God, it's good to be back. I had no idea how much I missed it until just this minute."

The place was lit with spotlights that angled up from the front yard, making it nearly bright as day. He'd never seen anything like it in his life.

"What do you call it?" he asked, still eyeing the house while he opened the hatchback for the luggage. "Victorian?"

"Uh-huh. Well, technically, it's Italianate. At least I think so. My sister is the authority on that."

Maybe it seemed so big because it sat—loomed, actually—on the crest of the sloping lawn. The sucker had to be ten or twelve thousand square feet or more, all three stories of it. A deep, columned porch ran around the first floor. All the windows were tall and arched and elaborately framed. Every possible surface was carved, or turned, or somehow decorated. Mick half expected to see a sign out front saying "Historical Society."

Shelby, standing beside him, seemed to be regarding it with an awe similar to his own.

"I haven't been back since my sister finished all the renovations. I can't believe how fabulous it looks." She squinted. "Beth must've used five or six different colors of paint. Amazing. It used to be just a flat, fairly boring white with green trim."

Not anymore. In addition to a basic pale gray, Mick picked out touches of navy blue, maroon, and even some gold.

"Well, the lights are on, so I guess they're expecting you," he said, pulling her suitcase out of the trunk.

"Actually, they're not. I couldn't reach them this afternoon to tell them I was coming. But that's okay. They're pretty good about surprises."

"Oh, yeah?" He angled his head toward the front door where a female figure had just emerged and stood, fists on hips, staring their way. "If that's your mother, I'd say she doesn't look all that pleasantly surprised."

Actually, the woman looked pretty much like a deer in headlights.

Surprise!

CHAPTER FIVE

"Shelby!"

Her mother looked great, absolutely stunning tonight in a pair of beige wool slacks and one of her own designer sweaters, this one a gorgeous turtleneck concoction of nubby beige yarn and black silk ribbon. Nobody ever said Linda Simon didn't know how to dress to show off her perfect size six figure and to set off her meticulous blond pageboy. Aside from her fabulous appearance, though, Shelby couldn't quite discern the expression on her mother's face.

Was she surprised?

Taken aback?

Flummoxed?

All of the above, Shelby decided as she ascended the veranda stairs with Callahan a few steps behind her.

"Shelby!" her mother exclaimed again, coming forward to kiss her. "My goodness! What a surprise! Why didn't you call, honey?"

"I did, Mom, but nobody answered. I didn't leave a

message because . . . Well . . ." She sighed. "It's complicated."

At the moment her mother was peering over Shelby's shoulder, apparently getting a good look at the complication. "Hello," she said in the gracious, almost musical tone that always translated to Shelby's ears as "Thank you so much for your interest in my unmarried daughter."

"Mom, this is Mick Callahan, my . . . uh . . . friend."

"Welcome, Mick!"

He dropped Shelby's suitcase in order to take her mother's extended hand. "Mrs. Simon."

"Oh, please. Call me Linda. It's so nice to meet one of Shelby's . . ." She paused, as if carefully considering the meaning and importance of her vocabulary. "Friends," she finally said with a faint sigh, making it sound like suitor or gentleman caller anyway. "Well, come in, you two. Let's find a place to put your bags."

Shelby trudged through the front door, thinking maybe this hadn't been such a good idea. All of a sudden she was *trudging,* for heaven's sake. Not just walking or even gliding across her parents' threshold, but coming through the front door like a dorky, slump-shouldered teen. Why did she always forget that despite the fact that she was a successful and independent thirty-four-year-old, her mother had this strange, almost Wiccan ability to turn her instantly into some sort of petulant spinster?

Behind her, she heard Callahan breathe a quiet "Holy shit" as he entered the foyer and encountered the full effect of Victorian grandeur from the massive walnut hall tree on the right, the huge porcelain urn filled with peacock feathers on the left, and the half acre of inlaid black and white marble beneath his feet.

"Welcome to 1880," Shelby said with a laugh.

"Yeah. No kidding."

Her mother was already upstairs, flinging open doors and shutting them again, talking to herself.

"This way," Shelby said, leading Callahan up the staircase with its oriental runner and heavily carved walnut banister.

"Why don't you put your things in your old room, Shelby?" her mother said. "Then Mick can take Beth's old room, and you'll have the bathroom between. Or . . ." She lifted her designer clad shoulders in a shrug. "If you prefer being in a room together, I don't have any objections. It's really up to you."

For some strange reason, Shelby glanced at her body-guard *slash* boyfriend. The look on his face was as neutral as any human being could possibly manage. Not even a tiny tic to suggest how he might feel about sharing a bedroom with her. And why her brain was even entertaining the thought was a complete mystery to her.

"Separate is fine, Mom," she said. "No big deal. Really."

Really.

Perish the thought.

She took her big suitcase from Callahan's grasp and shoved it into the bedroom where she'd spent hundreds of summer nights. "Your room is two doors down the hall." She pointed.

"Great."

"Well, I'm going back downstairs while you kids get settled," her mother said. "Have you had dinner?"

"Don't worry about us, Mom. Okay? If we're hungry, we'll find something in the fridge."

"All right." She sighed again and turned to go downstairs, almost as if she couldn't get away fast enough.

"Where's Dad?" Shelby asked. It wasn't like him to hide out during any sort of homecoming, expected or not.

"He's out in the carriage house," her mother said as she continued her trot down the staircase.

There was something odd about her tone of voice. Shelby couldn't quite put her finger on it. Her mother was usually pretty straightforward rather than veiled or ironic or downright shifty. Shelby was about to comment on it when Callahan cleared his throat and asked, "Did you say three doors down?"

"No, two. Here. I'll show you."

Once downstairs, Linda Simon paused in the kitchen only long enough to pour herself a glass of chilled Chardonnay before she slipped outside and made a bee-line across the lawn to the carriage house. Ordinarily, she didn't drink after dinner—why consume a few hundred extra calories in stomped grapes when she far preferred a midnight snack of Häagen-Dazs butter pecan or Belgian chocolate?—but tonight a little liquid fortification seemed like a good idea. A very good idea.

She stood at the carriage-house door a moment, debating as she always did whether or not to knock, willing herself not to be foolish or impetuous, and at the same time wondering what she'd do if she just barged in unannounced and caught her husband with another woman.

In the five months since they'd been "separated," Harry had managed to garner the sympathy as well as the attention of every female who wasn't tied down within a radius of twenty or thirty miles. They made sweet, sympathetic noises. They brought him god-awful casseroles. They vied to do his mending and cleaning and ironing. God only knew what else they'd offered him in the way of soft shoulders to cry on and other consolations.

Linda sighed out loud, dispensed with knocking, and walked into the large, loftlike space that had once been used as servants' quarters on her family's property. She went first to the big-screen TV, turned off the Golf Channel, then plopped on the sofa beside her husband of thirty-five years.

"Hello, Beauty," he said in the rich baritone that was partly responsible for his amazing success in the courtroom over the years. If he was surprised to see her on his turf tonight, he managed to hide it with his usual aplomb. "Is that Chablis?"

"Chardonnay." Linda handed him the wineglass. "It's pretty good, actually. Try it."

While he sampled it, she couldn't help but notice that he needed a haircut. His sandy hair was threaded with silver these days, and even though it was curling over his shirt collar in back, it was thinning dramatically on top. She'd even caught him once last year, in front of the bathroom mirror, experimenting with a comb-over. Just the thought of that made her smile for a second.

"Your daughter's home," she said, taking back her glass.

He blinked. "Who? Beth?"

Linda shook her head. "Shelby. Didn't you see the car pull into the drive a while ago?"

"What? That old beater? I saw it, but I thought it was

one of your knitters from town, delivering more sweaters or scarves or whatever it is you're peddling this week."

She bit her tongue, refusing to rise to the bait. In her heart of hearts, she knew that Harry was enormously proud of her midlife success and of the fact that her designs were now featured not just in assorted boutiques in Chicago, but in most of the major department stores in the country. In the past few years, she had taken what was essentially a hobby of designing and knitting sweaters for herself and her daughters and friends, and turned it first into a cottage industry and then into a multimillion-dollar corporation with no apparent limits on its fiscal horizons.

Harry could count. He knew how well she had done.

Not only was she raking in money hand over fist, but she employed fourteen women in the vicinity, eight of them full-time, most of whom were now able to earn fairly decent wages just by staying home and knitting. Her company, Linda Purl Designs, had increased the gross national product or whatever it was of this rural county by a whopping fifteen percent. She even belonged to the Mecklin County Chamber of Commerce. Harry was proud of that, too.

But Harry was still a stubborn ass. And so, Linda supposed, was she.

"I haven't said anything to her yet," she said. "To Shelby, I mean. About us."

"Chicken." He laughed softly and his brown eyes warmed as he reached out to finger a lock of her hair. "Afraid of what our daughter will say when she finds out you kicked her poor old daddy out of the house?"

"I didn't kick you out," she said defensively. "I just

suggested a temporary *détente* for the sake of our sanity, Harry. A little sabbatical for both of us."

"Same difference."

She ignored his irritating snort, and said, "And to answer your question . . . No, I haven't told her anything because she only got here a little while ago. With a man, Harry."

His eyes widened perceptibly. "What kind of man?"

"The kind who wears pants," she said. "For heaven's sake. How do I know what kind of man he is? I only just met him."

"What does he do for a living? Does he work with Shelby at the paper?"

"I have no idea." Now it was her turn to snort. "Don't always be such a lawyer. Frankly, I don't care what the man does for a living. I'm just glad Shelby finally brought somebody home."

"Is he old? Young?" He scowled. "What the hell kind of man drives an old rust bucket like that thing in the driveway?"

"He's old enough," Linda said. "And pretty cute."

"Oh, yeah?" Her husband waggled his eyebrows and slid his arm around her shoulders. "You're pretty cute. You want to spend the night out here, Beauty?"

"Not the night." She took another sip of wine, then leaned into him, smiling. "Maybe just an hour or two."

⌒⌐

Without the benefit of an alarm clock, Shelby slept past nine the next morning. Rather than having an encounter of the embarrassing kind with Callahan in the bathroom that separated their rooms, she showered and dressed in a bathroom farther down the hall, then trotted downstairs to the kitchen.

Where the hell was everybody? she wondered while she got a pot of coffee going. She assumed everyone was still sleeping since she hadn't heard a peep or a clank of plumbing anywhere in the house. It wouldn't be so surprising that her father was sleeping in now that he was retired from his law practice. But her mother? Linda Simon, aka Linda Purl, of Linda Purl Designs, the newly created captain of industry and queen of knitters? Shelby would be shocked if her mother didn't snap out of bed at the crack of dawn every day.

She hadn't even seen her father yet. By the time she'd unpacked her things last night, the lights in the carriage house had gone out, and here inside the house, her parents' bedroom door was closed. It was a relief, actually, not to have to field a hundred questions about her unexpected homecoming and her mysterious companion.

The lieutenant had retired early last night, too, pleading weariness from the day's drive, although Shelby half suspected he was just avoiding her. "I think I'll just read awhile and doze off," he told her, his U. S. Grant biography tucked beneath his arm. "You don't need to be afraid. Just shout out if you need me."

"I won't," she'd answered. She had no intention of being afraid or shouting out.

While she listened to the coffeemaker gurgle and drip, she considered her current circumstances, tried once more to get really worried about some vague and faceless letter bomber, and then gave up. It was hard, if not impossible, to be back here at Heart Lake, the place she loved, and to feel threatened at the same time. This was home, after all. It was the place she'd always felt so safe.

When the coffee was done, cup in hand, she wandered through the dining room, the foyer, the formal parlor, toward the sunroom where a wall of windows presented a stunning view of Heart Lake. It was absolutely gorgeous this morning, smooth as a mirror reflecting fiery red maples and flaming yellow birches and evergreens. The room itself was gorgeous, too, thanks to Beth's decorating talents. She had gotten rid of the ragged rattan stuff their grandparents had installed in the forties and fifties— the furniture first Linda, and then Beth and Shelby had abused over many a summer—and replaced it with wonderfully intricate wicker pieces and Tiffany-like lamps and an oriental rug that had the most amazing shades of crimson and navy and cream.

Settling into one of the deep cushions on the sofa, Shelby sipped her coffee and gazed out at the lake. All the summer people were long gone by this time in October. Their cottages would be battened down for the coming winter. That's what happened with this house every Labor Day weekend before her parents had decided to make it their permanent residence.

She was squinting, trying to see the Mendenhalls' place through the trees on the north side of the lake, when something vaguely purple flashed on the edge of her vision. Then, by the time she had turned to focus on the nearby shoreline, all she could see was a whirl of arms and legs splashing in the water. What idiot, she wondered, would even contemplate swimming at this time of year, much less run full tilt into water that couldn't have been more than a bone-chilling fifty degrees?

The splashing and the flailing body parts continued for a few seconds, moving from the shallows toward the deeper parts. Then there was a tremendous splash, and then . . . Nothing. Just stillness. The surface of the lake smoothed back to its former mirrored appearance.

Shelby put her coffee cup down and moved closer to the window, staring out, wondering if she'd only imagined the idiot swimmer. Maybe she was hallucinating, having finally succumbed to the stress of the last twenty-four hours. Maybe . . . Oh, God. She wasn't hallucinating. There really had been somebody out there. She was certain. Maybe the idiot in the lake had suffered a massive coronary the minute he hit the frigid water. Should she call 911? Or maybe . . .

Callahan came up out of the water like some sort of Greek god—half dolphin and half man. Sleek. Sexy as hell. Water sluiced down his broad shoulders and shimmered over his naked chest. He shook his head, and his wet hair shot beads of bright silver into the air around him. For just a second, Shelby thought that she might have her own massive coronary right then because her heart was sort of floundering inside her rib cage and her breathing seemed uneven, more in than out, as if the air had suddenly, somehow thinned.

"Nice," her mother's voice sounded just behind her. "A keeper, Shelby, if you ask me."

Startled, Shelby whirled around to see Linda Simon's gaze trained where her own had been a moment before. She felt like a kid caught with her hand in the cookie jar, or more exactly, like a kid caught under the covers with a flashlight and a copy of *Playgirl*.

"Mother! You shouldn't sneak up on people that way."

"I didn't, honey. You were just preoccupied." She smiled slyly and her blond pageboy bobbed as she gestured out the window with her chin. "He's very nice, your . . . uh . . . friend."

Shelby, her coronary now a mere flutter, reclaimed her coffee cup and took a gulp of the lukewarm brew. "That's all he is. Really, Mom. A friend. A friend who was *nice* enough to drive me up here. He'll be going back to Chicago today. Soon."

"Oh. That's too bad." Her mother's smile fizzled out. "I've just come from the market with some really nice steaks and a special wine for our dinner this evening."

"Well, you should have asked me first before you planned a menu." And there she went, sounding thirteen and petulant again. Worse, she sounded ungrateful. "I'm sorry, Mom. Hey. It doesn't matter if Callahan isn't here. You and Dad and I will enjoy the steaks and the wine. We'll have a wonderful dinner, just the three of us. I'll even cook, if you'd like."

Neither Shelby's apology nor the offer to fix dinner succeeded in removing the lines of anxiety in her mother's face or the worried slant of her mouth. "Have you talked to your father this morning?" she asked, using that odd tone again that Shelby had heard the night before.

"No," she said. "I haven't even seen him. I figured he must be sleeping in now that he's a gentleman of leisure." Her gaze drifted briefly, surreptitiously to the window in search of the wet Greek god. "Why?" she asked.

"Oh, no particular reason. I just wondered." Her mother shrugged. "Well, I'd better get those steaks into the refrigerator."

"What's going on, Mom? You've been sounding . . . Oh, I don't know. Weird. Kind of furtive."

"Furtive! Oh, for heaven's sake. Nothing's going on, Shelby. Don't be silly. I just wondered if you'd seen your father yet."

Shelby didn't press her, but rather watched her mother turn and pick up a bundle from a wicker table near the sun-room door.

"What's that, Mom?"

"This? Just mail. I stopped by the post office while I was in town. They don't deliver out here after Labor Day, you know. It's pretty inconvenient sometimes, I have to say, with all the mail I get for the company. Especially when the weather's bad."

While she spoke, her mother was riffling through the assortment of envelopes in her hand. One of them, Shelby noticed, was a large, lopsided manila affair with an ungodly amount of stamps attached to it. She suddenly thought about something one of the postal inspectors had mentioned the day before when cautioning her about letter bombs, about odd-shaped or lopsided packages with too much postage, ones that often emitted funny odors.

And no sooner had the thought flickered through her brain than her mother lifted the manila envelope to her nose and said, "Now this is odd. It smells just like . . . ."

Shelby didn't let her finish. With a speed she didn't even know she possessed, she grabbed the envelope out of her mother's grasp, threw it to the far side of the sunroom, and shoved her mother through the sunroom door.

"Shelby!" Linda Simon shrieked.

"Get out of the house, Mom. Hurry." She spoke on the

run, clutching her mother's arm, dragging the startled woman along through the parlor. "I'll explain outside."

"But, Shelby . . . !"

"Hush. Hurry. Faster."

She propelled her mother across the slick marble floor of the foyer and practically pushed her out the front door onto the veranda . . .

. . . and into Mick Callahan's wet, bare arms.

"Whoa," he said, trying to keep her balance as well as his own.

"There's a bomb in the house," Shelby screamed.

"Where?" Immediately he moved her mother aside, and started into the house. "Tell me where."

"In the sunroom. In a big manila envelope. Here." She took a step forward. "I better show you."

"Stay here, goddammit," he shouted. "Just tell me where."

"It's through the parlor. Just keep going left. The big room with all the windows that overlook the lake. I pitched the envelope in a corner."

"Okay. Stay here. Both of you. I mean it."

The last she saw of the lieutenant was a pair of bare feet, a glistening wet back, and damp, low-riding jeans with a suggestion of purple at the waistband as he went racing through the foyer.

"Shelby Simon!" Her mother's hand was splayed across the bosom of her beautiful alpaca sweater and she was leaning against a post of the veranda, breathing hard and blinking furiously. "What in the name of God is going on?"

All of a sudden Shelby realized that she, too, was blinking furiously while standing there with her heart lodged in her throat, fully expecting to hear a gigantic explosion coming from the other side of the house and then watching as little pieces of mail and little scraps of blue jeans and purple briefs rained down upon the lawn.

It was all her fault. If only she'd taken this all a bit more seriously. If only . . .

"Relax. It's okay," Callahan said as he came striding toward the front door with something in his hand.

"What the hell is that?" she asked, feeling relieved and confused and foolish all at the same time.

"Dunno. Some kind of yarn, I think." He lifted it to his nose. "Smells like Chanel No. 5."

"I'll take that." Her mother pushed past her and plucked the skein from his hand. "This is a very expensive linen and silk blend I ordered from Marseille, France. Shelby, what's wrong with you? What were you thinking?"

"Oh, I don't know," she sighed as she edged a hip onto the porch railing. *Maybe that somebody's trying really hard to kill me.* "I don't know what I was thinking, Mom. I guess I overreacted. That's probably why I need this vacation." She managed a limp little "Ha ha" for punctuation.

Her mother simply stared at her. "Are you all right, honey?"

"Yes. Jeez, I'm fine, Mom," she insisted. "I've just been working hard. It's nothing a little time off won't fix. Honest."

With a little *hmpf* to indicate that she didn't believe a word of it and had every intention of getting to the bottom of this later, Linda Simon took her fragrant yarn into the house, leaving Shelby and the lieutenant on the porch.

"Sorry," she said from her perch on the railing. "I guess I really did overreact."

He didn't say anything as he reached for the shirt he'd been using as a towel and had flung aside when all this madness began. "Don't apologize," he said, stabbing his arms into the plaid flannel sleeves. "Your instincts were good. That envelope did look pretty suspicious with all that postage."

Now she was quiet for a minute watching his strong fingers work the buttons on the front of his shirt. Then she sighed again and tried with all her might to keep her lip from quivering when she said, "Okay, Callahan. You win."

"Excuse me?"

"I'm scared. I'm really scared."

It seemed an odd time for him to smile, but that's what he did. And then he said, "Good."

CHAPTER SIX

To go or not to go. That was Mick's dilemma an hour after the exploding yarn incident as he was driving into the town of Shelbyville in order to alert the local postmaster of possible problems with the Simons' mail.

He didn't like doing a half-assed job at anything, but especially with police work, and he didn't feel good about just dropping Shelby Simon off up here on the evergreen fringes of nowhere with nobody around qualified to protect her. He hadn't met her father yet, but she'd mentioned that he was an attorney, and from Mick's experience with the legal system, he assumed that the man probably wasn't capable of much more than a good tongue-lashing when it came to defending someone.

The town of Shelbyville was barely the size of a square block in Chicago, so it wasn't hard finding the post office right next door to the volunteer fire department. The postmaster turned out to be the postmistress, Thelma Watt, a woman who looked about ninety-eight years old, fragile as a china teacup, and stubborn as a mule, at least when it came to procedures at her facility.

"Been doing this for forty years, sonny, and doing it damned well if I do say so myself," she told him while she poked letters into slots behind her counter. "Nothing gets past me. I'll tell you what else. I had a healthy respect for suspicious packages long before anybody ever even heard of anthrax, too."

He told her to keep up the good work, then asked where he could find the chief law enforcement officer in town, but it turned out they'd fired the last constable for embezzlement a dozen or so years ago, and the town now relied on the county force, headquartered in Mecklin, the county seat.

"What you want to do," Thelma told him, leaning across her counter and whispering as if passing along top-secret information, "is talk to the private security man the folks out at Heart Lake have hired. Fella by the name of Sam Mendenhall. He lives there in a little cabin on the north shore."

"I'll do that," Mick said. "Thanks."

He went back to his car, parked on Shelbyville's only street, thinking that even a rent-a-cop on the premises would make it easier for him to feel confident about returning to Chicago, leaving Ms. Shelby Simon to her fate. At least she was scared now. That was a step in the right direction. It would make her more cautious.

She'd been shaking like a little leaf and on the verge of tears in the aftermath of the yarn incident. Mick had almost reached out to take her in his arms, before reminding himself that such a response was pretty inappropriate for the Chicago PD. He'd done his job, after all, by getting her safely out of town. He'd alerted the local post office and felt more or less confident that no letter bomb would get past Thelma Watt. Soon he'd put this Mendenhall guy, the rent-a-cop, on notice to keep an eye out for anything or anyone suspicious around the Simon place. What more could he do?

Sitting in his car, he phoned his captain, Rita Bruzzi, to get an update on the investigation, but the only news was bad news. Apparently none of the letter bombs had any latent prints other than those of the victims who were the last to handle them before they exploded. One guy had died from his injuries in Buffalo. The other victims were stable. But basically, nobody knew anything more than they had the day before about the bomber or his motive.

Mick swore, and then suddenly, out of nowhere, he heard himself saying, "I've got some vacation time coming, Captain. Any problem with my taking it now?"

Rita nearly choked on the other end of the line. "Did I hear you right, Callahan? You want vacation time? Like the druggies won't take over the streets if you're not there to prevent it? Like Chicago won't burn to the ground again? Wait a minute. Hold on. There must be something wrong with this phone."

He could hear her fingernails tapping on the voice box and the sound of static rasping in her throat. Real cute. Very funny. A little humor in the workplace.

"Am I speaking to the same Mick Callahan who didn't even take a full day off for his wife's funeral?" she asked.

"Kiss my ass, Rita."

"I can't if you're on vacation." She laughed. "I'll fill out the paperwork for you as soon as we hang up. Take as long as you want, Mick. God knows you deserve it."

"Thanks. Listen. Keep my cell number handy, and

keep me apprised of any developments in this letter bomb case, okay?"

"Oh. I get it now. It's a *working* vacation." She laughed again. "I take it little Ms. Simon has gotten under your skin."

Mick swore as he broke the connection and then shoved the phone back in the glove compartment. It wasn't like that. It wasn't personal, for crissake. He was just trying to keep Shelby Simon from getting her pretty head blown off.

If it was personal—which it wasn't—then maybe it served as a kind of atonement for earlier sins, a way of doing penance for not being there two years ago to help Julie during a purse snatching that would probably have been pled down to a mere misdemeanor if his wife hadn't decided to fight back. She died instantly, damn her, still hanging on to the fucking purse that contained a grand total of four dollars and eighty-seven cents.

That old, undiluted anger boiled up inside him, and Mick slapped the heel of his hand on the steering wheel. He didn't think about Julie that often anymore. At least, he tried not to. As soon as a memory tempted him, he'd force it out of his brain, usually by drowning it with booze. For some reason, though, ever since he laid eyes on Shelby Simon, those memories were making a vicious and very unwelcome comeback. He told himself it was probably another pretty compelling reason to point the Mustang south and head back to Chicago.

Instead, he made a U-turn in the middle of Main Street, and drove back to Heart Lake.

The headquarters of Linda Purl Designs, its home office and veritable hub, was in the third-floor ballroom of the huge old house. Nobody had attended an actual ball there for eighty years or more, and to Shelby's knowledge, the last time anyone had danced on its beautiful inlaid parquet floor was when she and Beth had sneaked two boys and a boom box up there one summer during high school.

As she climbed the stairs to the third floor, she wondered who she had been with that long-ago night. Oh, yeah. It was Stuart Borman, who was on his way to Princeton at the end of that summer and who was currently doing time in a federal prison for some junk bond scam. She knew because he'd written a long letter to Ms. Simon two or three years ago, hoping she'd publish his arrogant, self-serving apology in her column. Fat chance.

Shelby didn't need to wrack her brain to remember who her sister's date was that night up here in the ballroom. It was Sam Mendenhall. For Beth, it was always Sam.

"Shelby!" her mother said, looking up from a yarn color chart on her worktable. "I thought you went for a walk."

She shook her head. She'd meant to do that, but then she got to thinking about her schedule for the fall and had decided it would be a good idea to cancel all her appointments and appearances at least for the next two weeks.

"Mind if I use your computer, Mom, to get in touch with the office?" she asked.

"Help yourself, honey. I might even put you to work since Terrible Tina, my assistant, took the whole day off for a half-hour dentist appointment."

"Tina Jensen? Does she still live around here? Jeez, I haven't seen her in—what?—twelve or fifteen years."

"She's Tina Cortland now. She married that boy who used to mow our grass. Remember? The one with the ring through his eyebrow?"

Shelby not only remembered, but she could feel her stomach turn at the mere mention of the Cortland boy's body piercing. She shivered. "Does he still have it?"

"I doubt it. He sells Toyotas in Mecklin now. Tina tells me he's doing rather well."

"That's good."

Shelby plopped into the leather chair behind her mother's big antique desk, swiveled around twice, and decided this was really a fabulous office. One entire wall was fitted out with wooden diamond-shaped bins where skeins of yarn in every possible color and texture were stored according to a system that probably made sense to the artistic Linda Purl but that completely eluded Shelby at the moment.

Her mother's treasured dressmaker dummies—Lucy and Ethel—stood in a corner, each of them wearing a gorgeous original design. In addition to several floor lamps and desk lamps, she was pleased to see that the old Venetian glass and brass chandeliers still hung from the high ceiling. Her great-grandmother had bought them in Italy and had them shipped home via the White Star Line to New York and then by train to Michigan. It was nice, Shelby thought, being surrounded by so many family heirlooms, even if she didn't appreciate them half as much as Beth always had.

She sighed and turned her attention to the computer screen, happy to see that her mother was already on-line.

It was easy to bring up the *Daily Mirror*'s Web site, but when she tried to log in to the restricted employees' section, her password kept coming up as incorrect.

"That can't be right," she muttered, typing the seven-letter, case-sensitive password again, more carefully, and once again being refused. "Dammit."

"What's wrong, sweetie?" her mother asked.

"I can't log in to the computer at work for some reason. Would you mind if I called them, Mom?"

"Go ahead. But use the third line. I'm expecting a call on line one any minute now about a late delivery to Neiman Marcus."

"I didn't know your stuff was in Neiman Marcus," Shelby said, sounding as impressed as she felt.

"There are a lot of things you don't know, dear." Her mother smiled inscrutably.

"Like what?" Shelby asked.

"Well . . ." her mother began, only to be cut off by the ringing of the phone. "That's Neiman's, probably. I'll take it over here." She picked up the receiver on her worktable and enunciated her name in the crisp, no-nonsense voice she tended to use for business.

With her curiosity put on hold, Shelby punched the button for line three and then the numbers for the *Daily Mirror*. It wasn't until the phone on the other end started ringing that it suddenly dawned on her that she had dialed her own extension. How stupid was that? But just as she was about to hang up, somebody answered. The female voice was familiar, but Shelby couldn't quite place it.

"Good morning," she said, her own crisp, businesslike voice reminding her more than a little bit of her mother's tone. "To whom am I speaking?"

"Kellie Carter," the voice, equally crisp, replied. "To whom am *I* speaking?"

Shelby's first instinct was to wonder why her intern was answering her phone. Her second instinct was gratitude that *somebody* was taking her calls.

"Kellie!" she said. "It's Shelby."

"Oh, I'm so sorry I didn't recognize your voice. How are you? *Where* are you? We've all been so worried."

"I'm fine, except I can't get my password to work. The server isn't down again, is it?"

"Gosh. Not that I know of."

Shelby couldn't help but smile. Kellie was the only person she knew who was capable of saying "Gosh" and having it sound perfectly unhokey.

"Okay," she said. "Well, I'll try again later. No biggie."

"Is there anything I can do for you, Shelby? Do you need anything?"

"No, thanks, Kellie. You're such a sweetie."

"I just feel so sorry for you."

"You're a doll," Shelby said. "I'll talk to you later."

She hung up, and then sat there biting her lip, feeling sorrier for herself than Kellie possibly could. Jeez. She felt once again as if she'd been fired, forcibly removed from her office, from her home, and even from her city. It just wasn't fair.

Twelve years of writing her column, of giving advice—all of it good, if she did say so herself—of working tirelessly to see that the name Ms. Simon Says became a household word similar to Dear Gabby, and now what? What was she supposed to do? Sleep late and take walks and live in fear of every envelope and package in the house? For how long?

Picking up the phone again, she carefully punched in Hal Stabler's extension.

"Stabler," the managing editor growled.

"Hal, it's Shelby," she growled back. "I hate this. I really, really hate it. I want to come back."

"You do, and I'll fire your ass," he said, "if it doesn't get blown up first."

"Well, how long is it going to be? Are they making any progress on this bomb thing?"

"It's only been twenty-four hours, Shelby."

That was twenty-four too many in her opinion. "What can I do to help?"

"Just stay the fuck away. You hear me? The police and the feds are on this, plus I've got four guys on the story, including Derek McKay, and nobody's as good as he is running down leads."

Shelby sighed "Well, that's good to know. Maybe I'll give Derek a call and . . ."

"He flew east to get a look at a couple of the other offices that were targeted. Probably be back tomorrow or the next day. I'll let him know you want to talk to him."

"Thanks, Hal. Oh. And one other thing. Is the server down? I can't get my E-mail or access my files."

"Relax, Shelby, will you? Just consider this a vacation. You've earned it. Where the hell are you, anyway?"

"In Michigan. At my parents' place."

"Okay. Stay in touch. Gotta go. Bye."

She sat with the dead phone in her hand, thinking there was something else she'd meant to tell him, but damned if she could remember what it was. Well, at least Derek was on the story. When the cops hadn't been able to crack the West Side Strangler case, it was Derek who uncovered the fact that the five victims had all lived in the same apartment building, going as far back as 1972. Except it took him four years to make the connection.

Dammit. Shelby didn't have four years to waste. Four days, maybe. Four weeks, tops. After that she didn't care what anybody said. She was going back to work if she had to write her column, print it herself, and sell it on a street corner.

It made her feel a little better, putting a deadline on this whole bizarre business. She stood up, stretched, and pantomimed to her mother, who was still on the phone, that she was going out for a walk.

Sam Mendenhall lived in a prefab log cabin on the north side of Heart Lake. The cabin sat well back from the shoreline in a grove of birch trees whose sunlit yellow leaves cast a mellow light through the kitchen window where Mick sat trying to finish a cup of warmed-over coffee.

The rent-a-cop turned out to be younger than Mick had expected. For some reason he'd pictured him as a potbellied geezer in his mid sixties. But this guy was probably Mick's age, thirty-eight, give or take a year or two. He was taller by an inch or two, probably six-two to Mick's even six feet, and probably outweighed Mick by twenty or thirty pounds. If he'd been a boxer, Sam Mendenhall would've been in the light heavyweight category. He had a nose that looked as if it had been broken enough to make boxing, or some other contact sport, a significant part of his past.

After his first sip, Mick had decided the coffee was shit, but he was still withholding judgment on the security guy himself, knowing full well that nobody could assess a man's skills and competence much less his courage after a mere ten-minute conversation.

Even so, he didn't need a thermometer to tell him that the guy's temperature spiked the second Shelby Simon's name was mentioned. The reaction was clear and visceral, but its meaning wasn't, and Mick couldn't tell if Sam Mendenhall had the basic hots for Ms. Simon or if he was pissed at her for some unknown reason. Great detective that he was, and having spent the past twenty-four hours with the woman in question, Mick guessed it could have been both anger and lust that was visible in the man's expression.

While he sipped the shitty coffee and gave Sam a thumbnail sketch of the letter bomb situation, Mick was still trying to make up his mind whether to stay here at Heart Lake or to return to Chicago. Just because he'd put in for vacation time didn't necessarily mean he was obliged to take it.

His inclination at the moment was to stay because he didn't have complete confidence in Sam's ability to protect Shelby if the need should arise. Mick didn't know what the problem was with the security guard. But there was definitely a problem. Sam looked fit enough, but the guy was slightly crippled and didn't seem to be able to walk without a cane or without a certain amount of hard-to-conceal pain. Mick knew that if something happened and if Shelby called the security guard in a panic, it would take him at least a couple critical minutes to make his way out to his battered Jeep, not to mention to drive the distance around the lake to the Simon place on the east shore.

"More coffee?" Sam Mendenhall hobbled from the stove to the kitchen table with the old-fashioned, dented metal coffeepot in his free hand, the one without the cane.

Mick shook his head, covered his cup with his hand, and then watched while Sam poured more liquid tar into his own empty cup. Jesus. The guy's taste buds were probably crippled, just like his leg. Then, while Mick watched him, the man wasn't able to fully suppress another grimace of pain as he lowered himself back into his chair. Curious about the injury, Mick was about to inquire, but Sam spoke first.

"So, when are you going back to Chicago?" he asked.

"Dunno." That was the truth, but Mick tacked on a convenient falsehood. "I need to talk to my captain and see if she wants to extend my assignment. Whenever I do go, I'll give you a heads-up. I can keep you posted on the investigation, too, from Chicago."

"Yeah. That'd be great. Don't worry about it if you don't have time. I've got a few contacts with the feds, so it shouldn't be too hard to stay on top of it."

Mick nodded agreeably even as he was thinking that those contacts were probably nothing more than a brief acquaintance with one or two lowly field agents in Grand Rapids.

"I've got some out-of-town business coming up," Sam said, "but I'll make sure she's covered in my absence. You don't have to worry about it."

"Great."

Sam angled his head in the direction of the eastern shore. "Linda and Harry need to be aware of this situation. Are they?"

"No. She didn't want to worry them."

"Let them worry," Sam said. "I'll apprise them of the problem if you don't want to do it."

"I'll do it." Actually Mick had been debating about that, too. He still wasn't sure if he wanted to override Shelby's wishes in regard to her parents.

"Good because . . ." Sam's eyes narrowed as he gazed out the window. "Speak of the devil."

Mick leaned forward to get a better view around the edge of the burlap curtains. The devil was dressed in skintight jeans and a turtleneck sweater that curved and clung and did things he never knew a sweater could do. In the yellow light, her hair took on a reddish cast. She was still far enough away that Mick couldn't discern her expression, but her walk was purposeful even as it was sexy as hell, enough to inspire a definite thickening in his blood.

He glanced at the man across the table to see if he was similarly moved by the approaching vision of Ms. Shelby Simon.

Nope. Sam Mendenhall just looked pissed, and sounded it as well when he swore under his breath and then said, "Guess we better go see what she wants."

⟋⟍

As Shelby approached the Mendenhall place, memories of past summers nearly brought tears to her eyes. My God. They'd been impossibly young and incredibly stupid back then. All of them. She and Beth and Sam and whatever young swain she might have had her eye on at the time.

She thought about that final summer they were all together, and wondered now if she'd do again what she did then—advise seventeen-year-old Beth to go to college rather than elope with nineteen-year-old Sam. He had signed up for the army and was headed for Fort Benning, GA, hot to make his little Beth his bride before he left until Shelby intervened, convincing her sister that it was in her best interest to wait at least a year or two.

"If Sam really loves you, he'll wait," Ms. Simon had said. She could still almost hear herself, such a wise big sister, so sure, so absolutely certain of her own rock-solid and sensible advice.

But then Sam didn't wait, did he? He'd barely gotten out of boot camp before sending Beth a Dear Jane letter, telling her he'd married a girl he met down there in Georgia.

Then Beth hated both Sam and Shelby, and Shelby hated Sam, and neither of them knew how Sam felt about anything because neither Shelby nor Beth ever saw him again.

What a big fucking mess.

The mere sight of the Mendenhall cabin up ahead brought it all back with a vengeance now.

And then the sight of two men coming out the door onto the cabin's little front porch made her stop dead in her tracks. Mick Callahan, of course, was a cinch to recognize, not only from his ratty jeans and stupid duct-taped vest, but also from the way her heartbeat stuttered the moment she saw him.

But the other man? Who . . . ?

Shelby squinted in the sunlight, bringing the man more clearly into focus, believing at first that it was Mr. Mendenhall because he looked a lot like Sam's father and because the man moved like a much older person. He even used a cane.

But wait. Hadn't her mother told her that Mr. Mendenhall passed away a few years ago?

She walked forward, stumbling once over a circle of stones outlining an old fire pit, still staring, beginning to feel oddly out of sync with the time and place.

Was that . . . ? No. It couldn't be *Sam*. It just couldn't be.

Could it?

The closer she got to the cabin, the more it seemed she was having an out-of-body experience or perhaps time traveling.

Up on the porch, he leaned on the cane and stretched out his right hand toward her. "Shelby Simon," he said, grinning. "Still giving advice, I see."

"Sam?"

"Yeah."

"Oh, my God."

His hand was still reaching out. "It's okay, Shelby. Come on up here. I'm not mad anymore." He laughed. "At least not enough to kill you."

CHAPTER SEVEN

"Mother, did you know that Sam Mendenhall is back? Here. At the lake."

Linda Simon looked up from the graph paper spread out on her worktable and saw her daughter's anxious face with its flashing eyes and flushed cheeks. Only seconds earlier she'd heard Shelby's footsteps stomping up to her third-floor office and Linda had thought the proverbial shit was about to hit the ballroom fan. Thank God this fuss was going to be about Sam, she thought, and not about herself and Harry.

"Of course, dear," she replied in her calmest, most maternal voice. "I know he's back. In fact, I was the one who suggested we hire him as our security person a few months ago. Why do you ask?"

"Why do I ask?" her daughter shrieked, lifting her hands toward the chandelier over her head. "Why do I ask? My God, Mom. Does Beth know about this?"

"About Sam being back? No, I don't think so," Linda said, knowing damn well that her younger daughter didn't have a clue. "I think Beth had already left for California when he arrived."

"And it never occurred to you that she might want to know?" Shelby asked accusingly. "That Sam's back after all these years. He's back and he's unattached."

"No, Shelby, it didn't occur to me. Furthermore, I doubt that your sister would be the least bit interested considering that she's living with someone at the moment."

"That painter guy," Shelby said with a snort and a dismissive wave of her hand. "She may be living with him, Mom, but she's still single. And so is Sam."

"Yes, and they don't need you poking your nose in their lives, either, Ms. Simon. Take *my* advice for a change, Shelby, and mind your own business."

Hoping to bring the conversation to an end, Linda returned her attention to the table and the sweater design she'd been drafting on her graph paper, as if to say *I'm working here.* Maybe her daughter would take the hint. Or not. God love her, Shelby could be pretty dense when she was on a mission, which she apparently was at the moment. She had inherited her perseverance, otherwise known as mule-headed stubbornness, from her father.

"What's wrong with Sam's leg, Mom?"

Linda looked up again. "Pardon me?" she said, pretending she hadn't heard the question perfectly.

"What's wrong with Sam's leg? He limps and uses a cane."

"Yes, I noticed that. I have no idea what the problem is."

Actually, she knew exactly what the problem was, but she'd promised Terry Mendenhall, Sam's mother, whom she'd known for nearly all of her fifty-six years, that she wouldn't breathe a word about his injury or the place on the other side of the globe where it had happened. Sam, it seemed, not only didn't want to talk about it, but also apparently wasn't at liberty to disclose any details.

"Shelby, sweetie, I've really got a ton of work to finish here." She glared down at her design in progress now, picked up a red pencil, and began coloring squares. "Can we talk about this later?"

Miraculously, just then the phone rang, and after Linda answered and began a conversation about fabric care and dry cleaning versus hand washing, she offered her daughter a helpless shrug, indicating that she would be on the phone for a while.

Shelby sighed, waved good-bye, and went back downstairs.

Undoubtedly to call her sister. She was such a buttinski.

~

Shelby sat sideways in one of the Adirondack chairs on the lawn, her legs draped over one of the flat wooden arms, while she entered Beth's cell phone number into her own cell phone. The two of them had never greeted each other with normal telephone etiquette. They just started talking. So when Beth said "Hello," Shelby replied, "Guess who's back at Heart Lake?"

"Shelby, I'm on a ladder right now, painting trim on a second-story window. I don't have time to play Twenty Questions."

"Guess who's back at the lake?"

"You," Beth said.

Shelby rolled her eyes and raked her fingers through her hair. "No, I mean other than me."

"What are you doing back at the lake?" her sister asked.

"It's a long story. Dammit, Beth. Guess who's here."

Her sister was silent a moment, and then said, "You know I'm up so high here that I can actually see San Francisco Bay. Which should give you a good indication of how badly I'll be injured when I fall off this fucking ladder, Shelby. Can we talk later?"

"Sam," Shelby said.

"What?"

"Sam's back. Here. At the lake."

Beth didn't respond, so Shelby asked, "Did you hear me?"

"I heard you," she muttered.

"He's not only back. He's not married anymore."

Again, there was silence on the other end of the line, but Shelby was pretty sure it wasn't because her sister had fallen off the ladder.

"Beth, he's back," she said softly, with just a hint of urgency, "and he's single."

"He's dead to me."

"Oh, for God's sake. Don't be so melodramatic."

"I don't want to talk about this now, okay? Don't call me. I'll call you when I have time. Give Mom and Dad my love. Hey, are they back together yet?"

"What do you mean, are they back together yet?" Shelby asked at the same time that her gaze drifted across the lawn to the driveway, where Callahan was climbing out of his Mustang. Her heart did that funny thing again, like stubbing its toe.

Meanwhile, in San Francisco, Beth was saying ". . . about five or six months ago. He moved into the carriage house. I figured since you're there, you finally knew."

Shelby was watching Callahan's lean-hipped, tight-jean progress across the lawn toward her, only half listening to her sister. "You figured I knew what?"

He edged a hip onto the arm of the adjacent Adirondack chair, cocked one leg, crossed his arms, and looked down at her while Beth was saying, "I figured since you're up there that you know that Mom and Dad are separated. Or at least they were. I haven't talked to either one of them in a couple weeks."

"Separated." Shelby echoed the word as if she had no idea what it meant or even what language it was. Portuguese, maybe. Or Urdu. "What do you mean?"

"Listen," her sister said, sounding more than a little irritated, "go ask Mom, will you? Or ask Dad. It's clouding up here and I've got to get this trim done. I'll call you later in the week."

Beth hung up, leaving Shelby blinking stupidly while she listened to the dial tone.

"What's the matter?" Callahan asked. "Bad news?"

"You could say that. My sister just told me that my parents are separated. Separated! Or at least that they were." She snapped her cell phone closed. "I can't believe this."

She swung her legs off the arm of the chair and stood up. "I don't know why nobody ever tells me anything," she muttered as she started up the lawn toward the house.

At her back she heard a chuckle, followed by "Maybe they don't want your advice."

Shelby would've flipped him the bird over her shoulder, but she wasn't sure whether or not that constituted threatening an officer of the law.

Her mother wasn't up in the ballroom. Instead, there was a note propped on her desk that read "Gone to town. Back around six."

Her father wasn't in the carriage house, where "Gone fishing" was scribbled on a small chalkboard near the refrigerator.

Thoroughly confounded now, as well as supremely pissed, Shelby stalked back to the grouping of lawn chairs where the lieutenant was still sitting, gazing placidly out at the lake.

She plopped in the chair beside his and muttered, "Nobody's home."

"They're probably avoiding you."

She aimed a glare at him, but then almost had to laugh in spite of her current mood. "You're probably right."

What did Beth know anyway? Unlike Shelby, she didn't spend much time worrying about other people's problems. Maybe she'd just invented that separation business to get back at Shelby for mentioning Sam or to punish her once more for the advice that broke them up. Bethie could be pretty unforgiving.

In an attempt to forget the whole thing, she forced herself to smile. "Hey! Want to go for a walk, Callahan? Or a drive? There's some pretty countryside around here." She leaned over to look at his watch. It was almost noon. "Oh, wait. I almost forgot. What time did you plan on leaving?"

"I'm not," he said. "I talked to my captain earlier, and they've extended my assignment. I'm going to hang around here for a while. A couple more days, anyway."

"Oh." Thank God that innocuous little word had popped out of her mouth instead of the "Woo hoo" that she was feeling. On the other hand, maybe this wasn't such good news. Maybe she should be feeling scared again.

"Does that mean that they think this situation's gotten worse?" she asked. "Do they know something?"

He shook his head. "Nope. Just taking the standard precautions under the circumstances. It's no big deal."

"Well, that's a relief." Phew.

He levered out of his chair and held his hand out to her. "How 'bout if I take you out to lunch? I'm famished."

"Oh, God," she moaned. "I haven't fed you. Some hostess I am."

"That's okay. I'm not exactly a guest. Come on."

∽

The restaurant Shelby Simon chose—The Blue Inn— overlooked Blue Lake, which was even more stunning in its reflected autumn colors than Heart Lake was. Maybe that was because this lake was smaller, Mick thought as he looked through the expansive picture window by their table. It was a cozy lake. That notion struck him as pretty funny since he wasn't an outdoorsman by any stretch of the imagination, or someone who appreciated pastoral landscapes. He was an urban animal. At least since the age of fourteen when he first came to Chicago and the concrete shores of Lake Michigan.

Shelby Simon, on the other hand, seemed as content up here in rural Michigan as she had in the Windy City. Well, maybe content wasn't the right word. She fit in here. She seemed at ease, as much as she had seemed at ease in Chicago. She looked even better here, in her jeans and that mouthwatering sweater and her long hair wind-blown from their recent drive.

She had ordered a margarita, and Mick had figured what the hell. He wasn't on duty. Not technically anyway. He was on vacation. So he asked the waitress to bring him a beer.

"Nice place," he said, putting the cold brown bottle back on the little square coaster with a line drawing of the rustic building they were sitting in right then.

"It is nice, isn't it?" She put her own glass down, but not before her tongue peeked out to catch a few big crystals of salt from the rim. "It's been here forever. I'm glad they're still open. Most places around here close right after Labor Day when all the summer people go home."

"Pretty good deal," he said, "being able to get out of the city every summer."

She nodded with enthusiasm. "Yes, it was. I didn't spend a summer in Chicago until I was nineteen or twenty."

"You were lucky." Even better, she looked as if she totally agreed. There was nothing in her expression that gave the impression of entitlement he so often witnessed with people who had money. Shelby Simon, of the big Victorian house and the recycled family name and the fancy Canfield Towers pad, struck him as surprisingly unaffected by it all.

"Mm." There went that pretty pink tongue again when she took another sip of her drink. Then she tilted her head to one side and fixed him with her glossy, cognac-colored eyes. "So, Mick Callahan, tell me about you. Have you always lived in Chicago?"

For a second, Mick had the damnedest reaction to her question. Maybe it was her earnest expression as she gazed at him across the table. Maybe it was the beer on his empty stomach, but suddenly he felt like telling her his life story. His true life story as opposed to the abridged and cleaned-up version he usually told everyone else.

What the hell was he thinking? That she'd somehow put all the details together and then tell him just where he'd managed to go wrong? Or point out things, moments, incidents that he should have noticed at the time in order not to have been flattened by the truth when he finally learned it? What was she going to do—give him advice on how not to screw up in the future? Not that he didn't need it, but . . .

"Tell me about your family," she said now.

He must've had an odd expression on his face, because Shelby immediately followed up her question with an apology.

"I'm sorry. I wasn't prying, Mick. Really. I just thought since we'll obviously be spending some time together, it would be nice to know you better. I didn't mean to offend you."

"You didn't offend me," he said. "It's just not a very interesting story. My father walked out on us when I was about two months old, and then my mother dragged me around the country for the next thirteen years until we finally landed in Chicago."

This, of course, was the abridged version. Even so, the look on Shelby's face seemed genuinely warm and sympathetic.

"Doesn't sound like such a great way to grow up," she murmured.

"Well, it was a great way to grow up fast."

"And cynical," she added.

"Yeah. That, too, I guess." Jesus. He was already tired of talking about himself, so he changed the subject. "What's the deal with you and Sam Mendenhall?"

She looked surprised, then picked up her margarita again, as if she needed a little liquid courage before she answered. "There's no deal," she finally said.

"I got the impression there was something between the two of you in the past."

Another sip. Another lick of salt. "Not between Sam and *me*. Between Sam and my sister, Beth."

Before she could elaborate, the waitress came to take their order. While Shelby debated aloud between the patty melt and the tuna salad, Mick found himself feeling strangely relieved that the relatively good-looking gimp on the north side of the lake wasn't going to give him any competition, and then realizing—son of a bitch—that for the first time since Julie died, he was actually interested in a woman for something more than a bleary, boozy hour or two of medicinal sex.

Something told him he was in trouble here, and it had nothing to do with letter bombs.

After lunch, Callahan was quiet, nearly grim, as they began their drive back to Heart Lake. Come to think of it, he'd been pretty quiet all through their meal, too. Even though he'd insisted that her personal questions hadn't bothered him, Shelby was convinced otherwise. It seemed pretty clear to her that Lieutenant Mick Callahan wanted to keep their relationship on a strictly professional basis.

Fine.

No problem.

She had a talent for picking the wrong men anyway, so the fact that she was attracted to Callahan served as a warning all by itself. It never ceased to amaze her that she could fix her friends up with people who turned out to be their ideal mates. There was terminally shy Stanley Feldman who suddenly discovered he had a personality in the company of Cathie White. On a hunch, Shelby had fixed up confirmed bachelor Michael Marvin with her old friend, Susan Kent, then a single mother of three. Michael proposed on their second date, and now Susan was a happily married mother of five with another one on the way.

The list went on and on. Sometimes Shelby felt like a fairy godmother. And yet when it came to her own love life, Shelby Simon was a flop. She should probably write herself about that, she thought only half in jest.

Dear Ms. Simon,
  I'm thirty-four years old, and all my friends are either married or hooked up while I can't find a guy

*I want to be with for more than two or three dates
much less a lifetime.*
   Signed,
   Always a Bridesmaid

It was letters like these that were the most difficult for
Shelby to answer. Usually she wrote something short and
uplifting.

   Dear Always,
   *Relax. And trust me. It will happen when you
least expect it.*
   Ms. Simon Says So

Not that finding her perfect mate was uppermost in her
thoughts all the time. When it came right down to it, she
spent so much time tending to her professional life that
she rarely gave her personal life a second thought. Maybe
that was her problem. She was just too damned busy to
fall in love.

Yeah. Right.

But she sure wasn't busy anymore, was she? She reminded herself that she still needed to cancel her upcoming appointments. Hopefully she'd be able to log into the
office computer when she got back to the lake.

That would be soon enough given Callahan's tendency
to speed even on this rural blacktop. She glanced at the
needle on the speedometer. Sixty! Good grief. The lieutenant, she noticed now, kept scowling in the rearview
mirror.

She turned to see a car moving up fast behind them.

Jeez. If they were doing sixty, the other car must've been doing seventy-five. The driver started honking now.

"Asshole," Callahan muttered, his gaze flicking repeatedly to the mirror.

"Maybe he's trying to pass," Shelby suggested.

He ripped his gaze from the mirror just long enough to give her a withering glare.

Shelby looked back again. The driver was waving his arm out the window, then pulled it back inside to honk again.

"Pull over, Callahan," she said. "I think he's trying to signal us or something."

"Oh, great. Is that what you'd do if you were alone right now?" he yelled over the sound of the Mustang's roaring engine. "Pull over?"

"Well, I wouldn't be going . . ." She leaned over to check the speedometer again and then screamed, "I wouldn't be going eighty-two fucking miles an hour on a narrow two lane road, I can tell you that. I'd rather take my chances with a homicidal maniac than commit suicide by car."

"Really," he shouted.

"Really."

Callahan hit the brakes, turning the wheel and muscling the car onto the weedy shoulder of the road, where it came to a dusty, diagonal stop. The car behind them squealed to a stop thirty or forty feet away.

Having just endured at least two Gs between her seat belt and the seat back, Shelby was trying to catch her breath when Callahan pulled his gun from beneath his vest and jumped out of the car.

Oh, jeez. A gun. Somebody was homicidal, and it

wasn't necessarily the guy in the other car. Okay. Maybe she'd been wrong. Maybe death by Mustang would've been preferable.

"What's your problem, buddy?" the lieutenant shouted at the other driver.

He had also exited his car. He didn't look like a homicidal maniac to Shelby. In fact, the elderly man looked slightly familiar. He had to be in his late seventies if not early eighties, and he was wearing a white cook's jacket.

"Didn't you hear me honking?" the man yelled, sounding slightly out of breath. "I've been trying to catch you for the last five miles."

"Yeah?" Callahan challenged. "Why?"

When the man turned to reach back into the front seat of his car, Shelby could see every nerve in Mick Callahan's body snap to attention. He widened his stance and was just raising his gun into position with both hands when the man turned back.

"Here," he said. "Ms. Simon left her purse behind at the inn."

That's who he was! Old Mr. Keeler who owned the restaurant at Blue Lake. Shelby's family had known him forever. She jumped out of her side of the car and walked toward him.

"Thank you so much, Mr. Keeler," she said. "I didn't even realize I'd forgotten it."

"There you go, Ms. Simon." He handed the black handbag to her. "I used to go hunting with your granddad, you know. A long time ago."

"Yes. I remember."

"And I want to tell you how much the wife and I enjoy your column in the paper."

"Thank you. That's very kind of you."

Out of the corner of her eye, Shelby could see that the lieutenant had holstered his weapon and was now walking toward them. Mr. Keeler saw him, too, and seemed none too pleased.

"Yeah, you give real good advice, Ms. Simon." He turned back toward his car as he added, "You might want to advise your friend here not to drive so fast, and not to be so damned suspicious of strangers."

～

Mick glanced toward the passenger seat. "You can stop laughing now," he said.

"I'm sorry." She could barely get the words out. "It's just that . . ." Once again, giggles overwhelmed her.

"Yeah. Yeah. I guess you wouldn't be laughing so hard right now, Ms. Simon, if that old man had produced an AK-47 from the front seat of his vehicle," he grumbled when, in all honesty, Mick was having a tough time not laughing at himself. There was reacting, and then there was overreacting. He had just been a prime example of the latter. A prime jerk.

She sighed and wiped the tears from her eyes. "Thank you, Mick. Really. I mean it."

Apparently she did because her goofy expression had turned quite sober.

He shrugged. "Well, we still don't know who's after you. It's smart to be cautious." He felt a grin cut across his lips. "At least you got your purse back."

"The turn to the house is just ahead on the right," she said, pointing.

"Thanks." He already had his directional signal on, but she probably hadn't noticed in her attempt to be helpful. That reminded him of something she'd said earlier when they were being pursued. "What did you mean earlier when you said you'd pull over rather than try to escape?"

"Well, it's probably better than winding up dead in a ditch."

He frowned. "So back there, when you didn't have any idea who was chasing you, you would've pulled over? Just to see who it was and what he wanted?"

"Probably." She didn't sound too certain until she added, "Yes. If I'd been alone, that's what I would have done."

Mick swore, and then muttered, "That's a really good way to get yourself killed."

"So would crashing a car into a tree at eighty miles an hour," she snapped. "Listen. Give me a little break here. I know a thing or two about self-protection, Lieutenant Callahan."

"Right."

"Well, I do," she insisted. "In fact, that's something I write about frequently in my column. Advising women on protecting themselves, especially against rape."

This was a subject that had always made him crazy, and it had made him even crazier since Julie's death at the hands of a purse snatcher. In Mick's opinion, a little female self-confidence went a long way in getting women in more trouble than they were physically able to handle. One or two karate lessons just wasn't good enough. Not nearly.

"What do you do?" he asked, unable to repress the vitriol in his tone. "Tell them to enroll in a martial arts class at some strip mall and then send them out like vigilantes on the streets?"

"No, I don't. I advise them to use their brains before they use their bodies in order to avoid those kinds of situations in the first place."

"And then what? A key across his cheek? A knee to the groin? A little shot of pepper spray?"

She was staring at him now. He could almost feel the heat in her eyes boring through his skull. He'd obviously managed to push one of her hot buttons, but he didn't care. His own hot buttons were sizzling right now.

"What's wrong with you, Callahan? Don't you think women have the ability to protect themselves? Oh, wait. Don't tell me. I know. You're one of the ones who think we should just quietly comply in order to stay alive, just lie back and enjoy it, right?"

"Maybe," he said. God. Why had he even broached this subject in the first place?

"You're such a jerk," she muttered.

He was clenching his teeth so hard that his jaw began to ache. At the same time he realized he was pressing way too hard on the accelerator, going far too fast for the road that snaked through the woods behind the Simon property. He eased his foot off the gas.

"Let's just not talk about this right now," he said.

"Fine with me." Under her breath she muttered again, "Jerk."

He turned into the driveway at the rear of the carriage house just in time to see somebody take a sledge hammer to a window on the side of the building. Mick was reaching for his gun almost before he shifted into park.

He had one foot out on the driveway already when Shelby pulled at his sleeve, screaming.

"Don't shoot him, for God's sake. That's my father."

CHAPTER EIGHT

~

Much to Shelby's chagrin, it turned out that she had inadvertently locked the door to the carriage house earlier when she'd searched for her father only to find his "Gone fishing" note.

"Why didn't you just go in the house and get the spare key?" Shelby asked him as she extracted herself with some reluctance from his warm, all-encompassing hug.

This gave her a better chance to really look at him. Retirement appeared to suit the high-powered attorney known around the Chicago area as Harry Harry Quite Contrary. He looked healthy and tan and trim. His brown eyes—the same color as hers—sparkled like a glass of fine aged bourbon sitting in the sunshine. His sandy hair was threaded with a bit more silver now, and it was longer as well as somewhat thinner than the last time she'd seen him, but that was probably to be expected since he was in his late fifties.

"Why didn't you get the spare key, Dad?" she asked again.

"Because your mother would probably have had me arrested for breaking and entering," he said.

That's when her sister's words came flooding back. *They're separated. Or at least they were.* Shelby wanted to tear her hair out. Her eyes felt as if they were pinwheeling, and it was all she could do not to scream.

"Breaking and entering your own house? That's just nuts. It's insane. I don't understand this at all, Daddy." She sounded six years old. Petulant. Confused. Helpless. And, yes, hurt. She even felt a little nauseous.

But her father wasn't paying attention to her at the moment. Rather, Harry Harry Quite Contrary's gaze was currently directed at Mick Callahan, who, for the second time in less than half an hour, had just packed away his pistol.

"I'm Harry Simon, otherwise known as Shelby's father," he said, smiling affably and extending his hand toward Callahan.

"Mick Callahan. Nice to meet you, sir."

"Harry," her father corrected. "I didn't mind people calling me sir before I retired, but now it just makes me feel old as hell. So, you're my daughter's . . . um . . . friend?"

"That's right."

Before her father started grilling the man about his intentions, Shelby intervened. "Emphasis on friend, Dad. Okay?"

"A friend with a nine-millimeter Glock, if I'm not mistaken," Harry Simon said, lifting a curious eyebrow.

"Well . . ." Callahan began.

Then Shelby stepped in again, saying, "He's a city boy, Dad. Through and through. The wilds of rural

Michigan make him really nervous." She managed a little nervous laugh of her own as she aimed a beseeching look at the lieutenant. "Right, Callahan?"

Help me out here, will you?

He looked really stubborn for a moment—like Francis the fucking Mule!—all granite-jawed and tight-lipped and steely-eyed, as if he had no intention whatsoever of playing along with her little charade, but then he shrugged his shoulders and said almost sheepishly, "I thought I read someplace that there were still bears around here."

"Only one," Shelby's father said with a sigh and a sidelong glance at the big house up the hill.

Then he looked rather helplessly at the carriage-house window he'd shattered a moment ago and murmured, "Well, it seemed like a good idea at the time. Shelby, baby, why don't you go up to the house and get me that spare key. It's in the kitchen drawer to the left of the sink."

"Fine."

Without another word, Shelby turned and stalked toward the house, grateful for the opportunity to leave the two of them. She was angry at her father and she didn't even know what lay behind this supposed separation, but it had to be half his fault. As for the lieutenant . . . She didn't know what she was thinking, but she knew she'd think a lot more clearly if she put a little distance between them. He'd made her furious with his take on women's self-defense, but then he'd come through for her by not disclosing his profession or reason for being here.

Dammit. How could a single human being be so irritating and so attractive all at once?

Mick didn't have the vaguest idea what a carriage house was, but its interior reminded him of the typical loft space in several gentrified neighborhoods of Chicago. There was a kitchen area, set off by a long granite counter lined with tall wooden stools. The living area contained an enormous curved couch and the biggest big-screen TV that Mick had ever seen. Damned shame the World Series had ended with an early four-game rout, he thought, and the Chicago Bears weren't scheduled to play this Sunday.

Once she'd returned with the key and let them inside, Shelby had immediately excused herself, saying something about the need to make phone calls and cancel upcoming appointments, but he got the impression that it was only partly the truth. She seemed on edge in her father's presence, and Mick wondered if that unease had something to do with the fact that her parents appeared to be living apart and that it was news—and not good—to their daughter.

"Have a seat," Harry Simon said, gesturing to the couch. "I'm about to open a beer. Can I get you one?"

"No, thanks."

Mick sat, staring at the blank TV screen, grateful for a brief reprieve while Shelby's father rummaged in the refrigerator. If he was supposed to lie about his occupation and his reason for being here in Michigan, what the hell was he going to say? And would he be contradicting something Shelby might already have told her mother about him? She'd introduced him as a friend. Well, hell.

At least she hadn't introduced him as "a student of military history," he thought bleakly.

Beer bottle in hand, Harry Simon came around the counter and settled on the far curve of the big couch. He leaned back, crossed one leg over the other, looked at Mick, and said, "So, what kind of trouble is my daughter in?"

Mick hadn't been ready for a fastball like that, so his face probably registered his surprise. "Excuse me?"

"I get CNN, even up here in the boonies, Mick." He angled the neck of his Michelob toward the gigantic TV screen. "I know about the letter bombs at the Helm-Harris offices. Does this have anything to do with Shelby?"

"Well . . ." He sighed softly and closed his eyes for a second. Okay. Shit. Shelby would be royally pissed, but this was the right thing to do. He'd known that all along. "She didn't want to worry you or Mrs. Simon."

"That's what I thought. And judging from the Glock and the way you handled it, young man, I imagine you've been assigned to protect her."

Mick nodded. "Yes, sir." He probably should have added, as long as he was 'fessing up, that his assignment was simply to get her out of Chicago safely, not to stick to her like glue up here in Michigan. But he decided against it, maybe because he didn't want her father to get any of the wrong ideas about his intentions. Whatever the hell those were. Assuming he even had any.

Harry Simon was nodding, too. "So you're . . . what? . . . Detective Callahan? Lieutenant? Officer?"

"Lieutenant. I've been working vice out of the Eleventh."

"The same Callahan who helped put Morris Pachinski away a couple years ago?"

"Yes, sir."

"Well, that's reassuring. My daughter seems to be in competent hands." He took a quick sip of his beer. "I gather, from what I've seen on the news, that the investigation hasn't turned up much of anything yet."

"Not yet. But it's only been a little over twenty-four hours. My captain is keeping me posted with any developments, though."

"Good. And you'll keep me posted, I presume," the attorney said.

"Absolutely."

"No need to say anything about this to Shelby or her mother, Mick." He gestured around the room. "I'm in the doghouse already, as you can see. No sense your being here, too."

Sitting cross-legged on the big brass bed in her room with her laptop and her cell phone, Shelby placed her first and most important call to Dave the Doorman at the Canfield Towers to find out if he knew how Joe the Mailman was doing. Poor Joe. It just didn't seem fair for him to get hurt when it was Shelby who was the actual target. If he was in the hospital, she was going to send him a huge arrangement of flowers and balloons. That was all she could think of to do at the moment. Perhaps, when this nightmare was all over, she'd devote a column to him and the unwitting sacrifice he'd made for her.

"They released him last night," Dave told her. "He got some pretty bad burns on his arms, but he's doing okay."

"Oh, thank God. That's really good news. Was anybody else injured?"

"Bumps and bruises. We lost a front window in the lobby, but I've got people fixing that right now."

Shelby sighed aloud. She'd really been expecting the worst.

"How long are you planning to be away, Ms. Simon?" he asked.

"Well, I'm not exactly sure, Dave." She couldn't imagine why he was asking her. In the several years she'd lived at the Canfield Towers, she'd traveled extensively, and the doorman had never inquired about her schedule. "Why?"

"Somebody was here early this morning, looking for you. He wanted to find out where you were."

He? A little warning signal went off in Shelby's brain. Nobody ever stopped by her apartment or dropped in on her unannounced. Not her female friends and especially not any of the men she knew and occasionally went out with. So who was looking for her? And why?

"Did he leave his name, Dave?"

"No, Ms. Simon, he wouldn't. I asked him . . . twice, in fact . . . but he was pretty unhappy with me by that time because I wouldn't give him your present whereabouts or a number where he could reach you."

Shelby's heart was beating a little harder now and her palms began to sweat. She felt threatened, which was completely ridiculous and even irrational because Chicago was 250 miles away and she was here, at Heart Lake, safe in the middle of the beloved brass bed she'd slept in since childhood. And Lieutenant Mick Callahan was around. Somewhere. All she had to do was scream.

"What did this guy look like, Dave?" She was already imagining a gigantic, drooling, bug-eyed monster who dragged one leg. No. Wait. To even get halfway through the lobby of the Canfield Towers, the guy would have to look relatively normal. He probably still looked vaguely chilling, like Christopher Walken, maybe, or Kevin Spacey, or Jack Nicholson at his most menacing.

"Well, let's see," Dave said. "He was tall. Over six feet. Maybe six-two or -three. He was heavyset. Kinda scruffy-looking, to tell you the truth, Ms. Simon. In a tan corduroy jacket with leather elbow patches. He had reddish hair—what's the word? Auburn?—and a big, sort of brushy red mustache."

"Derek!" Shelby let her breath out and flopped backward on the mattress. It was Derek McKay from the paper. Thank God. She probably should have known that the ace reporter and inveterate snoop with the brushy red mustache would come looking for her after she'd left the office so abruptly yesterday.

"So you know him, then, Ms. Simon?"

"Yes, I know him. He's a colleague of mine at the *Daily Mirror*. It's okay. I'll get in touch with him right away. I appreciate your concern, Dave."

"That's what I'm here for," he said. "Do you want to leave me your address, Ms. Simon, just in case . . . ?"

"No," Shelby said emphatically. "Thanks, Dave. Anybody who needs to know will be able to find me. And thanks for letting me know about Joe's condition. I'm so glad he's okay."

After she hung up, she lay there just breathing deeply

for a minute while she stared up at the ceiling fan. It was still, and Shelby was trying to be still, too.

She wasn't used to being wary and on guard. In thirty-four years, she'd never really been afraid of anything or anyone. Growing up in the suburbs, in the shady shelter of Evanston, and here on the quiet shores of Heart Lake, there had never been a single thing to fear. The sum of her caution as a kid had been looking both ways before she crossed a street and waiting half an hour after eating lunch before she dived into the lake.

But now, all of a sudden, the world seemed to have turned from a benevolent place to one where danger lurked on every corner, behind every tree, and in every single mailbox. And Shelby didn't have the slightest idea what she had done to bring such imminent doom and destruction down upon herself. She wrote an advice column, for heaven's sake. She tried her best to help thousands of people she didn't even know. What was so terrible about that?

Maybe she should ask herself for some good advice, she thought.

> Dear Ms. Simon,
> I seem to be sinking deeper and deeper into a pool of self-pity. Help!!
> Signed,
> Miserable in Michigan

> Dear Miserable,
> You need to worry about others. What about your parents? Worry about them. Self-pity sucks.
> Ms. Simon Says So

At the mere thought of her parents, Shelby rolled her eyes at the ceiling and sighed aloud. Well, that was one surefire way to forget her own problems. By focusing on theirs. Whatever they were.

She decided her call to Derek McKay and the other calls could wait while she stuck her nose in this separation business.

Her mother wasn't back from town yet, and her father was nowhere to be found. If Shelby hadn't known better, she'd think they were deliberately avoiding her.

As she strolled back from the deserted carriage house, she saw Callahan standing down by the dock, skimming rocks out into the lake. It struck her as such a little boyish thing to do that she found herself smiling in a goofy way and nearly laughing out loud. Then she remembered what the lieutenant had told her about being abandoned by his father and then dragged around the country by his mother, and she thought he probably never got to do too many little boyish things when he was a little boy.

She was feeling almost tender toward him when she suddenly stopped smiling and remembered how irked she was by their earlier conversation about women and self defense. What a macho jerk. By the time she'd made her way down the winding sidewalk that led from the house to the shoreline, Shelby had worked herself into a proper snit.

"Hey," he said, greeting her as he side-armed a small flat rock out across the water.

All of a sudden she noticed what a graceful athlete he was, and how beautifully proportioned his body was with its just right shoulders and just right waist and . . . oh, Lord! . . . buns that could put McDonald's out of business. She didn't ordinarily notice things like that.

Shelby almost stopped being mad at the patronizing pig for a second. Almost.

"Hey. We never got to finish our discussion about women and self-defense, Callahan," she said in a voice fairly dripping with honey.

"*I* was finished," he said, picking up another rock and skidding it across the surface of the lake.

"Well, I wasn't. You know, this is a subject I write about pretty frequently in my column so I've done more than just read about it. I actually took a course in self-defense a few years ago." Well, her schedule only permitted her to take half the course, but she didn't have to admit that.

Callahan just stood there gazing at her, his expression somewhere between irritation and condescension.

"Want me to show you?" she asked.

"No."

"Oh, come on. What're you afraid of?"

"Nothing. I just don't want to play your dumb little game."

"You're afraid of me," she crowed.

He lofted an agonized gaze skyward and then sighed. "Okay. Gimme your best shot."

Shelby shook her head. "That's not how self-defense works, you idiot. You're supposed to attack *me*."

"Forget it." He took a step away from her, then bent and snatched up another rock.

"Come on, Callahan."

"I don't want to hurt you." The rock went sailing out and did a triple skim across the still water.

"You jerk. That's the whole point," Shelby said. "You won't hurt me because I know how to counteract your moves."

Again, he just stared at her.

"Chicken," she muttered.

"You got that right."

"Come on." Shelby advanced toward him. She reached out and pushed his shoulder while she made a little clucking sound. "Brk. Brk. Brk."

He laughed, deflecting her hand when she tried to push him again. "Get outta here."

"Brk. Brk. Brk."

"Jesus, Shelby." He ripped the fingers of both hands through his hair. "Give it a rest, will you?"

"Not until you attack me so I can prove my point. What are you afraid of, Callahan? That I'll knock you on your ass?" She pushed him again. "Huh?"

"Yeah. That's what I'm afraid of, all right," he said, his voice thick with sarcasm.

"Come on," she taunted.

He dragged in a breath. "Okay. Shit. This is ridiculous, you know. What do you want me to do?"

"Attack me."

"Attack you. Okay. How? From the front? The back? Sideways?"

"The front's fine," she said, priming her biceps and her quads and her gluteus max along with all the muscles whose names she didn't even know, trying like hell to remember all the right moves she'd learned in class. "Go for it."

He swore again, then reached out to put his hands gently on her shoulders.

"Oh, for heaven's sake. What are you doing, Callahan? Dancing?"

"Okay," he growled. "Just remember you asked for this. On the count of three . . . One . . ."

The next thing Shelby knew she was flat on her back on the little strip of sandy beach, trying to catch her breath, blinking up at the autumn sky and Callahan's smirky face. "That's not fair," she howled. "You said on the count of three."

"You didn't say anything about being fair." He grinned as he held his hand out to her. "Here. Up you go."

She slapped the helping hand away and got up on her own, pulling twigs and leaves out of her hair. "Okay. Shit. I wasn't ready, but this time . . ."

He did it again. Whatever he'd done the first time, he did again. And this time, even as she was toppling, Shelby was aware of the smooth and efficient way he'd unbalanced her. Dammit. It was what she'd intended to do to him.

She hit the sand with a loud *oof* as the breath sailed out of her chest, then she closed her eyes a moment, not because she was in pain, but to block out the sight of Callahan, looming over her like some stupid, grinning colossus.

"You okay?" he asked.

"Ycp."

"Had enough?"

"Nope." Shelby clenched her teeth and summoned every ounce of strength that remained in her body, then blasted her left leg out in Callahan's direction, in the hope of cutting the son of a bitch off at the knees.

He must've seen it coming, though, because he leaped back just out of her range. God, the man had the reflexes of a snake! And then—before she could plan her next move—he was on top of her, his sudden weight forcing another little *oof* from her lungs. She raised her hands to push him away, but that turned out to be a big mistake when he linked his fingers through hers, stretched her arms over her head, and pinned her to the beach like a chloroformed butterfly.

"Say Uncle," he said, grinning down at her.

Fuck you.

Shelby didn't say it, but she thought it clearly enough as she forcibly wrenched her hips in order to shove him off. That was probably her second mistake—or was it the third?—moving like someone in the throes of passion beneath him.

His grin subsided and the light in his eyes altered from mirth to heat, from one sort of conquest to another. Or was his expression just mirroring her own?

Shelby's breath was gone again, but its absence had nothing to do with her fall. It was because Mick Callahan's mouth was mere inches from hers. Because she felt the strength of his erection where his jeans made contact with hers. Because she felt the sudden, hot, heart-stopping sweep of her own desire, which was a lot more than being turned on. It was more like being turned inside out.

Nobody had ever cursed her as the preamble to a kiss. Some men whispered her name. Some uttered a hoarse

"C'mere." Some didn't say a word. But Callahan muttered a harsh "Damn you" as his mouth came down on hers.

The kiss flared out of control the instant it began. It was as if they were both starving, trying to consume each other. Tongues. Teeth. Lips.

Instinctively, Shelby opened her legs and Mick groaned as he pressed harder against her. If it hadn't been for several layers of clothing, he would have been inside her, which seemed like the only thing in the world that she wanted at that moment. Boy, did she want it.

This was . . .

"Yoo hoo, Shelby." Her mother's voice drifted down from somewhere near the house. "Honey, will your friend be staying for dinner?"

Callahan broke the kiss, lifting his head and shifting his warm weight to the side.

It took Shelby a second or two to find her voice, and even then it came out sounding pretty sultry when she asked him, "Will you?"

He didn't answer immediately. Instead he just perused her face as if he were seeing her for the first time. His gaze moved almost leisurely from her eyes to her mouth, and then back to her eyes. A tiny grin played at the corners of his mouth. Shelby couldn't tell if it was bafflement or pleasure.

"Will you be staying?" she asked again, knowing full well she meant more than just for dinner, and knowing he knew exactly what she meant.

"Yes," he answered quietly.

Shelby tried not to smile too broadly as she turned her head toward the lawn and called, "Yes, Mother. He'll be staying."

CHAPTER NINE

~

At six that evening, Harry Simon came bearing gifts—two bottles of an outrageously expensive 1996 Merlot that he knew his wife would love. The side entry to the kitchen was open, but still he tapped one of the bottles on the frame of the screen door.

"Harry?" she called.

"It's me, Beauty."

He opened the door and stepped inside the old house for the first time in several months. Linda was standing at the sink, scrubbing potatoes with the same grace and enthusiasm she brought to almost everything she did.

Funny, he thought. His wife was fifty-six years old and she still looked to him the way she did in high school. Her hair was still as blond as it had been then, and she still wore it the same way, pulled back by a headband—usually of black velvet—and falling in a soft pageboy that perfectly framed her face. He'd never thought about it before, but she must've gone through scores and scores of black velvet headbands over the past forty years.

This evening she was wearing beige slacks that looked

very nice from his vantage point behind her, and above the slacks one of her own creations, or as he tended to think of them, the sweaters from hell that had driven a stake through the heart of his marriage.

He had retired early—the advance planning had taken a good three years at the firm—not just for his own amusement, but in order to spend time with his wife. Unfortunately, her business had begun to come out of the cottage at about the same time that he started winding down his caseload, and by the time he literally got his gold watch, Linda Purl Designs had gone ballistic and his wife was working twenty-six hours a day and traveling nine days a month.

At first he'd been a pretty good sport about it, if he did say so himself. Actually Linda's hectic schedule hadn't bothered him so much in the first months of his retirement when he was able to tee off at the club at eight o'clock on a Monday morning rather than fight traffic into his downtown office, when he was able to read fiction late into the night instead of legal briefs, when he was able to join his brother on safari in Kenya on one week's notice or to take off spontaneously for some fishing in Key West or some golf in South Carolina.

The thrill of it all wore off after a few months, though, and Harry began asking himself why the hell he'd retired if he couldn't spend his time with the love of his life. His moods darkened considerably. He muttered. He sulked. He turned into a goddamned martyr. Those were Linda's words, not his. In his opinion, Harry had a legitimate grievance. Even more, he had an unwavering desire to live the rest of his life in the company of the lovely Linda

Simon, not the perennially distracted and frequently absent Linda Purl.

Their marriage turned into a minefield.

When Linda had calmly but firmly suggested he move out to the carriage house, he'd indulged her in the belief that the so-called separation would last a few weeks, a month at most, and then they'd resolve their difficulties. In other words, she'd cut back on her professional obligations and spend more time with him, putting an end to his sulking and muttering and goddamned martyrdom. But that hadn't happened. Yet. His wife was as stubborn as she was talented and beautiful.

"Where's our daughter?" he asked, setting the wine bottles on a table by the refrigerator.

"Upstairs," Linda said. "She said she had some calls to make."

"And her . . . um . . . friend?"

She laughed. "He's taking a walk."

"Seems like a nice enough young man, don't you think?"

"I haven't had much time to talk to him, actually." She scrubbed her potato a little more aggressively when she added, "He and Shelby were going at it pretty hot and heavy a while ago down by the dock."

Considering their relationship as bodyguard and protectee, that should probably have surprised Harry, but nothing his daughters did surprised him much anymore. They'd inherited their unpredictability from their mother.

He was standing directly behind her now, looking down over her shoulder at the plain gold band on her wet left hand, the ring he'd slipped on that finger so long ago.

Sometimes it seemed like just yesterday instead of thirty-five years ago. He dipped his head to kiss her neck.

"Don't start, Harry," she said quietly but firmly.

"Can't blame me for trying." He sighed. "What's for dinner besides potatoes?"

"Steaks and salad." She turned off the water. "Let me get these in the oven, and then you can help me with the salad."

"This is nice," he said ten minutes later, standing beside her while she sliced a red onion and he pared a cucumber. "So, you think Shelby really likes this Callahan fellow?"

"Who knows? Shelby spends so much time butting in to other people's love lives that she doesn't seem to have any time for her own."

He nodded in agreement. "She's been doing that for a long time, hasn't she? Butting in, I mean."

"Yes, she has. I'd say she cut her teeth on Beth and Sam."

"Well, she wasn't wrong about that, Linda," he said, shaving the last of the dark green skin from the cucumber. "If I'd known that Beth was thinking about eloping, I would've locked her in her room and thrown away the key. And anyway, it wouldn't have worked out. Sam got married to somebody else a couple months after he left, didn't he?"

She put down the knife and turned to him with one of those *you really don't get it* looks on her face. "Sam *had* to get married to somebody else, Harry. He got a girl pregnant in Georgia or wherever he was."

"Oh," Harry shook his head in dismay. Sometimes it seemed he'd spent so much time at the office and in the courtroom that he'd missed half of what should have been his family life. Of course, now that he was retired and had all the time in the world, he still didn't seem privy to the inner workings of his harem. "Am I the only one who doesn't know that?" he asked.

"No. Beth doesn't know. Neither does Shelby. Sam's mother, Terry, felt so bad about poor Bethie when it happened that she apologized to me. I thought it was best not to tell the girls. I mean, what could they have done about it?"

"Nothing, I guess."

"Exactly. The marriage didn't last that long, anyway. There were complications in the pregnancy, as I remember. Both the mother and baby died. It was so long ago." She picked up her knife again and sliced a few more perfect, thin circles of onion. "I thought I'd told you, though, Harry. Are you sure I didn't?"

"I'm sure you didn't," he said. "Here's your cucumber, Mrs. Simon." He set the pale green vegetable on her cutting board.

"Thank you."

Harry leaned his hip against the counter, gazing down at his wife's lovely profile. "So, what else haven't you told me, Beauty?"

She smiled. "Not much, Mr. Simon. I think you know just about all of my secrets now."

"Do I, sweetheart?"

Sometimes he wondered. Maybe keeping secrets was a way of protecting each other, he thought. After all, he hadn't exactly rushed to tell his wife about their daughter's current situation with the letter bombs, had he?

As Linda had said herself, what could she do about it even if she knew?

～

Shelby glanced at the clock beside her bed. It was a little after six o'clock. Her mother had said dinner would be at seven-thirty, and no, thank you, she didn't need any help, so Shelby had gone upstairs to make as many cancellation calls as possible. Still annoyingly unable to log on at work, and irritatingly unable to contact her secretary, Sandy, by phone, Shelby had been forced to reconstruct most of her schedule for the next two weeks from her planner.

First, and quite happily, she called her dentist's office in Chicago to cancel her annual checkup. Then she canceled her appearance at the Women in Retailing convention in New Orleans. The specific woman in retailing to whom Shelby spoke didn't sound all that disappointed by the fact that her keynote luncheon speaker was forced to bow out on such short notice. "Maybe next year," the woman had said without warmth or conviction.

Next she called the Better Business Bureau in Des Moines where no one seemed to be in the office, and she was forced to leave her regrets and profuse apologies on voice mail. Finally, the woman on the phone at the Chamber of Commerce in Phoenix actually sounded as if she might cry.

"I really love your column, Ms. Simon," she said. "You're so much funnier than Ask Alice." Just for that, Shelby took the woman's name and address with the promise of an autographed eight-by-ten glossy and an autographed copy of her now out of print book, aptly named *Ms. Simon Says.*

Maybe she should write another book, she thought after she hung up. God knows she had plenty of time right now. She could call it *Ms. Simon Says More.* Still, the way things were going now, a better title might be *Ms. Simon Says Nothing.* Nada. Zip. Closed until further notice.

The final call she had made was to Derek McKay at the *Daily Mirror*, intending to leave her cell number on his voice mail in the hope that he'd call her from wherever he was in the East. Instead of voice mail, though, somebody picked up, and this time Shelby immediately recognized Kellie Carter's voice on the other end of the line. What was that eager little beaver doing? Running from desk to desk, making herself a one-woman message center?

Shelby wasn't in the mood for chitchat, and she debated about hanging up for a second, but she really did want to talk to Derek.

"Hi, Kellie. It's Shelby. I need to speak to Derek."

"Oh, hi, Ms. Simon. Shelby. Derek's not available."

"Any idea where I can reach him?"

"Sorry, no. I'd be happy to give him a message, though."

"Just ask him to call me, please." Shelby rattled off her cell phone number.

"Are you in Chicago?" Kellie asked.

"No, I'm . . . Well, it doesn't matter. Just give him the message, please."

After she hung up, Shelby felt bad about being so abrupt with the little intern. In the weeks that she'd been at the paper, Kellie Carter had proven herself to be not only enthusiastic, but smart as well. Even if it had turned out to be a case of nepotism on Hal Stabler's part, Shelby couldn't complain about the young woman's abilities. She wasn't hard to look at either with her long red hair and short little skirts. Derek had certainly noticed her.

Shelby gave a tiny gasp. Could it be? Was she jealous of this latest sweet young thing? But as soon as the question formed in her brain, she dismissed it completely. In fact, she laughed out loud at the very idea. She and Derek were history, and ancient history at that. Besides, even when it had been good between them, it hadn't been half as good as . . .

Callahan.

Shit. She'd been trying not to think of him for the past few hours. She didn't want to think about him now, but she couldn't help herself. That kiss had been incredible. And her physical response to it had been unlike anything she'd ever experienced before. It wasn't like her at all to just go for the gusto. On the beach. In broad daylight.

As she often wrote in her column, great sex was as much mental as it was physical. Get to know your partner first, Ms. Simon says. Don't rush. Take your time. Use your head. Be smart. Above all else, be careful.

That advice wasn't merely a posture for the column's sake. Shelby truly believed it, and she practiced what she preached. She'd never gone to bed with a man until she had a genuine sense of who he was. Well, not that there had been that many of them, truth to tell, but by the time they were horizontal, Shelby always knew far more than merely their names and occupations. She had at least an inkling, if not a solid handle on what made her lovers tick.

As for Lieutenant Mick Callahan . . . Hell, she didn't really even know his name, much less what made him tick, did she? Was Mick short for Michael, or was it his given name? Was he Irish? Catholic? Where was he born? How did his wife die? How long were they married? Were there any kids? Considering all the things she didn't know about him, she wondered why she'd responded at all to such a stranger's kiss.

She looked at the clock again to discover it was almost time to go downstairs for dinner. If she knew her mother, Shelby would be seated not only next to Callahan, but elbow to elbow, hip to hip. She could already imagine the sparks generated between them. Hot little blue bolts of electricity zapping back and forth under the dining-room table. God. The tablecloth would probably go up in flames.

A little groan escaped her lips. She'd come back home to feel safe. Now she wondered if, at the age of thirty-four, she was too old to run away.

⁓

Mick managed to extend his afternoon walk until almost seven o'clock. He made two complete circuits of Heart Lake, one clockwise along its narrow strip of beach, the second counterclockwise along the wooded path that snaked behind the houses and cottages. Actually, there was only one honest-to-God house—the monster Victorian residence of the Simons. There were a couple of A-frames, but the rest of the places looked like typical jerry-built summer cottages, most of them single story with one or two bedrooms in back and big front windows offering views of the lake.

Hardly any of the places appeared occupied now that summer was over. Aside from Sam Mendenhall's log cabin on the north side of the lake, Mick counted only three other cottages where cars were parked to show at least some signs of life. Out on the lake, he counted only three boats during his four-hour walk.

He was heading back to the Simon place now, not wanting to be late for dinner. "Nothing fancy," Linda Simon had said, sounding like an experienced and sincerely gracious hostess. "Just come as you are." Which was a good thing because even if he had time to change now it would only be into a cleaner version of his current faded jeans and flannel shirt.

They were nice people, the Simons. That was his first impression, at least. But Mick, who was used to making snap judgments on the street, wasn't often wrong about people.

Well . . . except for Shelby, maybe.

He'd only known her for—what?—barely thirty-six hours, but every time he thought he had her figured out, she'd do the unexpected. The woman who lived in the fancy Canfield Towers didn't bat an eye at the sight or smell of his crappy ghetto digs. The urbanite who resided in a boring sea of modern beige had brought him to an ancient, multicolored, frigging fairy-tale house deep in the rural woods, where the renowned giver of advice appeared baffled and tongue-tied in the presence of her very own family. And last, but hardly least, the professional paragon of female self-defense had melted like hot butter beneath his kiss this afternoon.

That kiss. His body quickened again at just the thought. He hadn't felt so out of control in years. Not since he and Julie were randy teens first exploring the hot, rich terrain of sex. From the look of surprise on Shelby's face, he suspected she'd felt the same. If her mother hadn't interrupted them, he had the feeling they would've progressed—at warp speed—to the obvious conclusion, neither one of them prepared for the act or its consequences or anything other than the white heat of the moment.

Mick shook his head in amazement as he bent down to snatch up a weed. When he clamped it between his teeth, he flashed on a vivid memory of when he and his mother lived in Tennessee. He must've been seven or eight when they lived in that trailer at the edge of a field outside of Murpheysboro. It was summer, hot as hell, and he'd get up every morning to race across those acres of tall weeds behind the trailer, scaring up crickets and grasshoppers and the occasional stray cat as he flew. Only the big chain-link fence on the far side of the field could stop him. Then he'd pick a weed, stick it between his teeth, and take his time returning, kicking beer cans and broken bottles and rusty hubcaps and whatever else might be in his path.

That was three decades ago, and he probably hadn't chewed on a weed since then, Mick thought. Hell, who'd put anything in their mouth they'd picked from a vacant lot in Chicago?

He usually only thought about his mother twice a year—on her birthday, June 15, and on New Year's Eve, which was when a cousin finally tracked him down and gave him the news that Carrie Callahan had perished in a motel fire six months before. But right now the memories nearly overwhelmed him.

He tried to remember how they'd gotten to that field in Murpheysboro in the first place, and then recalled that his mother had been a cocktail waitress at a Holiday Inn outside Baltimore when she hooked up with a country and western singer named Gary Gray. They'd followed him to his next gig in Tennessee and wound up stranded there for the next six months. And after that?

Oh, yeah. Roswell, New Mexico. But was that the trucker or the medical supplies salesman? Christ, it could have been an extraterrestrial for all Mick knew. His mother was as crazy as she was beautiful. Maybe if she'd had more kids they would've nailed her down to a specific place. Or maybe if the one kid she did have had ever complained. But he never complained—not until the end, anyway—because his mother was always so happy and excited to be going someplace new with someone new.

He swore harshly as he ripped the weed from his teeth. What was it about Shelby Simon that was making him dredge up all the things—the women—he'd been trying so damned hard to forget?

~

Callahan was coming up the stairs, two at a time, while Shelby was descending.

"How was your walk?" she asked, forcing a breezy lilt into her voice to counteract the sudden drumming of her heart.

When he answered "Great," she found herself looking at him from a wholly new perspective. No longer just a civil servant assigned to protect her, Mick Callahan was now a candidate for her bed. She must've been nuts, and the craziness must've shown in her expression, because he was staring up at her with a quizzical look on his face.

"What's your real name, anyway, Callahan?" she demanded.

"Excuse me?"

"Is it Mick? Michael? What?"

"Why do you want to know?" he asked suspiciously. It probably went with being a cop.

"Just curious."

"It's Michael."

"Michael what?"

"You mean my middle name?"

Shelby nodded.

"Forget it." He started to pass her on the stairs, but Shelby blocked his path with an outstretched arm.

"Come on. What is it?"

"I said forget it." He stepped up another stair, putting his chest in contact with the barrier of her arm.

"Consider it a password," Shelby said. "Tell me. Or do you want to stand here while I guess? James? David? John?"

He shot her a look of utter disgust, then muttered something under his breath that she couldn't quite understand. "Raymond?" she asked, thinking that was what it sounded like.

Again, he muttered, this time through clenched teeth, and Shelby heard something closer to Ramon. "Ramon?"

"Rainbow," he yelled. "Are you happy now?"

Oh, God! Was she happy? She didn't know, but laughter was roaring up her throat, threatening to explode. Rainbow!

He pushed her arm out of his way with a gruff "I've got to clean up before dinner" and then stomped up the rest of the stairs while Shelby kind of collapsed onto her own stair, sinking her teeth into the back of her index finger, trying to hold back a Vesuvius of laughter.

Michael Rainbow Callahan! Who knew? Who would ever have guessed? And he'd accused *her* of having a dumb name.

~

"What's so funny?" her mother asked when Shelby walked into the kitchen. "I haven't heard you laugh like that since you and Bethie were little."

"Oh, something just struck me as funny," she replied, suppressing another round of the giggles. "Shall I set the table?"

"Your father's already done it. He should be bringing in the steaks any minute."

Shelby plucked a piece of romaine out of the salad her mother was tossing, popped it into her mouth, and then asked casually, "Anything I ought to know about you and Dad, Mom?"

There was a moment of near silence when the only sound was the soft collision of bits of lettuce and cucumbers and onions before her mother said, "No, Shelby, there's not a thing you *ought* to know. Thank you for asking, though."

Speaking of cucumbers, Shelby thought, her mother's tone was even cooler. "Mother, I just mean . . ."

The big wooden fork and spoon clacked against each other. "I know what you mean, honey, but I don't want to discuss it now. All right?" She fashioned one of those strained smiles that always translated as *I love you, but shut up*.

"Well, when?"

"I don't know," her mother said irritably. "Slide those salad plates closer, will you? I don't want to drop this all over the counter."

Shelby picked up a plate and held it close to the big bowl while her mother loaded it with salad. After that, she held a second plate for her, and then the others, all the while taking note of the small, but distinct tremor in the agile and oh-so-talented hands of Linda Purl.

How the hell was she supposed to help if nobody would explain what was going on?

Before she could think of a different way to wheedle the information out of her mother, her father called "Here come the steaks" through the screen door just before he came in. Ah, God. He looked so handsome and happy just then that Shelby almost wanted to cry. Well, damn. Between laughing and crying and a burning tablecloth, she didn't know how she was going to make it through this meal.

As it turned out, Shelby had been wrong about the seating arrangement. Contrary to her expectations, her mother put her across the table from Callahan rather than adjacent to him, which was probably worse because now Shelby had to look at his infinitely appealing face instead of just brushing elbows. He had not only changed into a clean flannel shirt, but he'd also shaved and perhaps even showered. His hair had that slicked back, wet look that she always found devilishly attractive.

"Wine, Shelby?" her father asked, the bottle poised over her glass. She was sorely tempted to grab it all for herself and let the others do with water.

"Yes, please."

While he filled the other glasses, Shelby looked around the dining room. Beth had outdone herself in here with the dark and heavily patterned William Morris wallpaper. It looked as if she'd lightened the color of the woodwork, too, in order to perfectly match a particular beige in the paper. Little wonder it took her over a year to finish her renovations.

Her mother arrived from the kitchen a little out of breath, but still looking like the consummate hostess, and when her father pulled out her chair and gently touched her shoulder while seating her, Linda Simon didn't seem to mind. That was good, Shelby thought. A dinner here, a dinner there, and maybe soon they'd be back together again.

Her mother raised her wineglass. "Here's to Shelby and Mick."

"I'll drink to that," her father said.

Oh, Lord. Shelby glanced at Callahan over the rim of her glass to see his reaction to the toast. If it embarrassed him, nothing in his expression gave that away. He looked—well—almost happy, a far cry from his usual end-of-the-world demeanor. Or end-of-the-rainbow, she reminded herself, trying not to laugh.

After that, no sooner had everyone begun to dig into

their steaks than the phone sounded a shrill note from the kitchen.

"I'll get it," Shelby said, but her mother had already sprung from her chair and was sprinting toward the door, chirping, "That's probably for me."

And it was. Hardly a minute later, Linda Simon, aka Linda Purl, paused in the dining-room doorway just long enough to say, "I'm sorry. I have to take this call. It seems a truck has jackknifed in Colorado and my merchandise is being scattered all over the Rocky Mountains." Then she disappeared.

From the head of the table came a grim, fairly hostile silence, and for a brief instant Harry Simon's face said it all. This was a Maalox moment if ever Shelby had seen one. And suddenly she knew exactly what the problem was with her parents. Bingo! Eureka! How could she not have known? How could she not have guessed? It was just so obvious, and as plain as the nose on her face. Harry Harry Quite Contrary was now on the receiving end of a high-powered career, and he didn't like it one little bit.

Ha!

She picked up her wineglass and took a healthy swig. Instead of being upset by the revelation, Shelby was hugely encouraged. Now that she knew what was wrong—and she was sure she was right—it ought to be easy enough to fix.

Her father cleared his throat, probably of bile, and like a good host leaned forward and inquired, "So, are you originally from Chicago, Mick?"

"No, sir. I was born in West Virginia."

"Ah. I've never been there," her father said. "I hear it's pretty nice."

"I wouldn't know," Callahan replied. "I only lived there a couple of months."

Shelby sampled her baked potato, then picked at her salad. Sometimes it was nice having a lawyer for a father. Given the least opportunity, he'd grill her boyfriends so she didn't have to do it herself. But this time her father had barely framed his second question when her mother reappeared in the dining room with the phone in her hand and a look of concern on her face.

She handed the phone to Mick. "It's Sam Mendenhall. For you. He says it's important."

Callahan took the phone, and after a series of terse "Yeahs" and "Okays," he broke the connection and pushed back from the table. "There's somebody suspicious hanging around outside. Excuse me. I'll be back as soon as I can."

He glared across the table then. "Stay here. Inside the house, Shelby."

"Well, why don't I . . . ?"

"Make her stay here, Mr. Simon," he ordered. And then he raced out of the room.

CHAPTER TEN

~⌒~

Mick had grabbed his Glock from its hiding place beneath the mattress in his room, and then retrieved his flashlight from the car before heading into the dark woods behind the house. It crossed his mind that there might indeed be bears up here in the dense backwoods of this rural county. He swore under his breath, deciding he'd rather face a dozen gang bangers than a single mama bear playing defense for her cubs.

Edging forward, he swung the flashlight beam in a wide arc, expecting any moment to light up Sam Mendenhall, or if not to catch him in the light, at least to hear the guy limping through the underbrush.

But he didn't see or hear a thing. Not until a voice, only a foot or so from his right ear, softly spoke his name.

"Mick."

He pivoted, gun in one hand, flashlight in the other, and there was Sam, who'd apparently materialized out of thin air.

"Jesus H. Christ," Mick muttered. "You're lucky I didn't put a bullet in you."

Sam didn't appear to be either relieved or concerned. He angled his chin toward a distant spot in the dark woods. "Our stalker's over there," he said quietly. "Peeping Tom. Tell Shelby to keep her fucking curtains closed."

Mick looked in the direction the security guard indicated, but he didn't see a thing. "You recognized him?"

"It's a kid from town. Eric Shaler," he said. "The punk's about to get busted. Listen. I want you to go around that way, come up behind the little bastard, and chase him toward me."

Considering Sam's status as a rent-a-cop versus his own as a longtime member of the Chicago PD, Mick was about to countermand his order—for that's what it sounded like, as opposed to a strong suggestion—but then he figured it was as good a plan as any, so he nodded and then headed in the direction of the twisted little twerp. As he circled around through the dark, Mick was soon able to discern the boy's lumpy shadow against the trunk of a tree. Beyond the boy and the tree shone the soft yellow glow of Shelby's bedroom windows.

A flicker of pure and undiluted anger flared inside Mick's chest, a feeling far more personal than professional, as if this Eric kid were treading on Mick's home turf somehow. He'd been a cop long enough to know that feelings like that weren't just inappropriate. They made you careless. They could get you killed. Instinctively, he shut down everything that didn't pertain to the job and to the task at hand.

Angling silently between the trees, he decided to take up a position slightly up the hill behind the boy. That way, when he flushed him out, the kid would flee in the path of least resistance, back the way he had come no doubt, and straight into Sam.

"Police, Eric," he shouted. "Don't move. Don't do anything stupid."

Naturally, he did, taking off through the trees, crashing through the underbrush just the way Mick had predicted. By the time Mick and his flashlight beam caught up with the kid, Sam's cane was snaking out a foot above the ground to bring the idiot down. Panicky now, the boy tried to scrabble away on all fours. That was when Sam reversed his cane with the slick efficiency of a Big Ten baton twirler and he hooked the boy by the collar of his denim jacket.

"You need a ride home, Eric?" Sam asked him, his voice sounding utterly in control, infinitely cool, and maybe a little bit like God's.

"Y-y-es-sir," the kid stuttered. "You're not g-going to tell my . . . my mom, are you?"

God's voice warmed a degree or two. "Well, that might be negotiable. Why don't we talk about it on the ride to town?" He looked at Mick. "What do you think, Lieutenant Callahan? Care to come along and join the negotiations?"

"Sure. Why not?"

Sam's Jeep was parked on the gravel road just at the edge of the woods. The negotiations amounted to Sam telling Eric he expected him to keep his nose clean, his pants zipped, and if he ever caught him behind the Simon house again, he'd beat the shit out of him.

"So, you won't tell my mom?"

"Not this time. Next time, though, if there is a next time," Sam warned, "it'll be on the front page of the

Mecklin County *Times* and you'll be in a holding cell in the county jail with somebody looking at you like dessert. You hear what I'm saying?"

"Y-yessir."

⁓

Shelby was in the kitchen, covering Callahan's barely touched plate with a foot of plastic wrap when the telephone rang. She grabbed it on the second ring, not because she was faster than her mother or closer to the phone, but because her mother's hands were currently wet and soapy from rinsing dishes.

Hello was hardly out of her mouth when Sam said, "False alarm, Shelby. Your boyfriend and I are going to have a few beers. Don't wait up."

"He's not my . . ." Too late. Sam had already clicked off. Shelby swore as she slammed the receiver back into its cradle.

"What's up, kiddo?" Her father, who had been smoking a cigar out on the porch, appeared in the kitchen doorway, his forehead creased and his mouth drawn down with worry.

"Nothing," she said. "That was Sam. Apparently it was just a false alarm. He and Callahan are heading into town for a beer."

"Well, that's good," her father said. He pitched his cigar out onto the lawn before coming through the screen door and sauntering toward the sink. "It's getting late. Guess I'll head out to the carriage house and watch the Lopez-Casteneda fight on TV."

"Have fun," her mother said, coolly offering her cheek

for his kiss even as she continued to run a salad plate under the faucet.

Shelby, on the other hand, when it was her turn, threw her arms around Harry Simon's neck. "Good night, Daddy."

"Good night, little girl. It's nice having you home." Then he whispered, "You should probably stay inside tonight, honey, false alarm or not. Just in case."

"I will." She planted a loud *mm-wah* of a kiss, half on his shirt collar, half on his warm neck before letting him go.

"G'night, Beauty," he called to her mother as he went out the door.

Shelby finished securing the plastic wrap over Callahan's plate before putting it in the refrigerator. Hearing her father's favorite nickname for her mother nearly broke her heart. What did they think they were accomplishing with this ridiculous separation when it was perfectly obvious they still loved each other to death?

Frustrated, she closed the refrigerator a little harder than necessary, rattling all the bottles and jars on the inside of the door, and then turned toward her mother at the sink and launched a not-so-subtle trial balloon. "Dad's having a hard time coping with the wild success of Linda Purl, I guess."

Her mother reached for another plate to rinse under the hot stream of water. "Oh, I don't know about that," she replied, the Queen of Casual. Then she looked over her shoulder and added, "It sounds as if Mick and Sam have hit it off rather well, don't you think?"

Touché. Good one, Mom. Shelby didn't want to talk about Mick any more than Linda wanted to talk about

Harry, apparently. So, rather than answer, she asked if she could help with the rest of the dishes.

"I'm almost done," her mother said. "You go on and do whatever. Are you tired?"

"Maybe a little," Shelby lied. She looked at the half bottle of Merlot on the counter. "Want some more wine, Mom?"

"No, thanks, honey. I'm thinking about having a little dish of ice cream later."

Shelby reached into an upper cabinet for a wineglass. "Well, maybe I'll just take this upstairs for a little nightcap. Good night, Mom."

"Night, sweetheart. I guess we should leave the front door open for Mick. Chances are we'll both be asleep by the time he gets back."

"Yeah," Shelby said. Okay. One more try. "Unless you want to sit up and talk a while about . . . you know . . . things . . . sweaters at Neiman Marcus . . . sweaters lost in the Rockies . . . you and Dad."

"Not tonight, honey," her mother said in a voice that was as sweet as honey and as firm as concrete.

Shelby sighed. "Okay. Maybe later. G'night, Mom."

The Penalty Box in the little burg of Shelbyville was no different from any corner bar in Chicago that Mick had frequented over the years, with lighting provided by Coors and Anheuser-Busch, and warmth provided by too many bodies packed into too few square feet, pretty typical of a Friday night anywhere.

He and Sam Mendenhall sat shoulder to shoulder at

the bar. After one beer, the rent-a-cop had switched to coffee. Since Mick figured he had the benefit of a designated driver this evening, he was halfway through his third mug of draft.

Ol' Sam, it turned out, was a babe magnet. It had to be the cane, Mick decided as he watched women of every age and size stop to flirt with the guy on their way to and from the rest room. The blond, ponytailed barmaid had just leaned across the bar, refilling Sam's coffee mug and spilling a considerable amount of cleavage in the process, to ask the security guy if he wanted her to come out to the lake after she got off work. When he answered, "Maybe some other night, Rosie," little Rosie looked like she was going to cry.

"Got a date for the Masque?" she asked him then. "It's next Friday, you know. You're planning to go, right?"

"If I'm here," he replied. "I'll be out of town for a couple days. But if I'm here, babe, I'm yours."

Rosie fairly glowed with contentment as she went back to drawing mugs of cold lager.

"Out of town?" Mick asked.

He nodded. "Yeah. I wanted to talk to you about that. About making sure Shelby's covered while I'm gone."

"No problem," Mick said. "Looks like I'll be hanging around here for a while. Probably through next weekend, anyway."

"Great." He blew across the surface of the steaming brew. "Shelby will probably drag you to the Masque, you poor bastard."

"The what?"

"Masque." He spelled it. "It's the town's big annual blowout. Fourth of July, Valentine's Day, New Year's

Eve, and Halloween all rolled into one. Especially Halloween. Everybody wears a costume. There's even a queen."

Mick tried not to appear too jaded or indifferent. "Cute," he said, feeling his lip curl slightly in spite of his good intentions

Sam laughed. "Hey. It's something you have to grow up with, I guess."

"You grew up here?"

"Yep. How about you? Where are you from? Chicago?"

"Yep," Mick said without embellishment, then asked, "So, where are you off to?" Not that it was any of his business. Not that he even cared, really. He was just making Friday night bodega conversation, something that wasn't exactly his long suit. In all honesty, he figured he didn't have much in common with the rent-a-cop who hailed from Shelbyville, but his question was at least a rung or two above "How 'bout those Cubs?"

"Washington," Sam said. "I'm going to have some tests done at Walter Reed." His gaze strayed to his bum leg by way of explanation.

"That's the army hospital."

"Right. That's what I did before." He smiled kind of mournfully. "Before this."

Now Mick was genuinely curious. This put the gimp in a whole new light. "Infantry? Artillery?" he asked him.

"Special ops."

Ah. Well, that explained the earlier aura of command in the woods and probably also the facility with which Sam had wielded his cane to capture the fleeing perp. So, he wasn't just your average rent-a-cop. That was good.

Mick had a healthy respect for military training, and he admired the ingrained discipline of his fellow cops who'd come out of the army or the Marine Corps. There were times he thought maybe he could use some of that himself. At any rate, he felt a lot better about leaving Shelby up here in the backwoods, if and when he decided to go back home.

He lifted his beer mug in a toast to his companion. "Good luck at Walter Reed," he said.

"Thanks."

Then he was about to ask, "So, what happened to your leg?" when another highly perfumed member of the Sam Mendenhall Fan Club wedged herself between them, precluding further conversation.

Shelby refilled her wineglass with the last of the Merlot, and leaned back against the brass headboard. The house was as quiet as a mausoleum, which both pleased her and unsettled her. This way she'd be able to hear any intruder larger than a field mouse, but then she'd have to deal with it, and at the moment her self-defense skills were ... well ... wobbly at best, or nonexistent according to *some* people she'd rather not think about right now.

Gazing around her, she was glad that Beth had kept all the monster pieces of marble-topped walnut furniture that had always decorated this room. Thank heavens her mother had forbidden Shelby from turning it into a typical teenager's den with a white-laminated dresser and bookcases, black lights, BeeGees' posters, and a waterbed when she was in high school. This was so much nicer, not to mention a whole lot neater than when she was in summer residence here. Jeez. Just the sand on the floor back then could've contributed to a new shoreline for a man-made lake.

When people wrote to Ms. Simon complaining about their children's messy rooms, Shelby always responded with her laissez-faire advice. Let them have their space, she'd answer. Pick your battles carefully, moms and dads. A messy bedroom isn't a battlefield, after all. It's a son's or daughter's sanctuary.

Ask Alice disagreed. Bless his tidy, tyrannical, Neo Nazi little heart. Only last week he/she had written: "Organization is the true key to success, and it's never too early to learn." This bit of wisdom came in response to the mother of a four-year-old with a neatness disability.

Phooey. Shelby took another sip from her glass. Now that she was on the sidelines, more and more people would be turning to Alice for advice. It was a measure of Shelby's devotion to her column and her confidence in her own advice that the mere thought of awful Alvin Wexler becoming the country's foremost adviser nearly made her sick to her stomach.

"I gotta get back to work."

Oh, great. Ms. Simon was talking to herself now after a mere two days in exile. In another few days, she'd probably be writing Ask Alice herself, begging for advice. After that, who knew? She might strip off all her clothes and walk straight out into the lake until the cold water closed over her head.

On the upside, she supposed, was that after twelve years of doing her column, any tendency she might've had to take her career for granted was gone. She would be returning with renewed appreciation for every letter she read and every piece of advice she offered.

Feeling a bit less glum, Shelby swallowed the last of the wine, set the glass on the antique marble-topped nightstand, and reached to turn off the lamp just as a car door slammed in the driveway at the bottom of the hill.

That would be Sam dropping off Callahan. A quick glance at the clock told her that Michael Rainbow Callahan was twenty minutes shy of turning into a pumpkin at the stroke of midnight. Then she wondered what the two of them had talked about over their beers.

Well, two guesses what Sam had said about Shelby, the Evil Buttinski, and how she'd altered the course of his life with her "good" advice to Beth. She was surprised he'd been civil to her this afternoon, considering the grudge he bore her for something that really wasn't her fault. After all, Sam was the one who'd immediately gotten married to that bimbo in Georgia and had put an end to any future plans with Beth.

Of course, he was single now, wasn't he? And so was Beth. There was still time to fix things, to repair the damage she had done. If she could only get the two of them together and . . .

Oh, wait—wait a minute—hold the phone—why hadn't she thought of this before? Next Saturday would be Halloween, which meant that Masque was coming up. Masque, with the entire town in attendance and in disguise. Even a flock of summer people made it a habit to come back at Halloween for the festivities. It was the only time her parents had ever brought their daughters back here after the summer was over. To participate in

Masque, the celebration founded by Orvis Shelby, Jr., half a million years ago.

Legend had it—or rumor, in this case—that old Orvis, Jr., was a cross dresser who spent thousands and thousands of dollars on the annual affair in Shelbyville just so he could indulge his little lace-trimmed, high-heeled hobby in public once a year. Shelby suspected there was some truth to the rumors, especially since her mother's memories of the man always seemed deliberately vague and misleading. She hoped it was true, really. Didn't everyone want a horse thief up in the branches of their family tree? And if they couldn't have a horse thief, a cross dresser would certainly do.

She and Beth had attended Masque one year as the Olsen twins of television fame. One year they'd gone as Sonny and Cher, with the loser of a coin toss—poor Beth, naturally—having to be Sonny in a ratty faux fur vest while Shelby, aka Cher, got to wear a pink wig, false eyelashes, hip huggers, and platform shoes studded with rhinestones. That was the same year, as Shelby recalled, that her parents had dressed as Ashley Wilkes and Scarlett O'Hara. Talk about your mismatches of all time.

Okay. That settled it. Her mind was made up. She owed Beth and Sam a second chance, and Masque was the perfect way to get them back together. Tomorrow she'd call her sister, remind her about all the fun they'd had at the annual event, and offer to pay her airfare from San Francisco so they could celebrate again and play dress up together for what might be the last time in their lives.

It occurred to her then that the costume party might also be the perfect opportunity to reunite her parents.

Maybe if they attended the party as Rhett and Scarlett this time, the sparks would carry over into their actual lives. It was certainly worth a try.

So, in a single evening, nearly in the blink of an eye, Ms. Simon had solved the problems of two pairs of problem lovers. And once again, here she was alone, having paired up everyone in the world but herself. A typical end of a good day's work. It should've made her happier somehow . . .

She heard a creak at the bottom of the staircase, which meant that Callahan had come silently through the front door left unlocked for him and was on his way up to bed.

Or not.

She assumed it was Callahan, but what if it wasn't? People who've been threatened with death by letter bomb probably shouldn't make assumptions of any kind. Should they? What if it was someone else? What if . . . ?

With her heart thumping hard, this time out of fear rather than physical attraction, Shelby reached for the nearest weapon, the empty wine bottle on the nightstand. She slipped out of bed, then tiptoed to the closed bedroom door and listened almost fiercely to the squeaks of the treads and the creaks of the banister. Oh, God. It sounded way too spooky to be Callahan.

Her knees were turning to tapioca. Okay. Calm down. Let's be smart here, she told herself. What would you rather do in a situation like this—clunk someone over the head with a wine bottle, or just lock the damned bedroom door and be safe behind it?

Duh.

The only problem now was that this ancient and oh-so-familiar door locked not with a regular turn of a bolt but rather with a big, curlicued metal key, which was not currently inserted in the keyhole. Not on her side of the door, anyway. Shelby bent to peek through the ornate brass doorplate, possibly to glimpse whoever was coming up the stairs, but naturally her view through the keyhole was blocked by the big, curlicued, goddamn metal key that was stuck in the lock from the outside. Shit. She had to retrieve that key.

Twisting the knob and opening the door just wide enough to slide her hand through the opening, she felt for the key, hoping to whip that sucker out in the blink of an eye and then to close and lock the door from the inside.

Only . . .

The key, when her shaking fingertips made contact, wouldn't budge. She edged her arm farther out through the crack in the door, trying to get a bit more leverage on the damned thing, but when she stretched her fingers toward the key again, it was gone. God. She almost slammed the heavy door closed while her arm was still in it.

"Is this what you're looking for?" Callahan's voice rumbled on the opposite side of the door at the same instant that she felt the cool touch of metal against her palm. Shelby didn't know whether to sag to the floor with relief or to whip open the door and smack him. Clutching the key, she opened the door a few more inches to find herself staring straight into the soft plaid collar of his shirt. Her eyes jerked up and met the Grinch-like expression on his face.

"That was really a bone-headed move," he said.

Like she really needed him to tell her that, especially when the insult wafted through the space between the door and the frame on the wings of the Anheuser-Busch eagle. Angry now rather than frightened, she pushed the door with her shoulder and heard it thud against him. With any luck, she'd bruised something important.

"What were you going to do, Shelby?" he asked. "Stab me to death with the key?"

"No." She pulled the wine bottle from where she'd wedged it under her arm and brandished it. "I was going to brain my attacker with this. Of course, if I'd known it was you, Callahan, I wouldn't have bothered since you don't have one."

"Cute."

He jerked the door all the way open and blew across the threshold like some sudden storm, forcing Shelby to step back out of his way, and continued until he reached the windows on the far side of the room, where he began yanking on one of the long brocade panels that was swagged back against the window frame.

"What do you think you're doing?" she shrieked. "Stop that."

Callahan turned toward her, a wad of brocade fabric in his fist and fire in his hazel eyes. "I'm trying to discourage any more Peeping Toms is what I'm doing. There was a kid out there tonight who could barely wait for the Shelby Show to start."

"Oh, jeez." She felt her expression sort of flattening, almost sliding off her face, as she tried to recall where she'd changed out of her sweater and jeans and underthings into her long sleep tee earlier this evening.

God help her. Had she done anything stupid with her bra, like waving it over her head before she'd tossed it onto the dresser? Or had she performed a quick little Bob Fosse hip twitch in the buff? Or—oh, shit!—had she inspected various and sundry parts of her anatomy for sudden moles or discolorations or errant veins or patches of dry skin. Judas Priest. She was used to living on the twelfth frigging floor, after all. Now she wished she were twelve stories underground.

"Yeah. Oh, jeez," he said, mimicking her tone.

As he spoke, Shelby couldn't help but notice that Callahan seemed to be having a hard time maintaining eye contact with her. His gaze kept dropping to her bare feet, then wallowing at the hem of her pale blue cotton shirt, then sort of creeping back up with a pronounced lull at her chest. Talk about your Peeping Toms!

"Just pull down the shade, you jerk," she snarled at him.

"Excuse me?"

"Quit yanking on the curtains, Callahan. They aren't even supposed to close. Just pull down the stupid shades."

Now it was his turn to mutter a foolish "Oh." Ha! But then he reverted to full macho mode by nearly ripping the shades off their rollers when he whipped them down one after another on each of the tall windows.

Shelby, still miffed, would've crossed her arms over her chest with a proper amount of righteous indignation, but she had some concerns about that pose as it related to the length of her garment, so she placed her hands on her hips instead.

"I know I should thank you," she said, "but you make it almost impossible, Mick. You are without a doubt *the* most irritating man I've ever met in my life."

He turned from the now-secured windows and stared

at her, from her bare feet on upward, for a moment before he said, "That's because you want me."

Everything on Shelby's face that could form an O did so. Her eyes. Her nostrils. Most of all her mouth. "I beg your pardon."

"I said you're irritated because you want me." He stopped speaking just long enough to let his mouth slide into a goofball grin. "I feel the same way. You're the most irritating woman I've ever met, and it's all I can do not to toss you down on that mattress right this minute."

"It is? I mean, I am?" She swallowed. The sound was embarrassingly loud and vaguely reminiscent of a Disney character. She might as well have had a bubble over her head with the word "Gulp" printed in it.

"You are," he said, moving toward her the way a lion might move toward a shivering antelope. "And, yeah, I do."

"You do what?" she asked, having lost track somewhere, somehow, of the banter, of the you's and the I's and what they did or did not want. Pretty much all Shelby knew just then was what she wanted. Him. And here she was all of a sudden. Antelope on a stick.

"I want," he said, "you." The words had hardly left his lips before those lips made hard contact with hers, and his arms—they were hard, too, like young tree limbs— wound around her and pulled her against him. And speaking of hard . . .

This kiss was as astonishingly visceral as the one on the beach earlier that day. Shelby responded in every single cell of her body.

Then Callahan's radioactive mouth moved to her ear,

where his tongue made a hot circuit that sent jolts of desire through all of Shelby's bones.

"Dear Ms. Simon," he whispered, his lips at her ear.

It took her a moment to realize that his rasped "Dear" wasn't meant as an endearment, but rather a salutation.

He continued his wet, hot speech with "There's this woman . . ."

Oh, brother. Oh, damn. Shelby felt all of those sex-drunk cells of hers instantly sober up while her melting bones took on a distinct and rather unpleasant chill.

There's this woman, huh? Here it comes. Sadly, she knew this drill all too well, not just from letters she'd received, but from her own experience as well. He's involved with somebody else, but oh, you kid. She had to hand it to Callahan, though. Usually this little speech came accompanied by the mournful recriminations during the afterglow rather than during the foreplay. Apparently, the lieutenant liked to live (and love) on the edge.

She let him continue, although her ear suddenly didn't feel like an erogenous zone anymore.

"There's this woman," he whispered, "and I think she wants me as much as I want her, but it feels like it's too damn soon. I don't know. I just don't want to fuck this up. What do you advise?"

Her head snapped back. "You're talking about me?"

"Well, yeah." Callahan seemed to have a little trouble focusing on her face. He looked bewildered. Absolutely adorable.

"Omigod," she breathed. And then she laughed. "You were talking about me!"

He stepped back, abruptly releasing her from his embrace. "Well, who the hell else?" he exclaimed. Then he shook his head. "Okay. You know what? It's getting late here. I think I'll just . . ."

Shelby had obviously drenched his ardor with her laughter. But she couldn't help it. She was just so damned surprised. And pleased. Tickled, actually. Callahan was afraid of screwing up their relationship by moving too fast. That was so . . . It was so . . . Well, practically unheard of, for one thing. And . . .

"That's just so damned sweet," she said, lifting her hand to touch his cheek.

He swore and rolled his bleary eyes. "I'm going to bed. See you in the morning," he said gruffly. And just to prove to her that he wasn't all that sweet, he growled from the doorway, "And keep those goddamn shades pulled down, will you?"

"Yessir." Shelby gave a little salute in the direction of the slamming door.

Son of a gun.

CHAPTER ELEVEN

⌒

The next morning Shelby slept late. Well, that wasn't exactly true. It was closer to lollygagging than sleeping late. When she woke a little after seven, the room was still nearly pitch-dark because of the closed shades, which immediately set her to thinking—okay, dreaming—about Michael Rainbow Callahan.

His middle name didn't strike her as silly anymore, but utterly romantic. She must have been out of her mind.

But when had a man ever kept his gun in its holster, so to speak, when—quite clearly with another kiss or two, or with another hot, moist, sensual breath in the vicinity of her ear—he'd have had Shelby flat on her back with her legs wrapped like a pink satin bow around his waist?

Never. In her experience, admittedly somewhat limited, the majority of men were gunslingers, latter-day Wyatt Earps and Bat Mastersons, who stood ready—no, eager!—to whip out their forty-fives, their thirty-eights, or whatever size *pistola* at the slightest provocation. Hell, they didn't call it "banging" for nothing.

Shelby smiled up at the ceiling, and for a moment she

lingered over those images—Callahan's gun and her pink satin bow—and then she decided she was being pretty sappy, especially about a man who, when all was said and done, had walked out on her. She'd believed him completely last night, but what if he hadn't been telling the truth? What if his restraint hadn't been a fear of screwing up their relationship with premature sex, but fear of something else? Something entirely different?

Shelby's mind raced through a list of possibilities for his uncharacteristic behavior, from A for AIDS to Z for zipper deficiency. Well, she doubted that last one since she'd felt the strength of his arousal. Still, his behavior differed so radically from the typical male that she had to wonder.

In the end, though, she dismissed them all because Callahan had given her no reason not to believe him. Which brought Shelby back to his words—*It feels like it's too damn soon*—and to the remarkable conclusion that perhaps this man shared her view of great sex as the accompaniment to a great friendship.

She stretched, enjoying the darkness of the room and the warmth of the sheets, reluctant to begin a day in which she might discover she was wrong about her protector and his motives.

By eight-thirty, she had showered and dressed and trotted downstairs to discover her potential lover in the kitchen, wearing a chest-hugging, biceps-revealing black tee over his jeans, and helping her mother unload the dishwasher. Okay. There was "good," and then there was "too good to be true." Just her luck, he was probably the latter. She sighed softly as she entered the kitchen.

"There's my sleepyhead," her mother said. "Good morning, sweetheart."

Callahan's "Good morning" was accompanied by a fleeting grin and a quizzical tilt of his head, as if he were trying to gauge Shelby's mood.

"Good morning," she responded, padding toward the refrigerator while trying to gauge her own mood. It felt somewhere east of reason and slightly north of lust.

Over the clatter of silverware, her mother said, "Shelby, Mick has volunteered to run a few errands for me this morning. I thought maybe you could go along in case he has trouble reading my directions. You know how difficult it can be to make out my scribbles."

She was pouring a glass of orange juice while her mother spoke and she nearly spilled it at the part about the scribbles. Her mother printed so neatly it was less like penmanship than a damned font. Still, it was nice of her to play the eternal matchmaker. Too bad she didn't know her daughter couldn't wait to get Mick Callahan alone.

"Sure, Mom. I'd be happy to go along." She shoved the juice carton back onto its shelf and used her hip to close the door. "If Mick wants company."

"Absolutely," he said.

"Fine." Shelby took a long sip of her orange juice, wondering if anybody else was aware that the sexual tension in the room was so thick a person might need a snowblower just to get from the sink to the door.

Probably not. Her mother seemed blissfully unaware as she dropped the last fork into the silverware drawer and said, "Well, let me just go scribble down a few notes and you two can be on your way."

"Great. I'll run upstairs and get my jacket," Callahan said, making a beeline for the door. "Be right back."

The next thing Shelby knew, she and all that sexual tension were alone in the kitchen. She trudged through it to rinse her glass in the sink.

~

Mick fired up the Mustang. There was frost on the ground this morning and a bitter chill in the air, so he cranked the heater up all the way so the car would be warm for Shelby.

Just because he'd been an asshole last night didn't mean he had to be one today, he told himself. Ms. Simon had probably laughed herself to sleep after he fled her room like some kind of squeamish virgin.

It feels like it's too damn soon.

He must've been out of his fucking mind to say something like that with a woman like Shelby Simon in his arms and apparently in the mood. Christ. This courtship business was a mystery to him. Worse than a Rubik's Cube. There had never been anything resembling a courtship with him and Julie. They simply *were*. At least that was how it had always seemed. Considering the course of events, however, a bit of courtship might not have been such a bad idea.

He reached up to skew the rearview mirror his way, to see if he looked as idiotic as he felt. Yeah, idiotic. And tense. Wound way too tight. He passed his fingertips across his jawline, wishing he'd shaved this morning, wishing his life hadn't come undone two years ago, wishing he knew how to fix it.

Over breakfast this morning, Linda Simon had given him a couple interesting insights into her daughter. It seemed that Shelby was single-handedly responsible for pairing off most of her friends, while she herself rarely went out with any guy more than a few times.

"It isn't that she can't make a commitment," her mother said. "At least I don't think that's the problem. Well, on the other hand, maybe she can't commit to anything. Look at her apartment. You've seen it, haven't you, Mick?"

"You mean the House of Beige?"

"That's it exactly." The woman shook her head. "I just don't know. I've been shopping with Shelby, and she'll admire something in red or blue, but when it comes time to actually make a purchase, it's forever beige."

As he replayed the conversation in his head, he wondered about the wisdom of getting involved with a woman like this. Hell, if she found it impossible to commit to a blue couch, how would she ever make a commitment to a human being?

Of course, it might already be too late for him to consider being wise in matters of the heart.

"Dear Ms. Simon," he muttered. "Help. Shit. Signed . . . How about Bewitched, Bothered, and Bewildered in Bumfuck, MI."

He was jerked out of his little reverie by a succession of knocks on the passenger window. Shelby's pretty face was barely visible through the frosted glass. Mick leaned across to pull up the lock and open the door.

"Sorry I kept you waiting," she said, sliding into the seat, rubbing her hands up and down her arms. "Brr . . ."

"I've got the heater turned all the way up. It won't take

long once we're on the road. Where to?" He realigned the rearview mirror, then coaxed the shift into reverse and backed out of the driveway, while she consulted her mother's list.

"Well, let's see. First we go into town and pick up the mail." She laughed that wonderful, honey-dipped laugh of hers. "Well, there's some excitement, huh? Will there or will there not be more exploding yarn, sports fans? Stay tuned for the next exciting episode of . . ."

"Don't make a joke of it," he said, cutting her off, sounding far harsher than he intended, so he softened his tone when he continued. "I just mean that if you make too much of a joke about it, you'll let down your guard, and that can be dangerous."

"I know. It's just that a little humor helps me cope with this awful mess."

"That's my job," he said, taking his eyes off the road just long enough to meet her gaze, trying to smile in a way that she'd find comforting rather than a come-on. "To help you cope."

She didn't say anything in response, but Mick was aware of the fact that she'd turned sideways in her bucket seat and was leaning back against the door, staring at him. Staring a hole right through his right temple, as far as he could tell.

"What?" he asked.

"What was that all about last night, Callahan?"

He felt an immediate tightening in his jaw. "What was what all about?"

"When you . . ."

"Look, I don't want to talk about it now. Okay?" He was still weaving the car through the narrow, forested dirt road that led from the lake to the blacktop, so he decided it was reasonable to blame the driving conditions for his reluctance to speak. "I need to concentrate on the road here or we'll get wrapped around a tree."

"Oh, right. Like yesterday when you managed to go ninety miles an hour, glare repeatedly in the rearview mirror, yell at me, and whistle 'Dixie' all at the same time. Now you've suddenly got an attention deficit disorder." She clucked her tongue. "Give me a break."

He shouldn't have laughed. It undermined his credibility. But he couldn't help it. "We'll talk about it later. All right? Over lunch. How about that?"

"You promise?"

"Scout's honor." He held up two fingers, even as he felt as if he should be crossing his fingers behind his back and getting his lies, like his ducks, in a row.

As soon as Callahan parked on Main Street, Shelby was only too happy to jump out of the car. She'd practically had to bite her tongue all the way from the lake not to bring up the subject of last night. Lunch better be early, she thought as she pulled open the door to the little post office and heard a bell ring somewhere above her head.

"Hi, Mrs. Watt," she said, greeting the woman who'd been the postmistress here since before Shelby was born. Thelma Watt had looked about ninety-five twenty years ago, and today she didn't look a day over ninety-six in a starched blue dress with USPS patches sewn on the breast pocket and both sleeves.

"Hello, yourself," the woman replied, pulling her glasses down her nose to stare at her latest customer.

"I've come for our mail," Shelby chirped. "Simon."

"I know that," Mrs. Watt snapped. "Now which one are you? Shelby or Beth?"

"Shelby."

"Ah. The know-it-all."

"Well . . ." *Jeez.*

Shelby heard a barely suppressed chuckle at her back, and turned just in time to see Callahan wipe an asinine grin off his face. "Thanks a lot," she grumbled. When she turned back toward the counter, Mrs. Watt was peering over the rims of her glasses again, but this time over Shelby's shoulder.

"And there's your young friend who knows *all* about the U.S. Mail," she said.

Now it was Shelby's turn to chuckle.

Meanwhile Callahan maneuvered around her and stepped up to the counter, where he practically saluted the elderly postmistress as he asked, "Any suspicious packages, ma'am?"

She glared at him the way a drill sergeant might glare at a new recruit, then reached for a bundle of magazines and envelopes, which she slapped on the countertop. "Seems harmless enough to me, sonny," she said.

Shelby grabbed up the bundle and headed for the door before she fell on the linoleum floor laughing. "Thanks, Mrs. Watt," she called out.

"You're quite welcome, Shelby. Give my regards to your parents."

Out on the street, she leaned against the Mustang and flipped through the envelopes while waiting for Callahan, who had apparently remained behind to chitchat about the price of stamps or recent shootings in postal facilities. There was nothing suspicious in this batch of mail. Just something from State Farm for Harry, and everything else for Linda Purl. Poor Dad. All the bills and none of the glory these days. Maybe that would end this Friday night at the Masque.

That reminded her that she needed to call Beth ASAP about coming home next weekend. She dug in her handbag for her cell phone just as it started to ring. Beth was calling her, no doubt. It wouldn't be the first time they'd had phone synergy.

Shelby clicked on without checking the ID window. "You've got to come back here for Masque," she said instead of hello. "I absolutely insist."

"Uh. Shelby?"

She recognized Derek McKay's voice instantly. "Oh, Derek. I'm sorry. I thought you were my sister."

"You could've at least said brother," he replied, sounding as if he'd already had a few from his flask between breakfast and brunch.

"Sorry," she said again. "Are you still back East?"

"Yeah, but I'm taking the next plane out for O'Hare. They just got a break there in the letter bomb case."

Her heartbeat picked up major speed. "A break? Well, tell me."

"There's a guy at Northwestern. A chemistry major. He made some interesting purchases by credit card last week, including aluminum powder and iodine crystals, along with some other nasty little chemicals. The detectives are on their way to talk to him right now."

"So, this guy has a grudge against me or something?"

"Dunno. I'll find out more when I get back in town in a couple hours, and I'll let you know."

"Okay. Thanks, Derek. I hope he turns out to be the guy and they slap him in jail right away. I'm going nuts not working."

"Where are you, anyway, kiddo? I stopped by your place yesterday to console you if you were upset, and your doorman said you'd left town."

"I did. I'm . . ."

Wait. Callahan had told her under no circumstances to tell anybody where she was. Shelby went through a quick mental Rolodex of the people she'd talked to since she'd been in Michigan. Beth. Well, okay. That was her sister, for heaven's sake. And she remembered telling Hal Stabler she was at her parents' place when he asked, without identifying the exact location.

She'd talked to Kellie Carter, too, but had only given the intern her cell phone number to relay to Derek. Phew.

"I'm up north," she said, hoping he wouldn't press. "I'm glad you got my message and called me, Derek."

"What message?" he asked.

"The one I left with Kellie. I asked her to give you my cell number and to call as soon as you could."

"I didn't get any message. I called your Nervous Nellie secretary, Sandy, this morning to get your number. Listen, Shelby. They're announcing my flight. I gotta run. I'll talk to you later."

He was gone before she could say good-bye. She dropped the phone back into her bag just as Callahan came out of the post office.

"Ready?" he asked her.

"Yeah, but wait'll you hear . . ."

He held up a hand to silence her. "Is that my cell phone ringing or yours?"

"Must be yours," she said. "My purse is definitely silent at the moment."

Reaching through the open window on the passenger side, he pulled his beeping cell phone from the glove compartment. "Yeah," he grunted by way of a greeting, then began pacing back and forth on the sidewalk as he listened to whoever was on the other end of the line. Callahan's contribution to the conversation was pretty much restricted to "uh-huhs" and occasional curses that seemed to serve as punctuation marks.

He was a pleasure to watch, which Shelby did in a circumspect manner from her perch on the hood of the car. Today, in addition to his jeans and sexy black T-shirt, he was wearing a worn leather bomber jacket that looked as if it might have actually seen action in World War II.

If he was still here next Friday for Masque, she was going to insist that he wear it as his costume. Lieutenant Callahan, indeed.

Shelby was thinking about what she could wear to complement his Battle of the Bulge outfit when he snapped his cell phone closed.

"That was my captain," he said. "They've got a lead on your letter bomber."

"Let me guess," Shelby said. "A chemistry student at Northwestern made some suspicious purchases last week."

His lovely hazel eyes nearly popped out of their sockets. "Now how the hell do you know that?"

She smiled inscrutably. "I have my sources. Don't forget I was a journalist before I was an advice columnist."

He shook his head. "Frigging leaks between the police and the press. We might as well work out of the same offices."

"Half the time I think we do," Shelby said, then tilted her head and asked in all seriousness, "So, what do you think, Callahan? Is this the guy?"

"Could be. I guess we'll find out pretty soon."

He didn't sound too happy with the prospect of an imminent solution to the case. Come to think of it, neither was she. If they caught the letter bomber, her need for protection would be gone.

Along with Michael Rainbow Callahan.

For the next few hours while they criss-crossed the autumn-colored countryside around Shelbyville, picking up finished sweaters and scarves for Linda Purl Designs, Mick felt his mood descending into a full-fledged funk. It was probably the first time in his career in law enforcement that he was loath to see a case come to an end. Of course, he wasn't officially even *on* the case, but Shelby didn't know that.

But right now, worse than having the case closed and his services no longer required as a bodyguard, was what he'd stupidly agreed to earlier—their little tête-à-tête at lunch during which he'd promised—Scout's honor, his ass—to discuss *what that was all about last night*.

Sex, he'd tell her. He'd even spell it. S*E*X. He'd sound indignant and misunderstood. What the fuck did she think it was all about? But that wasn't going to work because he'd already pretty well given himself away with that dumbass remark about feeling like it was too soon for S*E*X. If he hadn't been driving at the moment, he would've bashed his forehead against the steering wheel.

Shelby looked up from the list. "That was our last stop," she announced.

"Great."

"Time for lunch, Callahan."

He glanced to his right. She was smirking. There was no other way to describe the peculiar slant of her mouth and the glint in her eyes. Jesus. He felt like a bigmouthed bass with a hook in his gut.

"Okay," he said, sounding as if lunch were just any old meal. "Where to? Back to the place where we ate yesterday? That was nice." And maybe the beautiful lake view would distract her enough to forget about her quest for knowledge. After all, she'd forgotten her purse there yesterday.

"It was nice, but I've got a better idea. Let's go on a picnic."

"A picnic," he echoed, sounding as if he'd never heard the word before.

"Yeah. A picnic, Callahan. You know. Outside. Food. Fun. Ants."

"I can't remember the last time I was on a picnic," he said.

"Well, then it's high time, don't you think? We can pick up some sandwiches and stuff at the little store in Shelbyville, and then I know the perfect little pine forest not too far from the lake. My sister and I used to take our lunches there all the time when we were kids."

"Okay. If that's what you want."

"That's what I want," she said.

And maybe, he thought, if all the planets were properly aligned, if he were suddenly the luckiest man alive, that would be all she'd want and the words "about last night" would never escape her lovely, lush lips.

⁓

Shelby balanced her salami sandwich on her knee because she needed two hands to lift the jug of screw-top Chianti and refill her paper cup. It wasn't quite the Martha Stewart picnic she'd had in mind when she suggested it, but it was wonderful nevertheless.

She'd been thinking along the lines of a baguette, some decent cheese, and a clever Bordeaux, but the best that Sneed's Quik Mart in Shelbyville could do was a loaf of sliced whole wheat, a package of Oscar Mayer salami best if used before tomorrow's date, a pillow-sized bag of Ruffles, and the five-liter jug of domestic Chianti she was currently wrestling with.

Their picnic blanket—instead of a Martha-ish blue-and-white checkered cloth with contrasting napkins, or even a dark tartan stadium blanket—was a navy flannel bedsheet, fitted no less, pulled from a stash of laundry in the trunk of the Mustang.

"Here." Callahan pulled the heavy glass jug from her hands and handled it as if it were a teacup, refilling her paper cup and then his, before he screwed the metal cap back on and plunked the jug down onto the rumpled blue flannel sheet. "Nothing wrong with Ripple, I always say." He grinned as he lifted his cup toward her in a toast.

Shelby laughed. Who ever had so much fun with bad wine, she thought. "Here's to . . ."

She had her cup in the air, ready to toast him, but her mind went blank all of a sudden. Well, not blank exactly. She'd been about to say "Here's to us," but that didn't seem appropriate. There wasn't any "us," for heaven's sake.

"Here's to picnics," she finally said, clacking her cup against his, spilling some wine over her fingers.

"Here's to us," Callahan said.

Oh, jeez. Was there an us, after all? Or was that just Mick Callahan's standard, all-purpose toast? Here's to us with the guys at the precinct. Here's to us with a blind date. Here's to us with the stranger down at the end of the bar. Shelby took a small, thoughtful sip of the Chianti, then figured what the hell, and knocked back half the contents of the cup.

"So, about last night . . . ?" she asked, peering at him over the paper rim.

He swallowed his wine audibly. "Well . . ."

She lifted her eyebrows by way of encouragement. Prompting him to speak. Daring him, actually. "Well?"

"Okay." Stretching out his legs, he leaned sideways, bracing himself on a leather-clad elbow. He contemplated the floral border on his paper cup. He took another sip from it. He lifted his gaze to study Shelby's face a moment. Her eyes. Her mouth. Mostly her mouth. He picked up a pine needle, bent it between his fingers, then dropped it. Then picked up another one. He cleared his throat.

Oh, for heaven's sake! Shelby was on the verge of screaming and telling him to just forget it—please!—when he spoke so quietly that she had to lean forward to hear.

"I got married when I was seventeen. I was married to the same woman for almost nineteen years, until she was killed two years ago. All . . . all of this feels pretty foreign to me." A mournful little laugh broke from his throat and his eyes suddenly glistened. "I feel like I'm in fucking Uzbekistan or someplace."

"Oh, Mick." She could hardly get the words past the lump in her own throat.

"So that's what last night was about basically," he said. "I . . . uh . . . hell. I just don't know how to play this game anymore, Shelby. Shit. I probably never did." He broke eye contact with her then and stared out through the rough trunks of the surrounding pines.

She thought that the lump in her throat just might be her heart. It didn't seem to be in its proper place at the moment. "Thank you for being honest," she said.

He rolled his eyes and continued to look away.

"No, I mean it. I . . . I feel the same way most of the time. As if it's all foreign. As if everybody else 'gets it' somehow. The hooking up, the moving in, the pairing off in couples, and then doing it all over again when it doesn't work out. People write me for advice, and half the time I just don't know what to say."

A tiny grin pulled at the corners of his mouth. "I find that hard to believe," he said.

"Well, it's true." She took another sip from her paper cup. "I keep waiting for the one letter that says 'Wait a minute. Wait a minute. If you're so damn smart, how come you're still alone?' "

He turned back to her now. The moisture was gone from his eyes, but the sadness was still there. "And what's the answer, Ms. Simon? How come you're still alone?"

Because I was waiting for you, she wanted to say. Fortunately, her cell phone beeped from the depths of her handbag just then, and no sooner had her phone sounded than Callahan's did, too.

Before she answered, she checked the caller ID and immediately recognized Derek McKay's number.

"Hey," she said. "What's up?"

"Hey, Shelby. Remember I told you about that chem student at Northwestern?" Derek asked.

There was a darkness in his tone that signaled bad news. "I remember," she said. "The police were on their way to question him. Was he the letter bomber? What did they find out?"

"Nothing," Derek said. "When they got there, the kid was dead."

CHAPTER TWELVE

Mick jammed his cell phone into his jacket, then walked back across the soft carpet of pine needles to the sorry blue flannel sheet where Shelby sat waiting for him.

"Bad news travels fast, I guess," she said as soon as she saw his face.

"That was your source? On the phone?" he asked, and pretty politely, too, he thought, for a guy who'd once been suspended without pay for two weeks for throwing a TV reporter's mike into Lake Michigan when the idiot got in the way of an investigation.

She nodded. "The chemistry student at Northwestern is dead. Derek . . . er, my source didn't know how."

"I do." He waggled his eyebrows. Cops One, Reporters Zip.

"How?"

He sat back down on the sheet. "They think it might have been poison, but they won't know for sure until the autopsy."

"Oh, my God. And that's why he bought those suspicious chemicals last week, I guess. To commit suicide."

Mick shrugged. He doubted that sincerely. It was too brutal, too slow and painful a way to go when eating a gun was a relatively quick and painless way to off yourself. There was little doubt, according to his captain, that the chemistry student had been murdered. They were going over his dorm room and his former life with a fine-tooth comb right now.

And all of that pretty much meant they were right back at square one as far as Shelby and her letter bomber were concerned. It also meant that his protective services weren't yet obsolete, and that he better start concentrating on Shelby's safety instead of her incredible mouth and her world-class assets. He looked around at the acres of pine trees that surrounded them, and decided this picnic hadn't been such a good idea. They were isolated at the same time they were exposed. Perfect targets.

"Let's get back to the lake," he said, levering up off the ground and offering Shelby a hand. "Come on."

"Oh, so soon? Let's stay and talk some more."

"Let's not." He reached for her arm to haul her to her feet.

"What's wrong?" she asked, her eyes widening as she stared up at him.

"Nothing. I just want to get you back to civilization. That's all."

She let him help her to her feet then. "You're scaring me, Callahan," she said. There was a distinct tremor in her voice.

"Hey." Mick put his hands on her shoulders and leaned forward so his forehead touched hers. "I'm not trying to scare you. I'm just trying to make sure nothing bad happens to you. That's my job."

She laughed weakly. "Such as it is," she said, echoing his words of two days before when he'd had no clue how quickly his professional and his personal lives would get scrambled.

"Such as it is," he whispered. "Now come on."

~⁓

They turned into the driveway, barely missing Sam's Jeep as he was backing out. Shelby jumped out of the Mustang and sprinted toward the rust-colored vehicle before its driver could take off.

He didn't seem too thrilled to see her.

"I just stopped by to tell your folks that I'll be gone for the next few days," he said.

"Gone?"

He seemed even less thrilled now. "Yeah, Shelby. Gone. As in not here. See ya." He reached to shift the Jeep into reverse again.

"No! Wait!"

The Jeep idled in neutral while Sam glared at her. "What? I've got a plane to catch, Shelby. Make it quick."

"Well, I was just wondering about your plans for next weekend. It's Masque, you know."

"Yeah. Every year. Funny how that happens."

She maintained a friendly, even charming expression, allowing his sarcasm to drift away on a cool lake breeze. This was for Beth, after all. If Shelby had to eat a certain amount of crow in order to reunite her sister with her true love, well, then she'd do it. Dammit.

"I was just wondering if you'd be back in time," she said cheerfully.

"I might. Why?"

"Oh, no particular reason. I was just curious."

He was practically skewering her now with his gaze. "Shelby, you've never been 'just' anything in your life."

She shrugged.

"If this has something to do with me and Beth, forget it. Neither one of us is interested in digging up the past."

"You don't know that," she protested.

"Okay. Then *I'm* not interested. You got that?"

"Well . . ."

"Good-bye, Shelby." He jammed the gearshift into reverse and nearly ran over her toes in his rush to get away.

"See ya, Sam," called Callahan. "Good luck."

Sam threw him a quick wave, and just for good measure he launched one more black look at Shelby before he sped up the road.

"Good luck?" Shelby asked, walking back to the Mustang where Mick was stuffing the sheet back into the trunk. "What did you mean?"

"Did I say that?" He slammed the trunk lid. "I meant good-bye."

No way was she buying that. "Why does Sam need good luck?"

Instead of answering right away, he picked up the wine jug and thrust it at her. "Here. Make yourself useful."

"Tell me," she insisted. "Why does Sam need good luck?"

"Probably because a certain know-it-all seems to have an agenda that he doesn't want any part of. At least that was the impression I got." He gathered the rest of their picnic stuff from the backseat, then started up the hill toward the house, calling back over his shoulder. "Or not. I dunno. Maybe he likes to have opinionated women pushing him around."

"Opinionated?" she shrieked. "I'm not opinionated, Callahan." The wine sloshed in the glass bottle as she struggled to catch up with him. "I'm not."

"Sorry. I meant to say forthright and candid."

"Well . . . yeah." She had to agree with that.

"Direct," he said, not slowing down.

"I guess so." It wasn't easy keeping up with his long strides uphill, but Shelby did her damnedest. "I am direct," she said. "And proud of it."

"Well informed."

"Extremely well informed." Where was he going with this? she wondered. She had the feeling, based mostly on an evil little slant to his grin, that the proverbial boom was about to be lowered.

"Articulate," he added.

"Very."

"And agreeable, too."

Okay. Shelby figured she'd spring this little trap before he did. "Okay. So I'm opinionated. But I get paid for it. Or at least I did."

He cupped a hand to his ear. "You're what?"

"Stop it." She slapped his leather sleeve. "You heard me."

That evil little grin turned into a brilliant smile as he wrapped his arm around her shoulder. "Did I ever tell you that I'm partial to pigheaded—oh, sorry—opinionated women?"

God, his arm around her felt so good. Still, she

couldn't resist. "Did I ever tell you to go jump in the lake, Callahan?"

The voices floated through the broken window in the carriage house where Harry and Linda Simon sat side by side, their hands entwined, in the center of the long curved couch. She'd come out only a short time ago to tell her husband about Sam Mendenhall's trip to the hospital in Washington.

"I like him, Harry," Linda whispered. "I think Mick is good for Shelby, don't you?"

"Yeah. Well, the kid can definitely hold his own. Your daughter has a tendency to run over young men like a locomotive."

"Not this one." She laughed softly a moment. "I had a nice talk with him over breakfast this morning. He was married before. For nearly twenty years, believe it or not. His wife was murdered two years ago during a purse snatching in the Loop. I remember reading about that in the paper."

Harry nodded. "One of our guys did the initial pro bono work on that case, I think. Damned shame."

"Mm," she murmured, tipping her head against his shoulder. "Why don't we take them out to dinner tonight? We could go to the Blue Inn. They always have a live band on Saturday nights."

"Are you asking me out on a date, Beauty?" His tone was amused while his thumb played over the back of her hand.

"If you want to look at it that way, then, yes, I guess I am."

"I'd be delighted. It's been a long time since we've danced." He drew back his head to look at her. "When was the last time? I can't even remember."

"It must've been at your retirement party at the club," she said, immediately regretting her words.

A frown sketched across his brow and his eyes darkened, and Linda imagined he was thinking the same thing she was—how they'd argued that night, Harry with all his grand plans for a life of leisure while she was a nervous wreck waiting to hear whether or not Nordstrom's would carry Linda Purl Designs.

Nordstrom's had come through, of course, as had Neiman's and several other stores, not to mention the Sundance Catalog. For a while, Harry seemed to be fine, jetting off with his pals to this macho place or that. But only for a while.

"Well . . ." She sighed and stood up. "I'll go ask Shelby and Mick about tonight. How does seven o'clock sound, Harry?"

"Fine. I'll be ready," he said with considerably less enthusiasm than he'd expressed mere moments ago.

"Fine." Sensing the imminent appearance of storm clouds, possibly accompanied by lightning and thunder, Linda made her exit without further ado.

~

Mick hadn't sat in the backseat with a date whose father was at the wheel since junior high when Julie's dad used to drive them to movies. Well, it wasn't a date so much as just going out to dinner with Shelby and her parents, but still . . .

He felt like a jerk in his jeans and leather jacket while Harry Simon wore a gray herringbone jacket and club tie over his perfectly pressed khakis, and Mrs. Simon looked equally well turned out, if not better, in a long suede skirt and a matching sweater and shawl or whatever the hell it was.

"They always dress like that," Shelby had whispered to him earlier, no doubt sensing his discomfort. That was probably why she'd worn jeans, too, to spare his feelings at being underdressed. "Hey," she said, nudging his arm, "we're just going to the Blue Inn, Callahan. Not Ambria or some other chichi place."

Amazingly enough, he'd been to Ambria, the upscale French restaurant on Lincoln Park West, numerous times, as well as countless other chichi places in Chicago with Julie and her doctor pals, although that all seemed a lifetime ago right now. Probably the fanciest thing he'd eaten in the past two years had been a pizza with anchovies. And he only wore a tie these days when he had to testify in court. Why he thought Ms. Shelby Simon would be even remotely interested in a guy who was such a sartorial mess was a mystery to him.

But she was. At least he thought so. In the confines of the Mercedes's backseat he could feel the warmth of her arm even through the leather of his jacket. She was wearing a different fragrance tonight, something musky and utterly feminine that was almost making his temperature spike. For whatever that was worth.

He'd meant what he'd said earlier today about feeling like he was in a foreign country when it came to the finer points of romance. He didn't know how to go slowly anymore. Between his impulse to make love to Shelby and the act itself, he had forgotten all the obligatory intermediary steps that told a woman she was special, that said this was more than just sex for its own sake, that showed her that her heart and brain and soul mattered to him as well as her body. Or maybe he'd never known those steps. His only frame of reference was Julie, and they'd pretty much grown up together, making courtship virtually unnecessary. Or so he thought for all those years.

Dammit. There was Julie again, intruding on his thoughts about Shelby. He would've distracted himself by starting a conversation with Shelby, but she was talking to her mother just then about the drill sergeant at the Shelbyville Post Office. He wished he could just erase his late wife from his brain, and he was trying to do just that when Harry Simon announced, "Well, here we are," as he slowed the car and turned into the parking lot of the Blue Inn.

Mick got out of the backseat, then opened the passenger door to help Shelby's mother. As they walked across the pebbled parking lot toward the front door of the restaurant, she leaned close and whispered, "If you ever want to get rid of that wonderful jacket, Mick, let me know. I've always wanted Harry to wear one. They're so . . . well . . . never mind."

"Sexy?" he asked.

She laughed. It was a sound similar to her daughter's, but deeper, throaty, as if she might have been a smoker at one time. "I wasn't going to say it for fear you'd think

I was a dirty old woman. But yes, sexy. It must drive Shelby wild."

Not that he could tell, he thought, while he responded to Mrs. Simon with a kind of *aw, shucks* lift of his sexy leather shoulders. They stepped through the door of the restaurant then and somebody grabbed him by his sexy leather sleeve.

"Aren't you the young man who broke just about every durn speed limit in Mecklin County yesterday?"

Instead of reaching for his gun, which was his first instinct, Mick stuck out his hand to the old geezer who'd chased him. "Yessir. Sorry about that."

The old guy laughed. "Oh, now that my heart's back beating properly, sonny, I can say I didn't mind at all. It was a lot cheaper than going to an amusement park and riding a loop-de-loop." He shifted his gaze to Mick's left and raised a ragged white eyebrow. "Evening, Linda. Haven't seen you in a while. This young fella your date? I heard you and Harry were having problems."

Linda Simon's mouth fell open, but no words came out. Other than punch the old guy out, Mick couldn't think of a thing to say or do, so it was a good thing that Shelby's father appeared right behind them and said, "Good to see you, Mr. Keeler. How's that little legal problem I helped you with last spring? Fine, I hope. We'll have a table for four by the window, if you please."

Within two minutes, they were seated at a hastily cleared table smack in the center of the big picture window where strings of amber lights were reflected in the dark waters of Blue Lake. A three-piece band—guitar, bass, and drums—was doing a pretty credible job with some oldies but goodies.

Ms. Curious finally got a chance to lean across the table and ask, "What little legal problem, Daddy?"

"It was nothing," her father said. "The man just—"

"Dance with me, Harry," Linda said, already pushing back her chair.

"Glad you finally asked, Beauty." Harry pushed back from the table, too. "Shelby, order us a couple liters of the house red, will you?" He winked and was gone.

Mick watched Shelby watch them as she sat with her chin resting on her clasped hands. There was an undeniable longing in her expression, one he wouldn't have minded being directed at him. He sighed softly to himself before he spoke.

"That doesn't look like a marriage in trouble to me," he said.

"No, it doesn't, does it?" She turned her whiskey and honey and amber gaze toward him. He could see the lake lights reflected in her gaze. "I just wish I knew what to do to get them back together once and for all. There ought to be something."

He was about to tell her to mind her own business in a veiled sort of way when the waitress appeared at the table.

"Can I get you folks something to drink before you order?" she asked just as casually as she'd looked at each of them, but then her gaze narrowed on Shelby. "Don't I know you?" she asked, pointing her ballpoint pen right between Shelby's eyes.

Once again Mick had a firsthand demonstration of this woman's high visibility, and it unsettled him. It worried the hell out of him, in fact. Shelby, however, took it in stride. It must've been same old, same old to her.

"I'm Shelby Simon," she said, smiling up at the waitress, making it sound no more impressive than Jane Doe.

Julie flashed in his brain again. Julie of the humble origins who had turned into the unapproachable Dr. Julie, even to him. His late wife would've cut this waitress off at the knees.

"Shelby! I *knew* I knew you," the waitress exclaimed. "I'm Kimmy Mortenson. I used to hang out with you and your sister at the lake. Remember? God, that was so long ago, you probably don't remember."

"No, I do," Shelby said. "You were the waterskiing maniac, right? You were great. I always thought you'd wind up in one of those water shows in Florida."

Kimmy sighed dramatically. "Yeah, well . . . Here I am, still stuck in North Overshoes. You're doing great. I read your column all the time."

"Thanks," Shelby said.

"I saw Beth a couple times when she was here redoing the house. Too bad she wasn't here when Sam came back. You know?"

While Shelby nodded, Kimmy's gaze shifted to Mick. "So . . . this must be your husband."

He was surprised, but he hadn't seen such an expression of astonishment on Ms. Shelby Simon's pretty face since the mailman's cart blew up in front of her apartment building the other day. Even in the dim light of the restaurant he could see her cheeks flush and she actually stuttered when she responded.

"N-no. He's m-my friend. This is Mick Callahan."

"Oops. Sorry." Kimmy laughed and flourished her order pad. "Well, before I step in it again, I guess I better take your order."

"We'll start with a couple liters of your house red," Mick said when it appeared that Shelby's mind had gone blank.

"Okay. Be right back with that."

After she hustled away, Shelby took a long drink from her water goblet. Mick got the distinct impression that she was stalling.

"That bother you?" he asked.

"You mean Kimmy's assuming we were married?"

He nodded.

"No, it didn't bother me," she said, still looking a bit flustered. "It was a natural mistake."

"Maybe she thought we looked good together," he suggested. "What do you think?"

"I think you'd look good with anybody, Callahan."

He laughed. "Oh, yeah?"

"Especially when you smile," she added.

"That's not my native expression."

"I've noticed."

"Well, I guess . . ."

He stopped speaking when something caught his eye on the far side of the dining room. Mr. Keeler, the old geezer, appeared to be saying something to a large party, all of whom immediately put their napkins on the table and rose to leave. Fast. Keeler then went to the next table. Same deal.

"What?" Shelby asked, looking across the dance floor.

"Let's get out of here," Mick said quietly. He was already half out of his chair.

"What in the world . . . ?"

"Come on. We'll cut across the dance floor and get your folks. Let's go."

"But—"

"Now, Shelby." He yanked her chair back from the table, grasped her arm, and pulled her up.

After so many years in law enforcement, his instincts were finely honed, especially in crowded public places. And he'd seen too damn many tragedies, too many dead bodies, either trampled or burned, in places where people had lingered too long. He didn't have to wait until old Mr. Keeler arrived at their table to tell them to make tracks.

With one arm around Shelby, Mick cut through the couples on the dance floor until they reached the slow-dancing, close-dancing Harry and Linda Simon.

"I hate to interrupt, folks, but I think we better step outside," Mick said.

"What's going on?" Shelby's mother asked, her eyes widening.

Harry, thank God, had taken one hard look at Mick's face and didn't need to ask questions. "Let's go, Linda. Come on. We'll follow you and Shelby, Mick."

Outside, he hustled his little flock across the parking lot to the far side of the big Mercedes, figuring that would adequately shield them if anything exploded. It didn't take more than a few minutes before the place was cleared out completely, including the help and the three members of the band. And just then a police cruiser, its blue lights flashing, peeled off the blacktop into the parking lot.

The officer jumped out, bullhorn in hand. "Just stay

calm, folks. There's been a bomb threat. We'll let you know when it's safe to go back inside."

Mick felt Shelby shudder beside him. He put his arm around her and bent his head to whisper, "Don't be scared. Ten to one, it's a coincidence. And more than likely it's just a prank."

She looked at him, her eyes big and glossy, as if she were trying with all her might to believe him.

Even as Mick was wishing he believed it himself.

CHAPTER THIRTEEN

Shelby and her parents sat in the elegant Victorian dining room in the house at Heart Lake over bowls of canned minestrone, and about the only sound Shelby could hear, other than the occasional clink of a spoon against the rim of a fine china soup bowl, was the incessant rattling of her own bones. She was already wrapped in her mother's wool and silk shawl, but the chill that ran through her had nothing to do with the temperature of the room.

Mick had stayed behind at the Blue Inn to help in the search for a possible bomb. Shelby had gotten the impression that he didn't have a lot of confidence in the local constabulary, and that if indeed anything suspicious was found, he wanted to make sure everything was done properly. Actually, his exact words had been "make sure these yokels don't fuck up."

Her parents were doing their best to keep her calm when calm was the last thing Shelby wanted to be. She just wanted this nightmare to end. After tonight's incident, she felt as if she were doomed to spend the rest of her life looking over her shoulder. God. She might even have to buy a bomb-sniffing dog.

Now that her mother was aware of the situation with the letter bomber, she didn't seem all that upset by it. Either that or Linda Simon was one hell of an actress. She was tilting her soup bowl now, spooning up the last of her minestrone, and saying ever so calmly, "I'll bet it's just as Mick said, sweetheart. Just some bored kid trying to spice up a Saturday night with a prank call to poor old Mr. Keeler."

"I hope you're right, Mother."

"I'm sure I am, honey."

Her mother's calm and confident tone made Shelby almost long to be a child again, one who thought her parents knew absolutely everything and that their every utterance was gospel. Pure, indisputable gold.

Lightning won't strike the house, honey. It's grounded.
Oh, good.
Lock the doors and you'll be safe.
What a relief.
Ssh. Nothing bad will ever happen.
Phew.

Her father, who had been unusually quiet ever since the bomb scare had forced them out of the restaurant, spoke up now. "Well, just in case you're not right, Linda," he said, "I'm going to spend tonight here in the house."

He spoke assertively, matter-of-factly, without even the smallest *by your leave, madam* glance down the table at his estranged wife. And much to Shelby's surprise and pleasure, there wasn't so much as a flicker of dissent from her mother. Well, hallelujah. Welcome home, Harry.

Maybe something good could come out of all this bomb business after all.

It was probably a good time to make her exit, Shelby decided. After kissing her parents good night, she climbed the staircase to the second floor, suddenly remembering how she and Beth had named each of these twenty-eight well-worn stairs for the first twenty-eight presidents of the United States. There had been some debate over whether or not to count the landing, therefore the list sometimes included number twenty-nine, Warren G. Harding, and sometimes stopped with Woodrow Wilson.

At the top of the staircase, or in this case atop Warren G. Harding, Shelby sighed, once again wishing she could go back to a time when it was important to know the names of the presidents in order, a time when it was a given that her parents would keep her safe forever.

Oh, great. She was regressing again, turning into a big damn baby. What was it about coming home that stripped her of her sense of self, her independence, and whatever amount of courage she possessed?

She flopped on her bed and stared at the ceiling. Anyway, she didn't need her parents' protection, did she? She was a grown-up. She could damn well protect herself, and if not, well, then, she had her very own card-carrying, gun-toting, bomb-sniffing bodyguard, right?

Callahan.

Jeez.

She hoped he was better at fighting crime than he was in the romance department.

There was no freaking bomb.

While the local cops waited for the arrival of a certified dog and handler from Grand Rapids, they stood around the Blue Inn's parking lot, talking about bass and bluegills and blowing away Bambi in the upcoming hunting season. Mick had nothing to contribute to the discussion. He'd never understood the sporting aspect of firearms, or maybe it was just that he'd seen too many seriously dead bodies. He was tuning the local yokels out when Kimmy the waitress had pulled him aside.

"I think I might know who made that call," she whispered, "but I don't want to get him in trouble."

"Better him than you," Mick told her, using the well-practiced evil eye he used on the street in Chicago.

Kimmy sighed. "My boyfriend and I had a big fight before I left for work. He's tired of me working on Saturday nights. Says it ruins his weekends. So, when I walked out, he yelled from the door that I might as well not go because I wouldn't be making any big tips tonight anyway."

She gazed at the front door of the deserted restaurant, and sighed again. "And he was right. I didn't."

Mick passed the information along to the sergeant in charge, and after the phone company confirmed that the call had indeed come from Kimmy's number, Mick didn't know whether he was relieved or not. He wanted Shelby's bomber apprehended, but at the same time he didn't want the guy anywhere near her or her family.

The sergeant gave Mick a ride back to Heart Lake where he found Harry Simon sitting on the front porch, blowing cigar smoke rings into the chilly night air.

"Cuban," Harry said, gesturing toward Mick with the stogie. "Care to try one?"

"No, thanks."

"Find anything at the restaurant?" her father asked.

"Nothing. It turned out to be just a prank. Some guy trying to close the place to make sure his waitress girlfriend didn't make any tips tonight."

"Asshole," Harry breathed through a cloud of smoke. "Shelby's scared to death. You better go inside and let her know everything's okay."

"I'll do that," Mick said, already on his way toward the front door. "Good night, sir."

"Good night, Mick."

Upstairs, Shelby's door was closed. Assuming she was asleep, he was about to continue down the hallway to his own room when she called out softly, "Callahan? Is that you?"

"It's me."

Mick heard the key twisting inside the lock, and a few seconds later the door opened. From the look of her eyes, Shelby had been crying. From the look of the rest of her, she was just about the most desirable woman on the planet from the top of her head to the dimples in her knees and the tips of her bare toes. He was suddenly aware that he was staring at her chest, not because he was ogling her boobs, but because he was trying to read what was printed on her T-shirt.

When Shelby realized what he was doing, her arms flew up to cover herself. "Don't read that," she said. "This shirt was a gift. Just a stupid joke."

"What does it say?"

"Never mind."

"I'll bet it says you're out of estrogen and you've got a gun."

She shook her head.

"Well, what then?" Her distress made him just that much more curious, so he gently grasped each of her wrists. "Come on. Let me see."

"Oh, all right." After wrenching out of his grip, she lowered her arms. "There. Satisfied?"

Mick read aloud. " 'What's wrong with always being right?' " Then he laughed out loud. "Boy, somebody really had your number."

"Very funny." Worry washed over her face again. Her eyes darkened. "What happened with the bomb?"

"Nothing." He told her about Kimmy and her disgruntled boyfriend.

"Well, that's a relief. I guess."

She didn't look all that relieved, though. She bit her lower lip and looked away. Aw, damn. Mick couldn't stand to see her cry.

"Hey," he said softly, reaching out his arms to bring her close against him, glad that she moved forward so willingly. "It's okay. You don't have to be afraid."

"That's not what you said before," she muttered into his collarbone. "You said I *should* be afraid."

"I said you should be cautious." He pressed his cheek to her warm hair and whispered, "Anyway, I'm here. So you don't need to do anything but relax and let me take care of you."

Her response was one of those skeptical little clucks of her tongue, so he tipped her chin up and looked directly into her face.

"I'm not kidding," he said.

When she started to turn her head away, he gently used his thumb to direct her gaze back at him.

"I'm serious, Shelby. I mean it. I won't let anything bad happen to you."

Well, damn. He meant to make her feel better, but now her eyes were flooding with tears.

"That's so sweet," she said, finishing her sentence with a very big and very wet sniff.

"I'm not being sweet, for crissake. I'm . . ."

"I know." She nodded, which loosened a tear from the corner of her right eye. Mick felt it plop onto his hand. "You're just doing your job," she said. "Such as it is."

"No!" he nearly howled. Jesus. He hoped her parents didn't hear him. Lowering his voice to a growl, he said, "That's not what this is about."

"It's not about protecting me?" Another big, wet sniff.

He was about to howl again that protecting her wasn't just his job. It was personal now. God, was it personal! But then a tiny switch suddenly flicked in his brain and he decided, rather than tell her, he'd show her just how personal this was. He stepped forward, and closed the door behind him.

Her mouth was soft and wet and salty, and for the moment anyway, it was completely his.

He wanted her so much his knees almost buckled.

And when Shelby's actually did, he picked her up and carried her to bed.

⁓

The master bedroom was the only room in the house where their younger daughter had allowed herself to relax her "strictly Victorian" credo. Beth had knocked out part of the west wall and installed enormous windows that offered a magnificent view of the lake through the treetops. Now, at nearly midnight, the yard lights were firing up the leaves of the sugar maple to an incredible, sensuous crimson just beyond the windowsill, and Linda thought it would be a glorious color for a tunic. One with bell sleeves, perhaps, and maybe a narrow scalloped or picot edge. She was staring at the leaves when Harry came into the bedroom.

His step was just the slightest bit tentative, which Linda appreciated since this wasn't his official bedroom at the moment. On the other hand, she wished with all her heart that it were. With that in mind, she had turned down the covers on his side of the king-size bed.

"Any news about the bomb?" she asked, levering up and adjusting the pillows behind her.

"You were right. It was a prank. Thank God."

"Amen to that." She sighed. "Are you sleepy?"

"Not too," he replied, lowering himself onto the mattress, stretching out his legs.

"Feel like talking?" she asked.

He rolled his head toward her, meeting her gaze. "What about?"

"Us."

His reaction was immediate. His mouth flattened. His jaw tightened. There was something verging on panic in his eyes. She'd obviously frightened him, which she hadn't meant to do.

"I want you to think about going to work for me, Harry," she said, dispensing with the preamble she'd rehearsed again and again.

He laughed, a sharp little explosion of sound that seemed propelled as much by relief as indignation. "Work for you?"

Linda sat farther up in bed. "Yes. Why not? With the business as big as it is and growing all the time, I need competent, full-time legal assistance."

"I do criminal law, Linda. For God's sake. Not contracts."

She'd anticipated an outright, knee-jerk, much aggrieved refusal. So far so good. And now she narrowed her eyes and crossed her arms over the bedcovers. "Well, you're not too old to learn, are you?"

For a long while, he didn't say anything, but simply stared past her, at the fiery leaves. "I'll think about it," he said at last.

Letting out the long, silent breath that she hadn't even realized she'd been holding, Linda said, "Good! Well, I can't ask any more than that, can I? I'm getting sleepy now, sweetheart. Let's turn out the light."

Quick. Before you change your mind.

⁓

Shelby was trying not to moan, but it wasn't easy. If she'd had any qualms about making love to this man, they'd all but disappeared when he kissed her. Then any remaining doubts were totally obliterated when he picked her up and carried her to the bed. No one had ever done that before. It was such a damned romantic gesture. She felt quite literally swept off her feet.

"Ssh."

Oh, dear Lord. She must've been moaning because

Callahan's fingers had just replaced his lips and he was shushing her.

"Sorry," she moaned.

"Ssh."

His lips returned to her mouth, tasting her, teasing, and tempting. He kissed her as if it wasn't just the prelude to something else, but important in and of itself. His hand reclaimed her breast. If this was foreplay, Shelby decided the most she'd ever experienced before was one-play, two-play at the very most.

Callahan's body was even better without clothes, with its warm flesh giving way to the hard, hot muscle beneath it. His shoulders were divine. His chest was smooth and perfectly sculpted. His abs were worthy of their very own infomercial. And when Shelby's hands roamed farther down, they encountered an erection that was damned near a miracle.

She moaned again.

It was dark in the room, but she could see the heat in his eyes when he levered up on his elbows above her and asked between kisses, "Are you sure you want this?"

Not *this*. Shelby wanted *him*.

"Speak now," he whispered, "or forever . . ."

"Hold your piece?" She lifted her head to kiss him as she reached for him again, and then it was Callahan's turn to moan.

He left her just long enough to lean down to grab his pants from where he'd tossed them on the floor, then Shelby heard the distinct sound of a little package being ripped open. Jeez. It sounded like he was using his teeth. For one scaredy-cat, what-am-I-doing, omigod second, she wondered if it was too late to change her mind.

But then his hard, wonderful body covered hers again and the only thing in the world that Shelby wanted was Michael Rainbow Callahan—on her, in her, especially in her, completely.

Then he was, and it was heaven. Such heaven that Shelby gave a little cry of lusty happiness. Unfortunately her partner took it as a cry of pain.

"Did I hurt you, baby?" he asked, pulling out and away.

"No!" She pulled him back and wrapped her legs around his waist. "Oh, God, no. Now, Callahan. I want you."

They might have missed a couple signals in the beginning, but their awkwardness melted away as they quickly discovered each other's innate rhythms and private pleasure zones. Shelby, in fact, was shocked that she had so many. She never knew! Callahan finally took her over the edge with a hot, harsh word in her ear, and he came tumbling after a mere second later.

Afterward, they lay side by side, their hands clasped, breathing deeply, letting their heartbeats settle back, at least one of them smiling up at the ceiling, hoping it was half as good for him as it had been for her.

Something fell on his chest, and Mick jackknifed up in bed only to discover that he wasn't sleeping alone and it was his bedmate's hand that had startled him awake. He fell back onto the mattress with a soft curse.

He'd fallen asleep on her last night. Way to go, bozo. You had the most incredible sex in your entire life, then rolled over and went to sleep. Christ. He probably snored like a ripsaw, too. Julie used to wear earplugs.

And here she was again—his late, great wife—right in bed with him. Mick closed his eyes and sighed in frustration. Maybe it made sense that he'd think about her now. After all, it was the first time he'd slept beside a woman since he'd last slept beside Julie in their bed. Other than that, though, the two women had almost nothing in common.

He turned his head to study Shelby's face, not that he hadn't already memorized it. A strand of her long brown hair curved over her cheek and fell across her mouth. Mick reached to gently brush it back, half expecting her eyes to open and then react to his presence in her bed. Would she be happy? Would her bourbon-colored eyes sparkle with joy and the remnants of their lovemaking? Or would the color of her eyes be closer to sour mash and her expression full of misgivings and regrets, a bit like a bad hangover?

He would've been crazy about her even if the sex hadn't been great. Or maybe it only seemed great because he was so accustomed to Julie's get-it-over-with-I've-got-early-rounds-tomorrow attitude and her bone-deep fear of getting pregnant. Hell, with their killer schedules—his when he went undercover, hers when she began an ER residency—they hadn't even slept together in what turned out to be the final three months of their marriage. Funny thing was, he hadn't missed it. Instead, it was a relief not to have to beg.

"Uh-oh." Shelby's voice was husky with sleep. "You look like a man suffering from recriminations."

He'd been so lost in his thoughts that he hadn't seen

her eyes open. They were searching his now, all warm and worried.

"Actually," he said, "you just caught me wondering whether or not I had any little soldiers, other than the Trojan I used last night."

"Do you?"

He shook his head.

"Too bad for you, Callahan," she said. Her eyes took on a topaz sparkle as she nestled against him. "I guess you'll just have to talk to me now."

It wasn't exactly like pulling teeth, Shelby thought, although it was pretty damn close. Mick Callahan didn't like to talk about himself at all, at least not at any length. But his reticence struck her less as a guy thing than a secret thing. She had the sense that there were some really dark and painful events in his past that he didn't want to bring out into the light.

She was, however, undaunted.

Even as he'd told her all the places his mother had moved to and from when he was a kid, he still managed to tell her very little about the woman herself.

"She must've been beautiful," she said, "to have had so many men just want to take her along with them."

"Beautiful? Yeah, I guess. I was just a kid. What did I know from beautiful?"

"Well, I always thought *my* mother was beautiful, even when I was in kindergarten." Shelby chuckled. "Actually, she looks pretty much the same as she did then."

"She is beautiful." He ran his palm along Shelby's naked flank. "So's her daughter."

It wasn't as if Shelby had never heard that before, but she never knew how to respond because—even though she was relatively comfortable with her appearance—she never felt beautiful. Attractive, maybe. Certainly not a bowser. But with a mother who looked like Linda and a blue-eyed, honey-blond sister like Beth, Shelby had always felt that she came in a distant third in the looks department. It had never really mattered to her, but suddenly she wondered just how important a woman's appearance was to this incredibly good-looking man.

"I'm okay," she said with a little lift of her shoulders. "So, tell me about your wife. Was she absolutely gorgeous?"

Uh-oh. Judging from the instantaneous scowl on his face, it was obvious that she'd hit a nerve.

"Sorry," she said. "I was just curious." Sensing that their little interlude had come to an abrupt end, Shelby started to move away, but Callahan's arm tightened around her.

"No, I'm sorry. I . . . uh . . . I'm just not all that comfortable talking about Julie." He sighed. "It's a long story."

"I guess it would be after being married so many years," she said.

"Yeah." He reached for her hand, brought it to his lips for a warm and lingering kiss. "I'm not being evasive here, Shelby. Trust me. It's just . . ."

She put her fingertips to his mouth, stilling whatever explanation he was struggling with. "I do," she said. "Trust you. You'll tell me when you're ready."

A little storm cloud seemed to have moved directly over the bed. In an effort to banish it, she grinned and said, "Speaking of ready . . . Maybe we should drive into town for . . . um . . . latex."

The light in his eyes rekindled. It was like warm hazel sunshine. "That's some pretty good advice, Ms. Simon."

"I thought so."

CHAPTER FOURTEEN

~

A few hours later, after finishing Linda Simon's world's-best omelet brunch and Harry's world's-best-and-stiffest Bloody Marys, both Mick and Shelby were ready for a Sunday afternoon nap. But first there was the little matter of protection.

Because it was a Sunday, the little burg of Shelbyville was locked up tight, including the closet-sized pharmacy, so they drove another eight miles to Mecklin, the bustling county seat, where the parking lot of DrugWorld was packed. Mick didn't say so, but he was grateful for the relative anonymity offered by the larger drugstore.

They roamed the aisles for a while. It had been years since Mick had done any recreational shopping. His shopping strategy lately had been simple. Get in and get it and get out. But now he found himself smiling as he trailed after Shelby in the cosmetics aisle.

She picked up a cologne bottle, studied it, sniffed it, then sprayed it lavishly on her neck. "What do you think?" she asked him, tilting her head to expose her pale throat.

"I think I vant to suck your blood," he replied in his best vampire accent, which Mick thought was pretty funny for a guy who was known more for his bad moods than his sense of humor.

She laughed, thank God.

The cologne was light and lemony, beckoning him, and it was all Mick could do not to wrap his arms around Shelby right then and there, and to start licking her lovely, long, lemony neck.

But apparently they were done in the cosmetics aisle. He followed her next to the large rack of paperback books, where she pulled one from its pocket, squinted at the blurb on the back, then opened her handbag. For one bleak second, Mick thought she was going to boost the book, and that he'd have to turn a blind eye to the crime, maybe even protect her from some overaggressive house dick. Yeah. Okay. He could flash his badge and tell the store detective he'd been following Shelby all the way from Chicago and now he'd caught her red-handed.

But, then, instead of dropping the book discreetly into her bag, she wedged the paperback under her arm while she fished in the leather depths of her purse and came up with a pair of glasses.

"Oh, damn," she said. "They're broken."

Mick offered a quick, silent prayer of thanks that she wasn't a klepto, then said, "Come with me, little blind girl." He took her hand, led her to the revolving eyeglasses display, and happily watched her try on at least forty pairs as she consulted the dinky little mirror, consulted him, once even stopped another shopper for an on-the-spot, unbiased opinion of a pair of tortoiseshell specs.

The guy liked them. Yeah. Well, who wouldn't on that lovely face?

He never knew a drugstore could be so damn much fun, comparable to an amusement park, and he wondered all of a sudden what his life would be like without Shelby Simon right in the center of it and how it was possible that after a mere three days she seemed indispensable. It was then that Mick figured he was in really big trouble, heartwise.

Wearing her chosen glasses with the price tag draped over her nose, Shelby grabbed his hand. "On to the important stuff," she said, pulling him along.

And there it was, on the wall next to the prescription window—the world's largest, most stupefying display of condoms.

He just stared, his arms crossed, his eyes nearly crossed, too. The few times he'd purchased rubbers in the past two years, he'd fed a handful of coins into a machine in a rest room and taken whatever the machine spit out.

"Any suggestions?" he asked.

"Well . . ." She peered over the top rims of the glasses. "First off, let's say nothing turquoise."

That narrowed it down somewhat.

Then she added, "And nothing with a helmet on the package. That's really offensive."

"Okay."

"No flavors," she said, leaning a little closer in order to read better. "And no—omigod!—no glow in the dark."

Mick continued to ponder the multicolored display, wondering vaguely about the advertised promises of extended pleasure and heightened feelings on several packages. What was that all about?

"Ribbed?" he murmured.

"Hm . . ."

While she was thinking that over, he asked, "How many?"

Shelby laughed and her glasses slipped down her nose. "A lot."

On the drive back to the lake, Shelby was peeking into the DrugWorld bag, reading the various claims and cautions about latex on the box of three dozen, and wondering how quickly they might need to make another run for the rubber, when a sharp jolt of reality punctured her happy mood. It had been hours since she'd thought about her situation. She wasn't even keeping abreast of the news. Of course, that could be remedied with one quick call to a certain Pulitzer Prize–winning guy. She fished in her handbag for her cell phone.

As soon as Derek McKay said hello, she sensed the urgency in his voice and cranked up the window on the passenger side so she could hear him better.

"What's up?" she asked.

"I'm onto something here," he said. "Listen. I don't have time to talk right now, but I'm pretty sure I know who's behind this letter bomb stuff, Shelby."

"Who?" The word came out with a gulp. She couldn't believe her ears. On the other hand, Derek was such a phenomenal investigator, somebody who could see patterns where often even the police were at a loss, that she probably shouldn't have been surprised.

"I just need to put a couple more puzzle pieces together," he said, lowering his voice even more. "Gotta go, babe. I'll call you back in a couple hours and fill you in."

"Okay, but . . ."

He was gone. Shelby snapped her phone closed and stared out through the windshield, gnawing on her lower lip.

"Bad news?" Mick asked.

"No," she said. "Actually, I think it was good news. That was Derek McKay, one of our investigative reporters. He's got a strong lead in the case, he says."

"What kind of strong lead?"

There was just a hint of disbelief in his tone. A tiny little whiff of sarcasm. A tincture of professional jealousy perhaps. Shelby really wasn't in the mood to debate the investigative merits of the police versus journalists. She didn't want to spoil all the fun they'd been having.

"I don't know." She shrugged. "He said he'd call me back later. It's probably nothing."

"Probably not," he said. "Want me to call the department and check?"

She shook her head. "No. I was enjoying not thinking about it, to tell you the truth." She reached across and put her hand on the soft denim covering his thigh.

"Me, too," he said as he took one hand off the steering wheel and placed it over hers. "What do you say we go home and take a nap?"

She grinned and waggled her eyebrows. "You read my mind, Lieutenant."

Alas, it wasn't to be. No sooner had they gotten out of the car and started up the hill, hand in hand, trying not to run, than her father's voice boomed out from somewhere behind the carriage house.

"Mick! Hey! Glad you're back. Come on out here and let me show you something."

Shelby groaned, and Mick gave her a quizzical look.

"What's up?" he asked.

"Oh, Lord," she said. "He's cleaning fish. He wants to induct you into the mysterious brotherhood of ripping out fish guts. He always does this. It's some sort of bonding thing." She groaned again.

"Guess I better go," he said without too much enthusiasm.

"You don't have to, Mick. Tell him you have a headache, or that you faint at the sight of blood. Tell him . . . tell him fish is against your religion."

"Nah. I'll go." He handed her the plastic sack from DrugWorld, and flashed her the sexiest grin in the universe. "Here. Guard these with your life."

"Absolutely."

Shelby watched him walk toward the carriage house, once again appreciating his athletic grace, the way his hair just brushed the edge of his collar, not to mention the way faded denim had a way of doing the most amazing things to the male posterior.

The Harry Simon Fish Indoctrination and Buddy Buddy School was likely to take the next hour or two, so Shelby went inside the house, tossed their purchases onto her bed, and then went up to the third floor in search of her mother, who would undoubtedly be working despite the fact that it was Sunday.

Linda was indeed upstairs in her office, but she wasn't working. Instead, she was gazing out one of the high ballroom windows with a look on her face that was so sad, so completely bereft that her daughter nearly couldn't breathe for a moment.

"Mom?"

The sad expression vanished in a heartbeat, replaced by a warm, welcoming smile. "Hi, sweetheart. I didn't hear you come in. How was your drive?"

"Fine," Shelby said, lowering herself into the chair on the opposite side of her mother's desk. "Lovely. I've never seen such gorgeous colors on the trees."

Her mother nodded in agreement, and said, "They really are spectacular this fall, aren't they? I think I read somewhere that it's because we had such a wet summer."

"Oh. I didn't realize that."

"It rained like crazy in June."

Trees, no matter how gorgeous, and the weather, no matter how wet, were the last things Shelby wanted to discuss just then. What about you and Dad? she wanted to shout. What about this stupid separation? And why were you just looking as if the world were about to end in the next fifteen minutes?

Obviously anticipating that sort of outburst from her opinionated offspring, her mother lifted up a sweater from her desktop, spread out its long sleeves, and asked, "What do you think of this?"

Oh, God. What did she think? It looked just like all the rest of them to her. Elegant. Colorful. Unique. Expensive. Another wonderful Linda Purl design. What was she supposed to say?

And that's when it suddenly hit her—the perfect solution to her parents' problem. Shelby wondered why she hadn't thought of this before. Linda Purl, captain of the chichi knitting industry, purveyor of unique designs, overworked female dynamo, ought to hire Harry Harry Quite Contrary, attorney currently sans portfolio and sans anything meaningful to do, to be her CEO.

It was positively inspired. Shelby couldn't wait to suggest it. She lifted one of the sleeves of the sweater. "This is so beautiful, Mom. It's really stunning. You know, if you didn't have to spend so much time on paperwork and sales and stuff, you'd have way more time to design."

Her mother nodded agreeably while she fussed with a loose thread on the front of the garment.

"If you had somebody you trusted to help you," Shelby continued. "Someone really smart, with plenty of experience and a certain—oh, I don't know—a certain savoir faire . . ."

Her mother glanced up at her. "Are you volunteering, honey?"

"Me? No. Jeez, I hardly have time to get my own work done. But . . ." Shelby leaned forward, her gaze zeroing in on her mother. "Here's a thought, though. This just occurred to me. What about Dad? He'd be perfect."

She was prepared for a minor explosion, for her mother to dismiss the idea right off the bat, and she was already lining up arguments to make her case when Linda just beamed at her and exclaimed, "What a wonderful idea, Shelby! Now why didn't I think of that?"

"Well . . ." Shelby sat back, so stunned by her mother's response that she barely knew what to say. For a second, she questioned her own hearing. She *had* called it a wonderful idea, hadn't she? "Well . . ." she began again. "You probably would have thought of it, sooner or later, Mother."

"Oh, I don't know about that, sweetie." Linda folded the sweater in front of her and set it aside, then smiled again across her desk. "After all, you're the one in the advice business. I think it's absolutely inspired. You should mention it to your father."

"Really?" She tried not to sound shocked that her mother was apparently taking her advice—and seemingly without a single grain of salt—for the first time in the history of the world.

"Absolutely," her mother said. "You should definitely mention it to him."

Shelby stood up. Jazzed. "Then that's just what I'll do. Right now, too."

Linda listened to her daughter racing down two flights of stairs, jet-fueled by the prospect of giving advice to her father.

"Shelby, Shelby, Shelby," she whispered, shaking her head, at the same time wondering if she'd just done something very foolish that would come back to bite her on the ass in about ten minutes.

It was the perfect solution, dammit, for Harry to become active in Linda Purl Designs in some capacity. If nothing else, it would give him a reason to travel with her, which was something he longed to do, and give her the incentive to fit a little golf, or sightseeing, or idle pleasures into her business trips. Of course, those trips wouldn't include some of the exotic destinations Harry might have on his agenda, but New York and San Francisco and Phoenix could be exotic in their own way. At

least they'd be together. And who knew? London and
Paris might not be out of the question if the business continued to thrive. They could do this, dammit, if each of
them could just compromise a bit.

Maybe it was wrong of her, sending Shelby like a sac-
rificial lamb to the altar of Harry's dented pride. But
maybe their daughter's well-meaning interference would
help him make the decision to finally come over to her
side, to accept the fact that his wife was not going to give
up this business she found so rewarding in so many ways.

Surely he would see that.

Or not.

My God. It was impossible to believe that they
couldn't work this out. Somehow.

Mick had never really had a father figure in his life.
His own father had walked out on him not too long after
he was born, and Mick had never seen the man again.
None of his mother's boyfriends took much of an interest
in Carrie Callahan's skinny kid. Even Julie's dad, in
whose house Mick had lived while attending high school,
hadn't paid much attention to him other than to watch
him like a hawk so he didn't get his teenage daughter in
trouble.

So even as he was enjoying Harry Simon's compan-
ionship this afternoon, this fish-cleaning business was
making him pretty queasy. It surprised him, considering
he'd seen his fair share of blood on the streets of Chicago.

Shelby's father was demonstrating his technique on
about the ninety-eighth bluegill, slipping his sharp blade

beneath a red-tinged gill before he sliced upward, removing the poor fucker's head, blank bluish eyes and all, and Mick was trying to keep from tossing his cookies.

"Think you're getting the hang of it now?" Harry asked, flicking blood off his fingers and lobbing another fish head into a half-filled bucket.

"Oh, yeah."

When the man offered him the knife, Mick demurred. "You're the pro," he said. "You go ahead. I'll just watch."

"Fine with me." He made short work of another fish, but this time he dispensed with the lessons in favor of another topic. "You and my daughter are moving along pretty fast, aren't you?"

Mick's queasiness took a whole new turn. "I guess you could say that, sir."

Harry flashed him a grin then, much to Mick's relief, and said, "I'm not giving you the third degree here, Lieutenant. Shelby's thirty-four. She's got a mind of her own, and it's a pretty sensible one as far as I can tell. You have my approval, unless, of course, there are some skeletons in your closet or bodies buried under your doorstep that I don't know about."

"Nothing like that." He shrugged. "I've got a couple reprimands in my personnel folder, but that's pretty standard for anybody who's been on the job as long as I have."

"So, you always wanted to be a cop?"

Mick shook his head. "No. I got married pretty young. My wife and I went to college together, then I joined the Chicago PD to support us while she went on to med school. I just stayed on in the job. Seventeen years now, give or take a couple months. That wasn't the original plan, but it turned out okay, I guess."

"What was the original plan?" he asked, slapping another fish on his worktable and positioning the blade.

Mick had to laugh. "Believe it or not, after she finished her residency and started bringing in some money, I was going to go to law school."

"Interesting," Harry said. "Well, if you're ever inclined to do it, I could be of some help. Just let me know."

"Actually, sir . . ." He didn't know how to tell Harry Harry Quite Contrary that most of the lawyers he'd encountered over the years were slimeballs, sleazebags, and ambulance chasers. Granted, his was the view from the gutter, but it had disabused him of any notion of pursuing a law degree. "Well, actually, I really like being a cop."

"I can understand that," Shelby's father said. "And you're lucky. I have enormous respect for people who enjoy their work. There's something . . ."

Mick guessed he'd have to wait to find out what that something was because Shelby came around the corner of the carriage house just then, looking beautiful and oddly determined. Maybe she was coming to his rescue. He could only hope.

"How's the fish gutting going?" she asked.

"Almost done," her father said. "We'll be having these babies for dinner in another couple hours."

"Great," Mick said, wishing he'd picked up some Pepto-Bismol while he was at the drugstore.

"Great," Shelby echoed. "I'll help you fry them, Dad. That way Mom can just relax."

"Sounds good, kiddo," he said.

Mick was calculating the time left between the fish

gutting and the fish frying, wondering if there were a few moments in between those events for the afternoon nap that had sounded so beguiling earlier. He was looking at his watch when his cell phone beeped in the pocket of his jacket.

One look at the district's number on the caller ID and he was pretty sure it would be important. They weren't calling just to ask how his vacation was going. He excused himself and walked a short distance away to take the call.

⌐

While she stood there and watched her father make short work of his final bluegill, Shelby remembered when he'd initiated her into his little private angler's society one summer when she was nine or ten, as soon as he felt she could be trusted to pay strict attention to a sharp blade. Beth, as she recalled, had preceded her by at least a year because of her advanced dexterity, quiet concentration, and keen attention to detail. In other words, Shelby talked too much and tended to think her ideas were better than anyone else's. Even then.

"This will be some feast, little girl," he said, winking at her the way he used to do so many years ago.

"I can't wait."

For one bleak moment, Shelby was at a loss for words, wondering how she could have the audacity, the unmitigated gall to suggest anything to this man. He wasn't an idiot, after all. He was smart and ambitious, and he'd accomplished everything he'd set out to do in his life. Maybe now he was finally reaping the reward of all that hard work and at last enjoying the simple pleasures. Maybe he deserved this.

Maybe—oh, God—convincing Harry Simon to go back to work would be doing him a terrible injustice.

And then, for just about the first time in her life, Shelby suddenly didn't trust her ability to give the right advice, so she was hugely relieved when Mick strolled back toward them, thus precluding any further father-daughter talk.

It took her a second to comprehend that the look on her lieutenant's face was not the one he'd worn moments ago when his phone had rung. Now he looked as he had when she'd first met him—his handsome face deeply lined with worry, his hazel eyes no longer twinkling, but filled with concern.

"Who was on the phone?" she asked.

"That was my office. It was about your friend at the paper. Derek McKay."

Shelby groaned. Journalists who competed with the law often ran afoul of the law. Derek more than most. "Oh, jeez. What's he done now? Does he need to be bailed out or something?"

Mick shook his head, and then reached for her hand. "I'm sorry to have to tell you this, Shelby. Your friend, Derek, is dead."

CHAPTER FIFTEEN

Chicago was the last place on earth where Ms. Shelby Simon—human target—ought to be, but nobody could keep her away once she found out that there would be a memorial service for Derek McKay on Tuesday morning. Nothing her mother or father said could dissuade her. Nothing Mick said could prevent her from leaving "with you or without you." God, she was stubborn.

And she blamed herself for McKay's death, which, according to Mick's sources in the department, was being treated as an accident or suicide. The reporter, a legendary drunk, fell from the platform at the Howard Station right in front of the oncoming Red Line train.

"Somebody pushed him," Shelby insisted.

"There weren't any witnesses," Mick said.

"I don't care."

So, since he couldn't very well handcuff her to the front porch of the big house at Heart Lake, they were on the highway headed south at seven o'clock the next morning, and with every mile Mick could feel himself winding tighter and tighter. By the time he parked the

Mustang in front of the Canfield Towers, he felt like a damn jack-in-the-box. One more little turn of the crank and he was going to go right through the roof.

"Hey, buddy, you can't . . ." The doorman took one look at Mick's facc and fell silent. "Welcome home, Ms. Simon. Hey, I read about your coworker in the paper this morning. I'm really sorry."

"Thank you, Dave."

"Anything I can do for you?" the doorman asked, rushing ahead of them to open the big glass door.

"No, thank you. That's really sweet of you, but I'm . . ."

"She's not staying," Mick said, his hand locked on Shelby's elbow as he hustled her across the lobby and into the elevator.

"Ouch." She yanked her arm out of his grasp.

"Sorry."

Once inside her apartment, Mick allowed himself to relax a notch or two.

"Shelby, listen . . ." He gathered her into his arms and pressed her head against his chest. "This is a really stupid and dangerous thing you're doing. You know that, right?"

She nodded. "I still have to do it. I don't believe for one second that Derek killed himself. You told them about his investigation, right?"

"Yep. They're checking out his office and his apartment, but so far they haven't found squat."

"And they probably won't. That was the thing about Derek. He hardly ever took notes. He kept all that stuff in his head."

Her voice got soggy again, and Mick just held her. He didn't believe McKay's death was an accident or suicide, either, but that wasn't his job at the moment. He needed to keep this woman alive. It was probably the most crucial job he'd ever have in his life.

While Shelby collected the things she'd need for the next few days, Mick sat in the living room on the beige couch next to the beige chair on the beige rug. He thought again about what Linda Simon had said about her daughter's inability or unwillingness to make a commitment, and hoped with all his heart that it wasn't really true. She was making a commitment right now, wasn't she, to a deceased friend and colleague? Putting her own life at risk in the bargain, too. That counted for far more than a plaid sofa or a brightly colored Persian carpet.

Jesus. He dreaded taking her back to his colorfully mismatched hovel, but it was safer than a hotel where there were too many strangers and too many opportunities for Shelby to get past him, whether it was a visit to the gift shop or a quick bite in the coffee shop. Mick was determined to keep her no farther than a foot away if it meant putting her on a damn leash.

Hoo, boy. When Shelby stepped over the threshold of Mick's apartment, the odor of faux pine nearly knocked her over.

"Sorry," he muttered from close behind her. "I'll open some windows."

The sight of his sunflowered couch, seat-sprung recliner, and the general disorder of the place made her smile. It seemed like a hundred years since her last visit here. She'd only known him a few hours then. And now . . .

Well, there was still a lot she didn't know about Michael Rainbow Callahan, but what she knew, she loved. She'd come to that conclusion on the drive from the lake. Somewhere around Holland, Michigan, Shelby had gazed at his hands on the steering wheel, remembered how those hands had felt on her body Saturday night, and wanted him enough just then that she almost suggested they pull off the road and into a motel.

They hadn't made love the previous night the way they'd planned. After the news of Derek's death, Shelby had been too upset. Mick had held her the whole night, stroking her hair, her cheek, her arm, and never once gave her any indication that he was interested in anything but comforting her and keeping her safe.

She had felt loved. Well, maybe that wasn't the proper word. Treasured and cared for. Safe. She had felt so completely safe in Mick's arms.

"Thank you for bringing me back to town for Derek's service, Mick," she said now. "Thank you . . . Oh, I don't know . . . Thanks for realizing how important it is to me."

He turned from the window he had just opened wide, leaned a hip against the sill, and said, "Well, I've always thought loyalty and bravery were fine qualities in a woman." Then he grinned as he opened his arms to her. "We won't even discuss your pigheadedness."

Shelby moved into his arms, against his warmth. "I prefer the word 'determined.'"

"I'll bet you do," he said while he kissed her neck.

Suddenly all Shelby wanted to do was burrow deeply

into this man's protectiveness, to get so close to him there would be nothing between them but skin.

"I haven't seen your bedroom yet, Callahan," she whispered at the same time she reached for his belt buckle.

"You're about to."

He started to sweep one arm beneath her knees in order to pick her up the way he had the other night, but Shelby stopped him by taking a small step backward. He looked confused for a second.

"What?" he asked.

"This."

Shelby stepped back toward him, and with a mighty hop, clamped her legs around his waist and her arms around his neck, thanking her lucky stars that his reflexes were quick enough to catch her and hold her there before she crashed to the floor.

"Now about that bed," she said, just before her mouth centered on his.

The bedroom was an even worse disaster zone than the living room, and the bed itself was just a mattress on the floor, but to Shelby it was heaven.

She didn't know the reason—perhaps because Mick had been married for so long—but he was the most wonderful and considerate lover she'd ever had. And leisurely. Oh, God. Maybe that was from being married, too, and from having plenty of time—years—to make love. Whatever the reason, Shelby thanked her lucky stars.

This time, before he had completely undressed her, Mick leaned back on an elbow, studied her face a long moment, and said, "We don't have to do this right now, you know. I mean, I know you're upset about your friend at the paper. If it would be better for you after the memorial service tomorrow . . ."

Shelby shook her head. "I don't want to think about death right now. Just life. Let's celebrate life, Mick."

And celebrate they did in every possible combination two bodies could explore. They rolled off the bed at least twice, so it turned out to be a blessing that it was just a mattress on the floor.

For someone who'd been offering advice about sex and relationships for a dozen years, Shelby discovered there was still a lot she didn't know about sex. Who knew that a hot word in her ear or a strong thumb pressed deeply into the arch of her foot could send her tumbling over the edge of the universe? Or that her being on top, taking control, could send her partner into literal paroxysms of pleasure? Or that twice was not nearly enough? Or thrice? She wondered if she'd ever get enough of this man.

Without their realizing it, the sun managed to set while they were dozing in each other's arms. When Shelby woke up, for a minute she thought all that explosive lovemaking had made her blind.

"That only happens from doing it alone," Mick told her.

"Very funny." She struggled up from the low bed. "I'm starving, Callahan. You probably don't have anything edible in your refrigerator, do you?"

"You're assuming this dump even has a refrigerator."

"Does it?"

"Amazingly enough, yeah, it does," he said. "But there's nothing in it except a couple beers."

"We could order a pizza," she suggested.

"Yeah, we could," he said, "if anybody delivered to this neighborhood."

"Hm. Well, that complicates things a bit. If you could find me a big shirt to wear and point me to the kitchen, maybe I can find something."

⁓

Mick didn't even know he had a box of saltines and a family-size can of chicken noodle soup in the cramped little pantry in the kitchen. He had no recollection of buying either one, but the crackers were still fresh and the date on the soup can indicated that the contents were still okay to consume.

He had no bowls, though, so they sat on his sunflowered couch spooning the soup out of coffee mugs.

"This is purely an observation," Shelby said. "It's not a criticism. But you're leading a really messy life, Callahan."

"Yeah. It feels like someone else's life half the time."

She wound her legs beneath her and leaned back against a cushion—beautiful body language for *I've got time. Start talking, buster.* "Tell me about before," she said.

He'd already told her a little about his life with his mother. That left Julie. Since her death, he'd tried very hard not to think about her much less discuss her. But he realized it was time, here, now, with this woman. If he wanted to know everything about her, it was only fair that he reciprocate.

He drank the last of the lukewarm chicken soup in his

cup, put it down on the cluttered coffee table, dragged in a breath, and said, "How about a beer for dessert?" Anything to stall for a little time. Anything to make this easier than extracting his own wisdom teeth.

They carried their beers to the bedroom where the only illumination was from a lamppost in the alley out back. The halogen beams came through the sagging Venetian blinds, casting slanted strips on the bare bedroom wall.

"What do you want to know?" he asked, tucking Shelby's head into the crook of his neck.

"Everything."

He told her *almost* everything. Things he hadn't thought about in years . . .

. . . beginning with the summer his mother took up with the Guatemalan jockey, Jaime Castillo, from Arlington racetrack, and then decided to follow the guy out to California, where he wanted to try his luck at Santa Anita. For the first time in his young fourteen years, Mick had said no to Carrie Callahan.

For the first time in his life, he'd felt something close to a normal homelife in Chicago, where he spent most of his time at the home of his ninth-grade classmate, Julie Travers. Even though her parents kept a wary eye out for their daughter's virginity, they seemed to take pity on the son of the woman they referred to—always behind his back—as The Gypsy, and invited Mick to stay with them if he chose not to accompany his mother to the West Coast. So Mick waved good-bye to Carrie and her four-foot ten-inch lover, and moved his few belongings into the Traverses' basement next to the Ping-Pong table.

Shelby gasped. "She left you? Your mother went to California and left you behind? Just like that?"

"Pretty much," Mick said.

"That had to have hurt you," she said, nestling closer, pressing her hand over his heart.

His first instinct was to utter a macho "Nah," but he took a deep breath and dispensed with the bullshit. "It did," he said. "But I was so damned glad to have a permanent home that I didn't let myself spend too much time thinking about it. The Traverses were good people, and Julie . . . Well, she became my whole life."

They did everything together, from eating breakfast to going to school to homework to brushing their teeth before bed. And it was fairly predictable that despite the eagle eyes of Mr. and Mrs. Travers, they eventually lost their virginity together during their junior year beneath that Ping-Pong table in the basement.

"What was she like?" Shelby asked him in a voice that was equal parts curiosity and dread.

Although he hadn't kept a single picture of his late wife, he couldn't excise the one in his head.

"She was blond," he said. "With blue eyes. Picture one of the Brady Bunch kids. And she was smart. Probably a lot smarter than I was, which was why I dropped out of college to support us while she went to medical school."

"But what was she *like*?" Shelby asked again. "Shy? Brazen? Funny? Finicky? What?"

Brazen in the end, Mick was thinking. Disloyal. Julie Travers Callahan devastated him, but she was already dead so there was nothing for him to do but be devastated and get over it. He wasn't ready to disclose the whole sorry tale. He wasn't sure he could do it without choking up, and as Shelby's Superhero protector, that didn't seem like such a good idea.

"She tended to be more serious than funny," he said. "She was a good doctor, as far as I know. And she collected antique toys for some reason I never understood since she wasn't interested in having kids."

"Never?"

"Not that I was aware of." He heard his own voice taking on a hard edge, and decided to put a capper on the subject of Julie before his mood curdled like month-old milk.

"Okay," he said, smoothing his hand over her wonderful, sleek-but-I-don't-spend-all-my-time-in-the-gym abdomen. "I don't want to talk anymore." His hand progressed downward. "I'm more a man of action."

Shelby made that murmuring sound, that hot fudge sundae with whipped cream and a cherry on top, warm kitten purr he loved to hear as she arched in response to his touch, then opened her mouth for his kiss.

It took him a full three seconds to forget about Julie and all that pain.

The next morning Shelby kept her eyes mostly closed in the shower in order not to see the mildew in every conceivable corner and crevice. She decided it was a measure of her growing attraction to Mick that she had the courage to step inside the tiled enclosure at all.

He showered then while she dressed in her basic black silk sheath with matching jacket. The memorial service was scheduled for ten o'clock, and she didn't want to be late. Just as she was putting on her earrings, the sound of a cell phone rang out from the living room. It took her a moment to figure out it was her phone that was ringing.

"Okay. You win. I just hung up from Mom, and I told her I'd come back to the lake for Masque."

"Beth! Oh, that's great," Shelby said. "It'll be so good to see you."

"You, too, kiddo. So what kind of trouble are you in with this mad bomber thing? Mom told me about that, too."

Shelby sighed. "I don't know. It's pretty scary, but . . ." She glanced toward the closed bedroom door. Callahan had apparently made his exit from the bathroom without her having witnessed it. "I've got a bodyguard who's gorgeous enough to make me want to stay in trouble for a long, long time."

"I heard about him, too. Hard Harry and Picky Linda, who never like anybody we bring home, liked him a lot."

On her end of the conversation, Shelby smiled. "I like him, too. A lot. I can't wait for you to meet him."

"Me, too, sweetie. Okay. Well, I'll see you sometime Friday afternoon. I'm flying in to Grand Rapids, and then renting a car to drive up to the lake, so I should be there around four."

"I can't wait, Beth. Oh, and . . ."

She was about to mention Sam, but her sister had already hung up. That was probably for the best, she decided. Beth could be easily spooked.

Just as she was reaching for the earring she had put down in order to answer the phone, the bedroom door opened and Shelby drew in a sharp breath. Where were the faded jeans and ratty flannel shirt? Where was the duct taped vest? For that matter, where was Callahan?

The man who stepped out of the bedroom wore a beautifully tailored navy suit, a snow white shirt with French cuffs, a purple tie that fairly screamed Hermes, and polished black Gucci loafers. His usually scruffy hair was slicked back. Sleek. Sophisticated. He looked . . . He looked . . . All of a sudden Shelby remembered to take a breath.

He lifted his arm and cocked his wrist, revealing a thin gold watch. "Ready? We'll be late for the service if we don't get out of here in the next few minutes."

"I'm ready," she said. "You look pretty spiffy, Callahan."

"Yeah?" He gave her one of those killer grins that always loosened her kneecaps. "You look pretty good yourself, Ms. Simon."

Shelby thought that in a million years, after a million makeovers, she'd never look as good as Callahan did to her just then.

When they arrived at the *Daily Mirror* building, the man actually turned heads in the lobby, but none as frequently as Shelby's. When they rode up in the elevator, hand in hand, she couldn't take her eyes off their paired reflection in the polished chrome door. This visceral response to him made her feel incredibly guilty, and she tried to clear her head of everything but poor Derek.

It made sense to hold the memorial service in the auditorium of the *Daily Mirror* building. Derek, in addition to being an ace journalist and a legendary elbow bender, was a card-carrying agnostic who would've spun in his grave if he were memorialized in a church. Shelby was going to miss his caustic wit and his skeptical eye. When she and Callahan stepped out of the elevator on the fifth floor, the first person Shelby saw was Kellie Carter, her face streaked with tears and mascara. Her sense of guilt deepened. She should have called and offered her condolences if not her advice to the bereaved young intern who had just lost her lover.

"Kellie, I'm so very sorry," she said, slipping her arm around the young woman's shoulders. "I know you and Derek were close."

"Oh, Shelby. I loved him so much. Why did this have to happen?" Her river of tears turned into a torrent.

Callahan, who'd been standing to one side, offered a neatly pressed handkerchief.

"Thank you, Mr. . . . ?" Kellie blinked at him wetly.

"Oh, sorry," Shelby said. "Kellie, this is Lieutenant Mick Callahan. Mick, this is my intern from Northwestern. Kellie Carter."

While they shook hands, Shelby couldn't help but notice a tiny, appreciative glint in Kellie's soggy eyes, and her immediate reaction was a rather petty *Well, so much for poor ol' Derek*. But that wasn't really fair to Kellie, when every woman in the building had looked at Callahan the exact same way.

Shelby looked around the crowd, hoping to see her longtime secretary, Sandy, who would undoubtedly be a nervous wreck in the aftermath of Derek's death. She should've called Sandy, too. It occurred to her that she'd been so wrapped up in her own problems that she'd overlooked some of the things she would've automatically done in these circumstances, like reach out to her bereaved colleagues. She'd been pretty wrapped up in Michael Rainbow Callahan, too, for that matter, and she warned herself not to get in worse trouble than she was already in.

"Kellie, have you seen Sandy Hovis?" she asked. "I don't see her anywhere."

"Sandy quit," the intern said as casually as if she were saying it's eleven o'clock.

"No one told me. When did she quit? Why?"

The little redhead shrugged, then asked, "Shelby, may I sit with you during the service? Please? I just can't be alone right now."

Shelby forced her concerns about Sandy aside in order to focus on poor Kellie.

"Well, of course, you may, sweetie. Come on. Let's go in. It looks like people are beginning to take their seats."

~

While another colleague of Derek McKay's eulogized the late reporter, Mick recrossed his legs, then picked a fleck of lint from the knee of his trousers. Goddamned suit. This was the third time he'd worn it, and he was considering burning it after today.

Julie had dragged him into Saks Fifth Avenue after they'd been invited to the wedding of some heart surgeon's daughter. He'd almost passed out when he saw the price tag on the suit, and then he'd almost puked at the price tag on the tie. When he protested, his wife had given him one of her frosty looks and said, "This is important to me, Mick."

"Right," he'd responded. "Well, I guess if this is how a student of military history dresses, what the hell, huh?"

The look she gave him after that remark was cold enough to freeze-dry his internal organs.

The next time he wore the suit—just a few months

later—was at Julie's funeral. He was actually surprised he hadn't soaked it in Jack Daniel's Black and dropped a lit match on it that same night.

Forcing his attention back to the present, Mick reached for Shelby's hand, the one that wasn't gripping the hand of the distraught little intern, Kellie. He could only guess, but it seemed pretty obvious that she and the dead reporter had something going on between them. Poor kid.

Shelby gave his hand a gentle squeeze. There were tears in her eyes, too, and they cut him to the quick. If it were up to him, she'd never cry again, by God. Ever. He'd never wanted to make a woman happier or keep her safer than pretty Ms. Shelby Simon.

After the service, Mick stood aside while she greeted her colleagues. He felt like a damned Secret Service lunk, watching out for the president, checking entrances and exits, eyeing the hands that reached out to shake Shelby's, checking for angry expressions, sullen demeanors, anything suspicious. He was wound so tight he was getting a headache.

"How's it going, Lieutenant?"

Mick recognized the managing editor of the paper in whose office he'd met Shelby last week, but he couldn't recall the guy's name.

"Hal Stabler," the man said, stretching out his meaty hand. "Thanks for watching out for Shelby."

"No problem," Mick said. "Sorry about McKay. He didn't leave any notes or tapes or anything?"

Stabler shook his head sadly. "Whatever it was he thought he knew about the letter bomb deal went to the grave with him. Shit. I've lost two of my best people in less than a week."

"Hey, boss." Shelby emerged from behind the portly editor. "We'll all miss Derek, won't we? I feel so sorry for Kellie."

Stabler gave her a quizzical look, and Shelby's face went a little pale. Apparently she'd let some sort of cat out of the proverbial bag by mentioning the young intern in the same sentence as the dead reporter.

She covered her error with a quick smile. "Well, I feel so sorry for all of us."

"Has Kellie talked to you yet?" Stabler asked.

Now Shelby looked confused. "Well, we've talked this morning. Did you mean something in particular, Hal?"

"Yeah," he said. "The column."

"What column?"

"The one she's going to write while yours is on hold."

That pretty face went even paler now and her finely sculpted jaw loosened a bit. Mick moved closer in order to grasp her arm.

"Kellie's going to write a column?" she asked, her voice obviously straining to stay out of the higher registers.

"Look, Shelby"—Stabler leaned toward her—"Helm and Harris don't want your readership to melt away just because you're out of commission for a while. I don't know if you've noticed or not, but that goddamned Alvin Wexler has suddenly started having Alice answer some pretty kinky questions. Anyway, Kellie wrote a mock-up column. I showed it to them upstairs, and they agreed it was good to go for a couple months."

"A couple months." She sounded like someone with part of a ham sandwich stuck in her throat.

"Yeah. It's just temporary. Once you're back, 'According to Kellie' will be history."

"'According to Kellie'?" Now the entire ham sandwich, pickle, little frilly toothpicks, and all seemed lodged in her throat.

It was probably a good thing that someone called to Hal Stabler just then from across the auditorium. He kissed her on the cheek, shook Mick's hand again, and turned to work his way across the room.

"Let's get out of here," Shelby said, pulling her arm from his grip, wheeling around, then walking faster than anyone ought to in heels that high.

He sprinted after her, ready to catch her or keep her from strangling somebody. Whichever came first.

CHAPTER SIXTEEN

⁓

They were in the Mustang, heading back to Mick's place, and Shelby had just chewed through her last manicure.

"If there's nothing else you need to do in the city," Mick said, "let's pick up our stuff at my place and get the hell outta Dodge. What do you say?"

"Fine."

She was almost afraid to speak for fear that long tongues of flame would come shooting out of her mouth. She'd never been so angry in her life. "According to Kellie." Jesus.

Okay. Sure. She could understand the dynamics of the newspaper business and the decision to run a column in place of hers. It made perfect sense. She agreed completely. It was a great idea. Fabulous. Fucking wonderful. Divinely inspired.

But "According to Kellie"? Kellie Carter was a twenty-year-old college junior. What was she going to advise people about? Where to get the most money for their used textbooks? Which Windy City bars had the longest happy hours and the best *tapas*? Which professors had a thing for undergrad females? Which ones had a thing for undergrad males? Which internships could lead to an affair with a Pulitzer Prize–winning journalist, not to mention a syndicated column of your very own?

Little Kellie didn't even know how to cope with her very own feelings of loss about Derek. She was such a mess at the memorial service that Shelby had quietly offered to take the young woman back to Heart Lake with her, believing that a bit of quiet time up there and a little guidance from Ms. Simon might help her significantly. When the girl didn't seem to be able to make up her bereaved mind about it, Shelby had sketched her a map on the back of a memorial service program and told Kellie she was welcome at the lake anytime.

"Just call first," Shelby had said.

"Thanks for being so kind to me," Kellie responded. "You're the best, Shelby."

During all their exchanges this morning, Kellie hadn't said a single word about the new column. Shelby decided the intern was either too upset or else—and quite properly—she'd considered it a breach of etiquette to mention business during a memorial service. At least that reticence under the circumstances showed some sensitivity.

But her own *column*?

At least now Shelby had a pretty good idea why Sandy had quit. Her secretary had probably gotten wind of the new column and had stormed out in a fit of loyalty. Maybe Hal had even asked poor Sandy to work for Kellie.

Okay. Shit. The girl had a leg up on the job with Uncle Hal as managing editor, obviously. And she's smarter than the average cookie, too. That's what Shelby liked about her. Kellie saw an opportunity, and she pursued it. You go, girl.

But . . . Dammit. If Helm and Harris wanted to run a bogus, temporary column that wouldn't draw the ire of the letter bomber, why didn't they just ask Ms. Simon to come up with something? Shelby would've said yes in a heartbeat, even if it meant she couldn't use her own name on the column.

Just as this thought occurred to her, Mick stepped on the gas in order to pass a westbound bus, and on the vehicle's side, in the frame where Ms. Simon's face should've been, was an empty space. Pretty soon there would probably be a photo of young Ms. Carter above the caption "According to Kellie . . . Everyone reads the *Daily Mirror*."

The longer Shelby stared at the empty space, the easier it was to picture Kellie's face there. If she'd had a Magic Marker or a grease pen in her purse just then, Shelby would've rolled down the window and reached out to sketch a big, fat, black mustache on the imaginary redhead's upper lip and one long, skanky hair on her dimpled chinny-chin-chin just for good measure.

According to Kellie, her ass.

She was still fuming and grinding her teeth when Callahan pulled up in front of his apartment building, and she was apparently still so engrossed in her own thoughts that she didn't realize that he'd opened her door and was patiently holding out his hand to help her out of the car.

Dear Ms. Simon,
What's a girl supposed to do when it seems like
everything is falling apart?
Signed,
Worried in the Windy City

> *Dear Worried,*
> *When somebody offers a helping hand, reach for*
> *it. Hold on tight.*
> *Ms. Simon says so.*

And that's just what Shelby did.

~

Mick wadded up the trousers and suit coat he'd just taken off and lobbed them into a corner of the bedroom. Good riddance, he thought, but then, suffering immediate recriminations, he picked up the clothes, folded them, and laid them on the mattress. A minute later he added the dress shirt and the purple tie. On the way out of town, he'd drop them off at the Good Shepherd Shelter, and by tonight there would be a wino, clad in Armani, picking through a Dumpster somewhere on West Division. The image brought a twisted smile to his lips as he put on his jeans and flannel shirt.

Before he went to the living room where Shelby was waiting for him, he put in a call to his precinct captain to get an update on the investigation.

"Nada," Rita said. "Zip on the kid at Northwestern. Not much more on the *Daily Mirror* guy. His blood alcohol level was enough to account for a swan dive under the train, though."

"Yeah. Well, I doubt it," Mick grumbled.

"How's the vacation?" she asked, her voice fairly embroidered with sarcasm. "Getting a lot of rest, are we?"

"Just let me know if anything turns up, Cap. Okay?"

He tossed a few more pairs of socks and underwear into

a spare gym bag, threw in the suit and tie, then walked out to the living room and stopped dead in his tracks.

"What the hell is this?" he asked.

While she'd waited for him, Shelby had not only picked up all the debris in the room, but she'd also re-arranged his furniture.

The smile that had been perched on her lips sagged a little bit. "You don't like it," she said. "Well, I can put it back. Here." She began to shove the couch, but Mick stopped her by wrapping her in his arms.

"I didn't say I didn't like it, Shelby. It just kinda surprised me. That's all. And it . . ." He fell silent, shaking his head.

"What?" she asked, tilting her face up to study his.

Mick had been about to say that it depressed the hell out of him that she seemed to care so much about his environment, the one he'd have to return to eventually. Back to this dump. This den of discouragement. Alone. It was enough to make him think that a swan dive under the El wasn't such a bad idea.

"What were you going to say, Mick?"

He kissed her. Just a sample. And then he lied to her. "I was going to say that you probably inherited your design skills from your mother. This room looks great." Then he forced a laugh. "At least it's not beige."

Shelby blinked. "Oh. You noticed that."

"What? That your apartment looks like it was decorated by Lawrence of Arabia? Nah. I didn't notice that."

Oh, shit. He'd meant it as a joke, but it was immediately clear, when Shelby wrenched out of his embrace, that she didn't think it was funny. At all.

"Hey." Mick tried to draw her back against him, but she wasn't having any of it.

"I *love* beige," she insisted.

"So do I. I wasn't criticizing you, babe. It wouldn't make any difference to me if your place was wall-to-wall black."

She just stood there glaring at him a minute, then her expression softened. "Well, I don't *love* it. I like it." She stared at the ceiling a second, then took in what turned out to be a long, confessional breath. "Okay. I don't really even like beige. In fact, I'm actually starting to hate it. Satisfied?"

Mick didn't know the right answer to that one, so he just gathered her against his chest again, where she seemed content to stay for the moment, muttering into the pocket of his shirt.

"I hate beige," she said.

"Okay. Well, that explains why you've surrounded yourself with it. Suicide by displeasure."

Again, she didn't laugh at his remark, making Mick realize that this was really important to her. "Tell me," he said softly.

After she dragged in a long breath, she did.

"Ever since I was a little kid, I've always had this mental image, this dumb vision, of the house I'd eventually live in with my handsome husband and our adorable 2.3 kids. It's a place full of color and patterns, with big comfy chairs and upholstered ottomans, sofas like down pillows, thick oriental rugs, and bookcases everywhere, the kind you need a ladder to reach the highest shelf, all of them filled with leatherbound classics and . . ." Her words dwindled to a soft little curse. "Well, shit. Just shit."

"Go ahead," he said. "I'm really into those bookcases."

"You're thinking I'm insane," she said.

"Nope." He tightened his embrace. "But I still don't get the beige." He didn't get it at all. If Shelby dreamed in a full palette of colors, why was her waking life monochromatic?

"I'm not sure I get it completely, either," she said. "My mother, God bless her, seems to think I have some sort of commitment problem. But it's not that. It's . . ."

He waited quietly for her to continue while he thought about her dream, especially the husband part of it and the 2.3 kids. He'd always wanted those 2.3 kids himself.

"It's not really a conscious choice," she said softly. "But I think maybe, deep down, I'm afraid to start accumulating those brightly colored dream house things. Like I'll jinx it all somehow. So I buy beige and neutrals, which can always fit in someplace."

"Makes perfect sense to me."

She leaned back and blinked up at him. "It does?"

Well, it didn't make *perfect* sense, but he loved the complicated little twists and turns of her brain and the quirks of her personality. Besides, goofy as her theory was, it did strike a somewhat familiar chord in him.

"I always wanted a dog," he said. "I mean really, *really* wanted one. And here I am, thirty-eight years old, and I've never had a dog in my life. It just never felt like it was the right time for some reason."

Shelby nodded and her face lit up. "That's it! You really do understand, don't you?"

"Yeah. I do." He grinned. " 'Course just because *I* understand, doesn't mean you get a gold star for Mental Health Week."

"Hey. I'll settle for a bronze."

He dipped his head, savoring the laughter on her lips, still thinking about those 2.3 kids. And now the stupid dog, too.

～

Her "beige problem" was something Shelby had never confessed to anyone. The fact that Mick hadn't looked at her and asked "Whaddya nuts or something?" kept a smile on her face and a twinkle in her heart long after their delicious kiss.

She followed him down the dank staircase of his building and out the front door, wondering if they'd keep seeing each other after this case was finally solved and she was out of danger. The only danger she felt in at the moment was losing her head completely, not to mention her heart.

A little while earlier, back upstairs in Mick's apartment, when he was kissing her, Shelby had almost blurted out an "I love you."

Did she?

Love him?

Omigod.

Her feet just stopped moving as if sudden paralysis had set in, and she stood on the broken concrete sidewalk, gaping at the man some twenty feet in front of her. She hadn't even known him a full week. If somebody wrote to her, asking if they could possibly be in love after such a short time, Ms. Simon would have said, "I doubt it."

So what was this? If it wasn't love, did it have a name? Lust with a side order of tenderness? The hots with care sprinkled on top? Physical attraction with complications of the heart?

"Callahan!" she yelled.

He spun around, his right hand poised in the vicinity of his weapon, his expression hard and alert.

Shelby gave a quick wave of her hand. "Sorry. I didn't mean to startle you." What had she meant, she wondered, by calling out to him that way? "I just . . ."

"What?" He walked back to her, stood looking down at her.

Shelby looked up, tilting her head to the side. "I just wanted you to kiss me again."

A slow smile worked its way across his mouth while a warm hazel light kindled in his eyes. "Lady, I'd love to." He dropped his gym bag and drew her into his arms and kissed her until her knees wobbled and she had half a mind to drag him back upstairs to the mattress on the floor.

When she finally opened her eyes, she was about to moan with pleasure, but instead she gulped and said, "Oh, shit."

"Excuse me?"

"Look who's coming up the sidewalk," she said, angling her head toward his two neighbors who were just then pulling their shopping carts along behind them. "Aren't I supposed to be your sister?"

"Jesus," he breathed.

Shelby couldn't help but laugh. "Boy, if they thought you were on your way to hell in a handbasket *before. . . .*"

"Need some help with your groceries, ladies?" Mick called to them.

Hattie, the short one, was shaking her head in a combination of dismay and disgust.

The tall Lena was glowering. "This is sister," she said sternly to Mick as she got closer, jabbing a finger toward Shelby. "No kissing."

He looked genuinely sheepish. "I'm sorry. She's leaving town and I just got a little carried away."

"I'll say you got carried away," Hattie exclaimed. She started shaking a finger at him, too. "Don't you be carrying on like that in this building, young man. You, too, sister woman. There's respectable, God-fearing folks living here."

Mick bent to pick up his gym bag, still apologizing profusely to his accusers, while at the same time Shelby could see that he was trying to keep from laughing. Oh, God. So was she.

"Come on, bro." She grabbed his hand and hustled him down the sidewalk to the car, while Hattie and Lena just stood there and stared, like two mismatched guard dogs, protecting the premises.

As he started the car, he was still trying not to break up. "I'm going to have to move, I guess."

"Probably," Shelby said. "Either that, or start going to church with them. If you want my advice . . ."

"I don't." He shot her a little glare. "Thanks anyway, sis."

"Don't mention it."

They had driven all the way across the border into Indiana before they could stop laughing.

~

This time the five-hour drive to Michigan seemed to go by in the blink of an eye because once they'd stopped laughing, they talked the entire way. After being somewhat reticent at first, Mick described his years crisscrossing the country with his mother and her succession of boyfriends. Shelby was amazed that a life like that didn't seem to have left deeper psychological scars. But Mick didn't appear to harbor any anger toward Carrie Callahan. Quite the opposite. He seemed to actually remember her rather fondly.

That didn't appear to be the case with his wife, however. Try as she might, Shelby still couldn't get him to really discuss his marriage or Julie in any detail. While he spoke of his mother in glowing language, his references to his late wife were mostly platitudes. She was a good doctor. She was a big spender. She was this or that. Shelby still didn't have a clue what the woman had really been like, or why it was so difficult for Mick to talk about her.

Well, she supposed if she'd lost a mate after almost twenty years, she might have a hard time finding the right words, too. Maybe it was less painful to speak of her in generic terms than specifics.

He also told her more about his career with the police department. Funny. She'd come to think of him as some sort of professional bodyguard, and pictured him doing that on the force, as well. But for the past two years he'd been working undercover, buying drugs in the worst neighborhoods in the city, putting together a regular Who's Who of pushers, slowly working his way up from the guys on the street to the major players. He didn't name names.

Shelby did. She told him all about the mess she'd made for Beth and Sam, all about her plans to end the estrangement of Linda and Harry, all about her less-than-professional resentment of her up-and-coming young intern, Kellie Carter.

"I'm a meddler," she finally confessed.

"There's news." He chuckled softly.

"Do you think I'm a horrible person?"

He shook his head. "No. You can meddle with me anytime you want. Just not in front of Hattie and Lena."

Shelby laughed again, and then sighed. "I'll really miss you, Callahan, when this is all over."

"I'll miss you, too, babe."

He kept his eyes on the road as he spoke, so Shelby couldn't tell whether or not he really meant it.

⁓

The big house at Heart Lake was all lit up, exactly the way it had been when Mick had first seen the place. Only tonight, in some odd way, all those lights seemed to be welcoming him home. It was a nice feeling, even if it wasn't true.

Once inside, Shelby called out to her mother. Once. Twice. After the third yoo-hoo, she looked pretty alarmed and began to tear through room after room in search of the elusive Linda. Mick followed her just in case something was really wrong. When she turned on the lights on the third floor and found the huge space empty, she became really alarmed.

"Your dad's probably out in the carriage house," Mick said, trying to calm her. "Maybe your mother's out there with him."

"Oh, I hope so."

He followed her downstairs, across the lawn and into the carriage house, where she hadn't paused long enough to knock.

"Shelby!" Harry looked up from his book. "I didn't know you were coming back tonight, honey. Hello, Mick."

"Mom's not out here?" she asked, looking a little wild-eyed now.

"No, honey. She left this morning for Denver. Something about that truck that overturned with all her merchandise in it. Then she's flying on to Los Angeles for a day. She'll be back Thursday night."

Mick could hear Shelby's sigh of relief as she wilted onto the long curved couch. There was nothing he wanted more just then than to put his arms around her, but it seemed like a good time to let father and daughter have a private moment.

"I'm going to go unpack a few things, and then hit the hay. Good night, Harry."

"Glad you're back, Mick. Maybe we can get some fishing in later this week if the weather holds."

"Great."

On his way back to the house, Mick consulted the stars in the clear autumn sky. With any luck some clouds, big ones, would roll in early tomorrow.

Shelby felt pretty silly for panicking when she couldn't find her mother, and she was extremely grateful to both her father and to Mick for not making her feel more like a fool than she already did.

Her father was sitting at the counter that separated the kitchen from the rest of the space. There was a goose-necked lamp beside him, casting its light across the open pages of a big fat book. If she wasn't mistaken, it looked a lot like one of the old law books that used to line the walls of his office downtown.

"What are you reading, Dad?"

He looked up at her over the rims of his glasses. "Contract law," he said. "I called Myra Phipps, our office manager, and asked her to send me the best text she knew of. Myra probably knows more about the law in general than any six attorneys in the firm put together."

"Contracts! Since when . . ." Shelby bit her lip and told herself to shut the hell up. If Harry was boning up on contract law, that just might mean . . .

"Don't say anything to your mother about this, Little Big Mouth. You hear me? I'm just taking a look at this, you might even call it a refresher course, in case your mother needs some help expanding her business." He narrowed his eyes. "And this is none of yours, Shelby. I want you to understand that."

"You haven't called me that in at least twenty years," she said, grinning at his use of her childhood nickname. She had been Little Big Mouth while Beth had earned the monicker Stands With Hammer because she was always building things or tearing them apart.

"Well, you haven't changed much," he said. "And I don't want your mother to get all excited only to be disappointed if I can't stomach this contract and merger stuff. So keep it zipped, okay?"

She pantomimed a zipper closing across her mouth. "Mum's the word," she said. "Mom's going to be so . . ."

He pitched her a glare that silenced her immediately, and Shelby promised herself that she wouldn't say a word to Linda Purl because she, too, didn't want her mother to be disappointed if this business alliance didn't pan out.

But it would. Shelby had a really good feeling about it. And the amazing thing was that she didn't even have to offer a single word of advice to Harry about going into business with Linda. Her advice seemed to have gotten through telepathically or by some weird osmosis.

Boy. She was *good*.

She kissed her father good night, and headed back to the house with a smile on her face and every intention of being just as good, or even better, with the man who was waiting for her there.

Then, just as she reached the top of the stairs—good ol' Warren G. Harding—she heard Callahan's curse reverberate along the second floor hallway.

She knocked on his door, then opened it to find him swearing again as he twisted up the navy blue suit he'd worn earlier today.

"What in the world are you doing?" she asked.

"I meant to drop this off at the Good Shepherd Shelter on our way out of town. I feel like the goddamn thing is stalking me."

"Okay." Well, what the hell. She couldn't buy anything but beige, and he had a personal vendetta with a suit. They were probably perfect for each other. "Do you want to tell me about it, Callahan?"

"No," he said, drop-kicking the wadded-up trousers across the room and pitching the purple tie right behind them.

"Suit yourself," she said, trying unsuccessfully to suppress a grin that was begging to become a full-blown laugh.

"*Suit* myself?" He glared at her, but in a matter of seconds he was grinning, too. "Okay. You win. Get your jammies on, Ms. Simon, because if you want to hear about this suit, it just might be a very long night."

CHAPTER SEVENTEEN

⁓

They snuggled in the big bed in her room. Shelby had lit a couple candles that created an amazing effect with the old-fashioned furnishings. She had also donned a not-so-old-fashioned, oversized T-shirt whose front was a replica of her *Daily Mirror* bus poster, so Mick found himself looking alternately at two versions of the same lovely face.

He was in no rush to tell her his sad little story, although he had come to the conclusion that it was indeed time for her to know the truth. From various comments she'd made, especially on the drive today, he thought she had a really mistaken impression of his marriage. Well, hell. So had he until it was over.

It wasn't easy knowing where to begin, but when Shelby's warm body moved closer to his and she spread her hand over his heart and pressed her lips to his shoulder, he somehow found the words.

"In the beginning," he said, "Julie was my lifeline. We were just kids, but wanting to stay with her gave me the courage to tell my mother I'd had enough of traipsing all over the country. And the Traverses, her parents, were good to me. It felt like I had a family for the first time in my life."

Shelby made a soft little sound. She probably knew better than to make an actual comment, for fear she'd ruin his momentum.

"We got married the summer after we graduated from high school," he said, almost leaving it there, but then deciding he cared enough for this woman to not hold anything back, no matter how it reflected on his character. For better or for worse. "She was pregnant, so that hurried things up a little. Well, a lot."

"Did you have a big wedding?" she asked.

"The whole nine yards. The church. The white dress. The bridesmaids. My mother didn't come, but she sent us a check that covered a weekend honeymoon at a cottage on Lake Michigan, which was where Julie miscarried."

"Oh, Mick."

"Save your tears, kiddo. She was thrilled. It meant that all her plans for college and med school were back on track. And I have to admit I was pretty relieved myself. We were just kids ourselves, and nowhere near ready for a responsibility like that."

"Then what happened?" She kissed his shoulder again.

Mick boiled the ensuing eight years down to a couple sentences about how they'd scraped for scholarships and part-time jobs in college while living in Julie's parents' basement, and how he'd finally dropped out in favor of the Police Academy, not to mention a bit of privacy in a place of their own.

And then, mostly because he was just so damned tired of talking about Julie, he cut to the chase. "Those last couple of years it seemed like we never had any time to spend together. We had a nice place on Rush Street, but she started a new residency and I started working undercover, and we were hardly ever home at the same time. I was ready for kids. She wasn't. Plus . . ."

He started wishing he'd never gotten into this in such detail.

"Plus what?" Shelby asked.

Shit. Acknowledging this to himself was one thing, but saying it out loud was something else.

"Plus, Julie seemed to be embarrassed by my job. Our deal originally had been for her to go to med school, and then to help finance me through law school. Only when we finally had some money, I didn't want to quit the force. I liked my fucking job. I liked being on the street. No, I loved it, and she just couldn't seem to understand that. To her it was comparable to working in the sewer."

Trying to tone down the harsh resentment in his voice, he took in a deep breath, then said, "And then two years ago she died."

"What about the suit?" Shelby asked.

"What?"

"You were going to tell me about the suit. Why you hate it."

"I wore it to her funeral," he said.

"Well, no wonder you have such bad feelings about it, Mick. And so many sad associations."

"Sad? No, not sad," he said. "Try mad."

"I don't understand."

"Yeah, well . . ." He filled his lungs with another shot of air, let it out slowly, and proceeded to tell her the story he'd never told anyone else. And as he told her, he felt as if he were living through it, dying through it, all over again.

He could almost smell the flowers in the funeral parlor. His were a spray of white and pink lilies directly in front of the closed bronze casket. The florist had asked him if he wanted a ribbon with "Beloved Wife" in gold lettering, and Mick had almost puked on the poor old guy. No. No gold letters. The flowers, her favorites, were expressive enough.

It was hard to feel bereaved and numb and angry at Julie for clinging to her purse instead of her life all at the same time, so he probably looked like a zombie in his navy blue Armani suit. He barely recognized people as they reached for his hand and expressed their condolences.

At some point, he'd been staring vacantly across the room when a man in a similar blue suit stared back at him, then slowly made his way toward the casket and Mick. The closer the guy came, the more Mick realized there were tears in his eyes and his expression more grief-stricken than somber.

He extended his hand to Mick and introduced himself. "Dr. Solomon Fellows. We haven't met yet, but I can tell from your expression that you know who I am."

Mick didn't know what the fuck his expression had communicated or who the fuck this guy was, but he stood there as the stranger droned on.

"I gather Julie told you, Mick. We didn't plan for it to happen, you know. It just did." He paused to gaze at the coffin, then cleared his throat and said, "Christ, I miss her. The baby was a boy. Did she tell you that?"

Mick had mumbled something. He didn't know what.

He hardly heard his own words for the thundering inside his head.

"No question that the child was mine," Solomon Fellows said. "The amnio results came in last week. Julie and I thought we could take care of things—the divorce, our marriage—next month in Las Vegas." His gaze strayed to the casket again, and his voice broke. "But now . . . They're both gone. I don't know what I'll do."

Mick didn't know what he'd do either until he found himself drawing back his fist and smashing it into Solomon Fellows's nose. The good doctor took out the spray of lilies and two other huge bouquets on his way to the carpet. Whatever transpired after that, Mick didn't know because he walked out.

"My next lucid thought," he said now, concluding the whole shitty tale, "was three or four days later when I woke up in the Eleventh District's drunk tank, still wearing the goddamned suit."

"Aw, Mick."

That was all Shelby said. Just a soft "Aw, Mick," her breath warming his skin as she moved even closer to him.

Then, as they lay there in the golden, flickering candlelight, Mick felt every muscle in his body melt with relaxation and every nerve unwind and smooth out. And damned if he didn't feel something shift inside his chest, some kind of weight that he hadn't even known was there. He turned his head to rub his cheek against Shelby's forehead, so grateful for her presence beside him.

Her soft, *quiet* presence. Maybe it should have surprised him that Ms. Simon, the High Priestess of Help and Advice, the Monarch of Meddlers, considered a whispered "Aw, Mick" sufficient commentary on his plight. If she'd wanted to discuss it at length, if she'd wanted to discuss it *at all,* Mick wasn't sure that he could've refrained from snarling at her or shouting shut up.

But her silence didn't come as a surprise somehow, and it pleased him that she seemed to sense his mood, and seemed to know that all he needed right now was to hold her close.

Mick blinked. All *he* needed? That didn't say much about his sensitivity to *her* needs, did it? The heaviness in his chest came back, even more oppressive now, and he wondered about all the opportunities he might have missed with Julie. As he had for the past two years, he wondered what he'd done wrong.

"Shelby?" he whispered.

"Hm."

"If you want to talk about all this, it's okay with me."

She edged her leg over his and pressed the rest of her body harder against him. "I just want to hold you," she said. "Are you okay?"

"I'm better than I've been in a long, long time," he said.

He could feel her lips curl into a smile against his shoulder just before she said, "I'm here if you want to talk about it more."

"Maybe tomorrow," he said as he was thinking *probably never.* All that misery and pain seemed truly behind him now.

The next morning Shelby woke before Mick. The pillar candles were still flickering and she was still in his arms, as she had been all night long. No wonder she'd slept so well.

Asleep, he looked so peaceful and relaxed. For a moment it seemed that their roles were reversed, and that she was protecting him. It was a good thing Julie was dead, Shelby thought, because otherwise she'd have to hunt the woman down and strangle her for the hurt she'd inflicted on Mick. Ms. Simon, in her wisdom, always said there were two sides to every story, but in this case she didn't give a rat's ass about Doctor Julie's version.

How could she not have wanted to have children with this man? He was bright and strong and funny and loyal and far more sensitive than Shelby ever had imagined.

She closed her eyes and sighed.

> *Dear Ms. Simon,*
> *How will I know if this one is The One?*
> *Signed,*
> *Hopeful at Heart Lake*

> *Dear Hopeful,*
> *He is. Ms Simon says so.*

In her mother's absence, Shelby took it upon herself to feed the two men in her care.

It turned out badly.

The shopping part of it was fun, though. Mick pushed the cart along the aisles of the grocery store in Mecklin while Shelby consulted her list, agonized over one type of cream versus another, wished she'd brought a ruler to measure the thickness of the pork chops, and discovered that she knew absolutely nothing about onions. Who knew there were so many varieties?

And who knew that among Callahan's many talents was a pretty good working knowledge of wine? The store's selection wasn't vast, but he seemed absurdly happy with a California pinot noir. When he confessed that he'd boned up on the subject of wine in order to please his wife, it was all Shelby could do to stifle an indignant snort. She vowed once again to be careful about those reactions. The man had loved his wife, after all, for a long, long time, and even after her betrayal, he refrained from speaking ill of her. Mick's gallantry made Shelby love him all the more.

Well . . . She respected him for his restraint. She was still waffling on the love thing.

After they came home and put the groceries away, with no one in the house to hinder them, and dinner still hours away, they raced upstairs to make love again. And again.

Shelby decided she was a lot better in the bedroom than she was in the kitchen. Her mother's pork chop with onion cream sauce was one of her father's favorites, but Shelby's version was nothing like Linda's even though she followed the recipe step by careful step.

"How long did you cook these pork chops, honey?" her father asked from his seat at the head of the table.

She was still sawing hers as she replied, "An hour and a half. Just like the recipe said."

"The sauce is great," Mick said.

"Oh, good." She hadn't sampled it yet because she was still trying to cut her first bite of pork.

"Great wine," her father said.

Shelby didn't comment because at last she was chewing the entrée that she'd slaved over.

"It's a little fruitier than I usually like in a pinot noir," Mick said, contemplating the pale liquid, "but not too bad."

"Nice and dry," Harry said.

Speaking of dry, Shelby thought morosely. She put her fork down and lifted her napkin to discreetly get rid of the chewed over chunk of meat in her mouth, then gulped down half the wine in her glass, and asked as cheerfully as she could, "Who's up for a grilled cheese sandwich?"

"Sounds good, honey," her father said, putting down his knife and fork with what appeared to be monumental relief.

Mick, bless his heart, insisted on finishing what was on his plate, but didn't put up much of a fight when Shelby grabbed it out from under his nose and took it into the kitchen.

She looked at her mother's recipe card again. "Well, no wonder," she exclaimed.

"What?" Mick asked while he scraped their plates into the trash can.

"I was supposed to cook the chops for half an hour, not an hour and a half."

"So, next time you'll know."

"Next time I'll order out," she said.

The phone rang just then, and Shelby picked it up and answered with a crisp "Simon residence." After a moment of silence, she said, "Hello?" And then somewhere in the silence, she heard somebody breathing. Or didn't hear it exactly, but sensed it. A presence on the other end of the line. How creepy was that!

"Hello." This time she didn't say it like a polite greeting. It came out more as an accusation.

All of a sudden, Mick was standing beside her.

"Who is it?" he asked.

She shook her head.

"Hang up," he said.

"But . . ."

"Hang the fuck up, Shelby."

She did.

Mick was glowering at the telephone now. It was an ancient rotary device, harvest gold, and nearly as big as and as obsolete as a bread box. The thing had sat on its little wrought-iron stand in the kitchen for as long as Shelby could remember. It had never been threatening, though. Not until this evening.

"No Caller ID on this damned thing," he muttered.

"What about the extension in my mother's office?"

They raced up to the third floor to discover that the call had come from a pay phone with a Chicago area code. Mick placed a call to his office while Shelby went back to the kitchen to put together a second dinner.

"The pay phone was at O'Hare," he said when he joined her after a few minutes.

"O'Hare!" Shelby exclaimed. She pictured the airport, once the busiest in the country, and still a welter of travelers nearly twenty-four hours a day. "Well, that narrows it down to about ten thousand possible suspects."

"Yep. No sense even checking for prints in a case like that. If the calls keep coming, I'll see what I can do about putting a trace on your line. But, you know . . ." He came up with a tiny, hopeful grin. "Maybe it was just a fluke, Shelby."

She narrowed her eyes. "What are the odds of that, Lieutenant Callahan? Tell me that. What are the odds of some tired, confused traveler wandering through O'Hare, picking up a pay phone, and dialing these ten digits by mistake?"

With each word, Shelby heard her own voice begin to tremble more as it climbed into higher and higher registers. The call hadn't been a mistake or "just a fluke." It was deliberate. She had felt the malice across several hundred miles. She could still feel it.

Mick wrapped her in his arms. "Nothing bad is going to happen to you. I promise you."

A few days ago, Shelby would have been eager to believe that. But now she wasn't quite so sure.

CHAPTER EIGHTEEN

⁓

It rained the following day, one of those chilly all day deals that usually depressed the hell out of Mick, but not this time. He built a crackling fire in the fireplace beneath the watchful eye of Shelby's great-great-grandfather's portrait. He whipped up a pot of hot chocolate from scratch, impressing Shelby with another one of his hidden talents. He sat next to her on the big Victorian sofa in front of the fire, sharing an enormous Linda Purl designed afghan, reading his Grant biography while Shelby dinked around on her laptop.

"This is nice," he said, probably for the tenth time. It was just that whenever he looked up from his book and took in the fire and the rain on the windowpanes and Shelby beside him, a palpable feeling of contentment would course through him and he'd have to acknowledge it out loud. It was better than nice. It was heaven. He wished he could think of a way to prolong this day for the next forty or fifty years.

The phone had only rung once so far today, but the sound nearly paralyzed Shelby. Mick answered it, relieved to hear Linda Simon's voice and happy to know that she'd be returning earlier than expected from her trip. He promised to pass the news along to Harry, who was somewhere out on the lake, fishing.

"Is everything all right there?" Linda had asked.

"Everything's great," he lied.

The call the night before worried him a lot more than he'd let on to Shelby. If there was still an aura of coincidence about the letter bombs, the death of the chemistry student at Northwestern, and that of Derek McKay, Mick had a bad feeling about the phone call. While the other incidents had been aimed *around* Shelby, the call had been directed right *at* her. It wasn't good news. And the fact that the call was made at a pay phone at O'Hare was a pretty good indication that they were dealing with somebody who put some thought into his malicious business and wasn't anxious to get caught.

Mick found himself staring into the flames, wondering not only who but why? Shelby had wracked her brain again and again, but hadn't been able to come up with a reason somebody might want to kill her. Without any sort of motive, the investigation was pretty much dead in the water. And Mick had to suspect everybody.

He closed his book and reached for Shelby's hand. "It'd be nice to get away to someplace warm and sunny, wouldn't it? What do you say we fly down to Cancun for the weekend? We could leave tomorrow. Does that sound good?"

"It sounds great, except my sister's coming back for the Masque tomorrow night. Remember? I told you."

"Yeah," he said. "I forgot. Well, Saturday, then."

"I hate to leave when she'll only be here a few days. Maybe next weekend?"

"Yeah. Okay. Maybe next weekend."

He had a sinking feeling that would be too late.

Linda arrived at dinnertime with an enormous bucket of extra crispy fried chicken plus all the trimmings that she'd picked up on her drive from the airport in Grand Rapids. God, it was good to be back. She felt as if she'd been away three months instead of just three days.

In her absence, not only had dismal weather settled in at Heart Lake, but Harry had acquired the beginnings of a cold, while her daughter and Mick Callahan seemed to have acquired the appearance of two people with a distinct case of the hots.

"Her lieutenant is a wine connoisseur," Harry said when Linda commented on the two of them after she joined him out in the carriage house for an espresso after their fried chicken dinner.

"That's nice." She took a tiny sip of the dark, rich brew. "Good wines will help distract from Shelby's inedible meals. She told me about her pork chops."

Harry rolled his eyes, which were beginning to look a little glassy with fever. "I'm worried about her," he said.

"Oh, Harry. Women don't have to be good cooks these days. That's why God invented freezers and microwaves."

"It's not the cooking. Do you know that your daughter hasn't offered me so much as a crumb of advice the past couple of days." He sniffed. "Hand me one of those tissues, Beauty, will you?"

Linda plucked one from the box on the coffee table and handed it to him. "So I guess she didn't tell you not to sit out in a rowboat in the freezing rain for six hours without proper clothes."

"Nope. Can you believe it? Our little Ms. Simon is slipping."

"She's distracted."

He reached for her hand. "*I'm* distracted, Beauty."

"You're also contagious, Harry, so don't get any ideas about exchanging fluids of any sort. Anyway, I'm exhausted." She sighed and put her feet up on the coffee table, then leaned back while balancing her diminutive cup and saucer on her leg. "I hardly had time to stop and breathe on this trip. It was just grueling."

He moved closer in order to rub her neck and shoulders. He could always zero in on just the right spot, and when he did, Linda couldn't stifle a moan.

"Oh. Now down just an inch. Mm. Oh, yes. Right there."

"Maybe I should go with you on your next trip," he said quietly.

Linda turned her head toward him. He'd already said that Shelby hadn't been hounding him about anything, so she had to assume there'd been no mention of his working for her. If Shelby hadn't nagged him, then maybe he'd had a change of heart about working for Linda Purl Designs all on his own? She was almost afraid to ask in case she jinxed it. After thirty-five years she knew Harry wouldn't be pushed. The man would cut off his nose to spite his face with very little provocation. But she couldn't *not* ask about this. "Does that mean . . . ?"

"No," he said, continuing to knead her shoulders. "It doesn't. Slow down, sweetheart. It just means I'm volunteering my services as a baggage handler and part-time masseur for a while. Don't jump to any conclusions or read too much into it, okay?"

"Okay." She searched his expression. "But you haven't ruled it out, have you? Actually working for the company."

"I haven't ruled it out," he said. "See those books up on the bar?"

She looked at the big stack of thick volumes at which he was pointing.

"That's contract law, Linda. About thirty pounds of contract law, give or take a few pounds. And I want to tell you that after three decades in criminal law, it's about as exciting as reading the goddamned phone book."

"Well, Harry, there are other ways to get excited, you know. I'd be more than happy to show you once you're over your cold." She shimmied her shoulders beneath his hand just a bit. "Oh. There. That's perfect. Now just a half inch to the left. Mm."

When Shelby awoke the next morning, the first thing she noticed was that it had stopped raining. The second thing she noticed was that her bedmate was gazing at her with a warm smile on his face.

"Happy Halloween," he said, dropping a kiss on her forehead.

"Omigod."

"What?" Mick jerked up on his elbow, looking over his shoulder as if he expected to see someone standing there with a knife.

"It's Halloween," Shelby said.

"So?"

"Masque! I haven't even thought about a costume."

He swore softly and lay back down beside her. "The last time I went trick or treating I was eight years old and a gang of skinheads beat the shit out of me and stole my candy."

"Poor baby." Shelby smoothed his rumpled hair back from his forehead, then kissed his eyes, his nose, and each corner of his mouth. "This will be better. I promise. Masque isn't trick or treating. It's just a big party where everybody dresses up and has a good time."

"Right." He raised a skeptical eyebrow. "So then there's no bobbing for apples, or trying to eat marshmallows on a frigging string, I guess?"

"Well . . ." She laughed. "It *is* Halloween."

After breakfast, she left him cleaning up the dishes while she trotted up to the third floor where her mother sat staring at her computer screen.

"Mom, where's that big trunk we used to keep our costumes in? Beth didn't get rid of it, did she?"

"No, sweetie. I think it's in the closet in the sunroom. Shelby, I don't think your father and I will be going to Masque tonight. He's running a fever this morning, and he feels like hell."

Shelby couldn't hide her disappointment. "This will be the first one you've missed in years," she said. "I could come home early and stay with Dad, if you want to go."

Her mother shook her head. "No. You three go and have a wonderful time." She looked at her watch. "Beth should be here in a few hours."

"I wonder when Sam is getting back," Shelby said, trying to sound offhand and not too obvious.

"He's not."

"Excuse me?"

"Sam's not coming back for another month or two. I thought I told you. He called your father Tuesday and said he'd decided to go ahead with surgery on his leg, and then, assuming all goes well, he'll have to stay a month, maybe two, for rehab."

"No, you didn't tell me, Mother." Shelby felt her best laid plan suddenly unraveling like an inferior Linda Purl sweater. "Did you tell Beth, by any chance?"

"Of course not." Her mother let out one of her well-practiced, beleaguered sighs. "Your sister isn't coming back to see Sam, Shelby. For heaven's sake. That's water under an ancient bridge. I wish you wouldn't interfere."

"Well, I guess there's no chance of that now," she said. "Is there?" She turned on her heel, attempting to walk out of the ballroom with a certain amount of dignity when what she felt like doing was stomping like a nine-year-old who'd just been told that Halloween had been canceled.

⁓

"I'm not going to wear this," Mick said when Shelby tossed something from the trunk in his direction. "What the hell is it, anyway?"

They were in the sunroom, where he had lugged the

huge old trunk from a closet and Shelby had promptly dived into it headfirst.

"It's a vest," she said, her tone implying an unspoken *you idiot*.

He glared at the thing. "What's it made of? Squirrel? Rat?"

"Oh, for God's sake, Callahan. It's rabbit. Just try it on, will you? It probably won't even fit."

Lord willing, he thought as he shrugged it on, feeling the lining strain across his shoulders. "Too tight," he said.

"Well, damn. I was really hoping we could go tonight as Sonny and Cher."

"Which did you have in mind for me?" he asked.

"Very funny." She threw something else at him. "Here. Try this."

It was a black pirate's hat, complete with a red plume and a black eye patch attached to the brim with a safety pin. "I'm not wearing this," he said.

Clearly frustrated now, Shelby turned toward him and yelled, "Well, you have to wear something. It's a rule."

She might've looked forbidding if it hadn't been for the pink feather boa around her neck. Mick reached out, grasped both ends of it, and pulled her against him. "If I wear the pirate deal," he whispered, "do I get to rip your bodice later?"

"Argh," she said, but the grumble quickly gave way to a laugh, and a moment later the laugh gave way to his kiss.

"Oops." Someone cleared her throat not too far away. "Mom said you guys were fooling around in the sun-room, but I didn't know she meant *fooling around*."

Mick lifted his head. The woman standing in the doorway looked like a blonde version of Shelby. She was nearly a clone, from the shape of her face to the slant of her shoulders and the length of her legs, and the way she stood with one foot turned slightly to the side. If her eyes were a whiskey brown, the woman easily could've been Shelby in a blond wig. But Mick couldn't see her eyes because she was wearing dark sunglasses.

"Beth!" Shelby extracted herself from his arms and rushed to greet her sister. "You're early, aren't you? I didn't expect you till later this afternoon."

"So I see." The blonde grinned toward Mick. "I took an earlier flight. This must be your bodyguard." She extended her hand that he immediately noticed was shaped just like her sister's. "I'm Shelby's little sister, Beth."

"Mick Callahan," he said. "I can see the resemblance between the two of you."

"You think so?" Shelby asked. "Wait'll you see this."

She snatched the glasses from her sister's face, and then let out a little gasp at the shiner she'd uncovered. "Oh, Bethie. Sweetie, what happened?"

"Oh, this?" Beth lifted her hand to touch the bruise. "It's nothing, Shel. I walked into a door the other day. What a klutz."

Mick couldn't help but notice that it matched the bruise on her wrist, and he'd seen and heard enough battered women to know that Shelby's sister was one of them, and that the door she'd walked into had a fist.

Shelby hugged her sister then, and seemed to accept her story. But if Mick knew Shelby even half as well as he thought he did, his little meddler would be sniffing out the truth sooner than later.

Shelby managed to keep her mouth shut—just barely—while she and Beth, sporting her dark glasses once again, paid a quick visit to the infirmary in the carriage house, but once they were back in the big house, Shelby hooked her arm through her sister's and briskly ushered her up all twenty-nine presidential steps, including the landing, and slammed the door once they were inside her room.

"Okay," Shelby said. "Take those shades off, look me straight in the eye, and tell me again how you walked into a fucking door."

Of course, Beth couldn't do it. Her one blue eye and the other black-and-blue eye flooded with tears the second she took off the glasses.

"He hit you?" Shelby asked. "Danny hit you?"

"He was drunk," Beth said, as if offering an excuse.

"I don't care if he was high on heroin, angel dust, airplane glue, and Dom Perignon, all at the same time," Shelby yelled. "Men don't hit women. Period. End of story."

"Well . . ."

"Well?" Shelby dropped on her knees in front of her sister, who had sagged upon the bed. She took Beth's hands in hers. "Bethie. Sweetheart. You don't have to take abuse like that. My God."

Beth pulled her hands away and sat up straighter, so straight that Shelby thought someone had suddenly shoved a steel rod up her spine. "I don't want to talk about this right now. Will you just leave it alone?"

She drew in a breath. "Beth, I don't think I'm genetically capable of leaving it alone. You're my little sister, and somebody—that creep!—hurt you."

"He's not a creep, Shelby. He's not. Danny's a really good person. He . . . He just . . ."

"He slugged you, for crissake!"

"He was upset. Insecure. Jealous, if you want to know the whole truth. Somehow he got it into his head that I was coming back here to hook up with Sam."

"How would he even know that? How would he know what happened with you and Sam a million years ago?"

Beth looked at her as if Shelby had the I.Q. of wallpaper. "Danny lived here with me for almost a year while we were working on the house. Don't you think every time he went into Shelbyville or Mecklin for paint or spackle or turpentine that somebody somewhere had a little something snide to say about the little Simon girl and good old Sam Mendenhall?" She ripped her fingers through her long blond hair. "Jesus, Shelby. Use your head."

Shelby sat back on her heels. "Well, but . . . But that was a million years ago."

"Not to Danny," Beth said.

"Obviously not." Shelby snorted.

"Listen, big sister. I know you mean well, but I don't want to wallow in all of this now. Maybe Danny was right. Maybe I did want to see how I'd feel if I saw Sam again. But he's not here, so it doesn't matter anymore. Let's just have a good time this weekend, okay? Let's just drop this, okay? For now, anyway."

Shelby thought about that. It wasn't in her nature to just drop stuff, particularly when a black eye was involved. But she'd already ruined one of Beth's relationships, and she wasn't eager to repeat that performance. Besides, other than flying out to California and socking Beth's significant other in his eye, there wasn't much she could do about Danny at the moment. Beth deserved a wonderful weekend away from the creep. At least Shelby could offer her that.

"Okay," she said, forcing a smile. "Consider it dropped. Temporarily. And now, kiddo, on to the important stuff. What are we going to wear tonight for Masque?"

Beth laughed at that, and Shelby decided she'd done the right thing. For now.

⁓

At six that evening, Linda stood in the front hall, inspecting and photographing her costumed crew.

Beth had turned herself into a ravishing Lady Pirate, no doubt because the costume allowed her to wear the black eye patch to cover her own black eye. Linda had already decided that she'd stay with Beth and Danny, rather than in a hotel, next month when she attended a meeting scheduled in San Francisco, and if she witnessed anything the slightest bit abusive, she was going to bring her daughter home if she had to handcuff her to a plane seat. Good Lord. Linda wondered if she was getting as bad as Shelby.

Shelby had come up with a slightly moth-eaten bowler hat and cane, and penciled on a thick black mustache, combining those with an oversized navy blue suit that . . .

"My, God!" Linda exclaimed, on closer inspection of the petite Charlie Chaplin. "Is that an Armani?"

"On loan from Mick," Shelby said, twirling her cane.

Linda looked at the young man she was already considering a prospective son-in-law. "You're just full of surprises, aren't you, Lieutenant Callahan?"

He grinned. "Well, it's Halloween, ma'am."

He was wearing not Armani, but the clothes he'd been wearing when Linda had first met him, the night he and Shelby had arrived last week. Ripped jeans. A faded flannel shirt. The down vest with the god-awful duct tape. "And what are you disguised as?" she asked him.

"An undercover cop."

"Gee, who'd ever guess?" Beth said.

Shelby twitched her mustache. "Well, we better hit the road. Are you sure you don't want me to come back, Mom, so you can go? You could just put this on." She gestured to the blue suit.

"No. I'm going to share some chicken soup with your father, and then go to bed early. Just tell everybody I said hello. And don't drink too much orange punch, children."

"Orange punch?" Mick made a face.

"They have it every year," Linda told him. "No other beverages allowed. I hate to admit it, but I think it's actually an old family recipe of the Shelbys." She grimaced. "Maybe this year they'll float some orange sherbet in it. That always seems to help cut the taste of the rum a bit."

"Rum!" Beth, the Lady Pirate, smiled and hooked her arm through Charlie Chaplin's. "Let's be off, matey."

CHAPTER NINETEEN

~

Shelbyville was as crowded as Rush Street in downtown Chicago on a Friday night. There were so many cars that Mick had to park the Mustang in a field just east of town, where some enterprising kid was collecting a buck a car and two bucks for RVs. After the heavy rain the day before, Mick only hoped the little entrepreneur would be around later to help get vehicles out of the mud.

It was a clear, crisp night. Perfect for Halloween. On their walk to the VFW Hall, he counted five witches, four ghosts, a Spiderman, a Batman and Robin duo, and one six-foot six-inch Abe Lincoln. In addition to the costumes, he also counted at least a score of out-of-state plates on cars parked along Main Street, mostly from Illinois and Indiana. When he commented on that, Shelby didn't seem at all surprised. She said that a lot of summer people made it a point to come back for this Halloween deal every year. But that didn't keep Mick from brooding about all those out-of-state tags. The beauty of staying up here with Shelby in the boonies had been not having a bunch of strangers around that he had to worry about.

Still, he tried to keep those worries to himself because his little Charlie Chaplin was so happy tonight. His suit looked a hell of a lot better on her than it would have on some bum in the city. Her sister, Beth, seemed happy, too. As for him, he'd be glad when this Masque deal was over and they were headed back to the relative safety and quiet of Heart Lake.

They walked through the door of the VFW Hall, where Mick had never seen so much orange and black in one place in his life.

"Isn't this great?" Shelby exclaimed.

"Great," he muttered.

There must've been a thousand pumpkins scattered around, grinning or leering or looking just plain goofy. Instead of chairs, people sat on hay bales. The dance floor was covered with straw, and the band was comprised of three skeletons and a creepy dead guy on drums. There was orange and black crepe paper strung everywhere, and he kept having to swat the stuff out of his face as he followed along behind Shelby and Beth.

Silly as this whole thing seemed to him, he had to admit that he envied their sincere enjoyment of tradition. He bet Christmas at the Simon house was something special, full of antique ornaments and decorations that had been in the family forever, and recipes for stuffing and mince meat pie that had been served since the 1880s. For a kid who had never even known his own grandparents, that had a lot of appeal.

Mostly it was Shelby herself who appealed to him. It was nice, standing back, watching her swing her Charlie Chaplin cane and wiggle her penciled-on mustache, seeing her greet other costumed guests with so much warmth and enthusiasm. She hugged the Statue of Liberty with so much gusto that she knocked the aluminum foil crown right off the woman's head.

He started wondering about his life after Ms. Shelby Simon, and found himself settling into a profound orange and black funk.

In the kitchen of the big house, Linda hung up the harvest-gold phone and then refilled Harry's mug with hot chicken noodle soup. He was still running a fever, although it was down from this afternoon's high of 102.3. He insisted he was fine out in the carriage house.

"I'm sure you've got better things to do than hand me Kleenex, Beauty," he'd said grumpily.

But in truth she didn't. She felt like taking care of him, so she'd made him trek over here in his pajamas, and settled him under an afghan in front of the fire in the living room.

"Who was that?" he asked when she handed him the steaming mug of soup.

"Some friend of Shelby's. I didn't get the name, but she wanted to know what Shelby was wearing tonight so she wouldn't miss her at Masque."

Harry slurped the hot broth. "What is she wearing?"

"An Armani suit," Linda said with a laugh.

"Sounds like Shelby."

Linda laughed again as she reached over to dab at her husband's chin with a tissue. "I wonder if I should call her, just to let her know somebody's looking for her."

Harry leaned forward and put his mug down on the

coffee table. She noticed he was frowning, apart from his *I feel like shit* expression. "Give her a call, Linda," he said.

She stared at him. Her heart squeezed like a fist. "You're not worried that . . . ?"

"Just give her a call. Now."

Responding to the urgency in his voice, Linda hurried into the kitchen to dial Shelby's cell phone number. She let it ring ten or twelve times, until Harry called out to her. "She didn't take her cell. I hear it ringing upstairs."

⁓

"So, tell me about Mick," Beth said after the two sisters found a quiet corner where they could perch on a bale of hay along with a floppy scarecrow.

Shelby looked across the crowded room, just managing to catch a glimpse of him in the long line at the refreshment table.

"What about him?" she said, sounding absurdly casual about the most gorgeous man in the room.

"Shelby!" Beth the Pirate bashed her shoulder against Shelby's. "Don't give me that *what about him* shit. You're crazy about the guy. It's pretty obvious."

"I like him," she said, her gaze still pinned on the spot she'd last seen him. Then she saw him again, and had to smile at the ferocious patience carved into his face as he was buffeted by clowns and ghosts and assorted storybook characters. "Okay. Okay. I like him *a lot*."

"And?"

She turned toward her one-eyed inquisitor. "And

what? I've only known him a week, Beth, for heaven's sake."

"Well, excuse me, Ms. Simon. I may only have one eye, but I believe there is something called love at first sight."

Shelby snorted, but even as she did, she thought at the very least that she'd been wildly attracted to Callahan at first sight that day he'd scared her to death when he walked into Hal Stabler's office, looking like somebody who ought to be wearing handcuffs instead of carrying them. She'd been more attracted to him then than any other man she'd ever met. That physical attraction had only increased as she'd gotten to know him.

"I don't know what will happen with us," she said now, aware of the underlying sadness in her tone.

"What do you want to happen?" Beth asked.

"Hey! Who's the world-famous, highly overpaid advice columnist here? You or me, little sis?" Shelby nudged her with an elbow. "You know how you didn't want to talk about Danny? Well, that's how I feel about Mick Callahan right now. Okay?"

Beth nodded. "I hear you. I guess we don't want to talk about Mom and Dad, either, huh?"

Shelby groaned.

"What do you think they're going to do? This separation has been going on a long time. Five or six months, as far as I know. Do you think we should do something? Has either one of them asked for your advice?"

"Are you kidding me?" Shelby clucked her tongue. "Although, I did suggest . . ."

"Shelby? Beth?" Somebody in a skimpy little French

maid's outfit was suddenly standing next to their bale of hay. "Is that you?"

Both sisters blinked at the woman, who proceeded to whip off her black-feathered mask and exclaim, "It's me! Kimmy! I've been looking all over for you. Oh, it's so good to see you guys together."

Shelby recognized the waitress from the Blue Inn, and Beth immediately jumped up to hug her.

"This is fun, the three of us being together again," Kimmy said, then she turned to Shelby and lowered her voice, "Hey, I'm sorry about ruining your dinner the other night."

"Oh, don't worry about it," Shelby said. "I was just glad it was a prank instead of the real thing."

"What real thing?" Beth asked, looking from one to the other.

"I'll tell you later," Shelby said.

The Lady Pirate rolled her one visible eye. "With all the things we've got to talk about *later*," she said, "there's nothing to talk about now."

"Let's talk about the time we drove your father's fiberglass speedboat over the rocks," Kimmy suggested.

Shelby and Beth replied as one. "Oh, let's not."

⁓

Harry had gone back out to the carriage house for another jolt of cold medicine, but when he returned to the kitchen he was wearing a pair of khaki slacks with his pajama top, and a trench coat over that.

"Get your coat, Beauty. We're driving into town." He jingled his car keys.

Linda didn't have to ask why. "You're that worried about Shelby?" she asked.

"I just want to check up on her," he said. "I tried calling the VFW Hall, but it's a madhouse. Whoever I talked to had never even heard of Charlie Chaplin. Get your coat."

Two minutes later, as they walked down the lawn to the garage, Linda reached for the keys. "I'll drive, Harry. You've been slugging that cold stuff all day, and they always caution that you shouldn't operate heavy machinery."

He held steadfastly onto the key ring. "A Mercedes isn't a goddamn piece of heavy machinery, Linda. And I'd like to go faster than fifteen miles an hour, if you don't mind."

She sighed in capitulation. She really didn't like to drive at night, anyway.

As they headed toward Shelbyville, she could tell just how worried Harry was from the deep creases in his forehead and the way his fingers gripped the steering wheel. Ordinarily he was an elbow-out-the-window, one-palm-on-the-wheel sort of driver. But not tonight.

"Mick's with Shelby," Linda said, as much to reassure her husband as herself. "He'll keep a watchful eye out for any problems. I think he cares for her beyond his professional capacity, Harry."

"I know. I think so, too. I'll just feel better touching base with our little girl."

They had only driven another quarter mile or so when Harry said out of the blue, "If I do decide to sign on with Linda Purl Designs, Beauty, I've got a few non-negotiable demands."

She tried not to sound thrilled beyond belief. And rather than scream, "Oh, boy. Oh, boy," she kept her voice level and replied, "Such as?"

"I'd want to be the CEO," he said. "Not some vice president or flunky legal adviser. My manly pride dictates that I at least have the title of head honcho."

"Done," Linda said. Then she smiled. "Of course, you realize I'll have to kick myself up to chairman of the board, then."

"And when we travel," he said, "I want my days off for golf or fishing or whatever. And unlimited access to the minibar in our room."

"I don't have any problem with that," she said, still trying to keep the "yippee" out of her voice. "Anything else?"

"Just one more thing."

"What's that?"

He reached across the center console for her hand, brought it to his lips, kissed her knuckles. "I love you, Beauty." He sniffed. "And I still feel like shit."

"I love you, too, Harry. I'll fix you a hot toddy when we get back to the lake."

～

Mick had waited longer to get to the refreshment table than he'd ever had to wait for a table in some of the busiest restaurants in Chicago. That was probably because everybody was chitchatting. Jesus. You'd think most of these people didn't see each other on a daily basis.

It was probably the costumes, he decided. Everybody

had to comment on what everybody else was wearing. Abe Lincoln, ahead of Mick in line, had to quote the Gettysburg Address continually, getting it wrong every damn time. George Washington was wandering around, not telling a lie. Clowns—there must've been a hundred of them—felt compelled to juggle and spray seltzer and tell bad jokes. There was a mime, and if Mick saw the guy feel up an invisible wall one more time, he was going to punch him into permanent silence.

Between all the clowns and his funk over Shelby, when he finally advanced along the refreshment table groaning with Jell-O molds and thirty-seven kinds of potato salad and enough brownies to feed an army, he nearly bit off the head of the masked Little Bo Peep who hovered behind the punch bowl.

"You look like a man who's really thirsty," she said in a kind of breathless, Marilyn Monroe voice.

He growled in the affirmative and told her he needed three cups of the orange stuff.

"Oh, I know who you are," she breathed. "You're here with Shelby Simon and the Pirate, aren't you?"

"That's right."

"I've known Shelby ever since we were little," Bo Peep said as she ladled out another cup of punch. "We used to . . ."

"Yeah. Okay." Mick didn't want to be rude, but he'd been waiting half an hour for these three dinky paper cups of Day-Glo liquid. "Thanks a lot, Bo," he said, picking up all three cups and wondering how he was going to make it to the other side of the big, crowded hall without spilling half their contents.

He started back, holding the cups aloft, out of the way of tricorn hats and huge multicolored wigs.

⟜

Out of the corner of her eye, Shelby spied Mick making his way across the crowded room, and her heart did a little tap dance in her chest. She told herself to tamp down on it, not to get carried away. He was, after all, just doing his job. Who knew? Maybe he just considered their great sex one of the perks.

Rather than get depressed, she turned her attention back to Beth and Kimmy, who were having such a good time reminiscing. The only thing that would've made this evening perfect would be seeing Sam limp through the door right now. But since that wasn't going to happen, Shelby decided she'd have to come up with another plan to get the two of them together.

Maybe Christmas when Sam would be home and fit as ever after finishing his rehab. Beth could fly back from San Francisco, without Danny, of course. Shelby would drive up from Chicago, with Mick, of course. Well, maybe . . .

"Ladies." Mick was suddenly beside her, his hands full of paper cups. "Take these before I spill any more."

"Thanks, Mick." Beth took two, and gave a cup to Kimmy.

"Here's yours, Charlie." He winked as he offered Shelby the last cup.

She was just taking it from his hand when somebody shouted, "There they are. Yoo hoo, Shelby Simon. Yoo hoo, Beth. Come over here, you two."

The shouter was Thelma Watt, the postmistress, who was decked out in full postal regalia, including gold-fringed epaulettes on her blue jacket.

"Oh, Lord," Shelby moaned, echoing Beth. "I guess we better go see what she wants." She handed her cup back to Mick. "Hang on to this for me for a sec, will you?"

"Mine, too," Beth said, putting her cup in his other hand. "Thelma will have a fit if she sees us drinking. She still thinks we're teenagers."

"Hurry back," Mick said, then he leaned down to whisper in Shelby's ear, "I want to get you out on the dance floor so I have a good excuse to hold your hot little bod."

She laughed. "You just want to see what it's like to dance with a guy in an Armani suit, Callahan."

Then she grabbed Beth's hand. "Come on, Pirate Pete. Let's get this over with."

"Argh," Beth groaned.

~

Mick put the cups of punch down on the bale of hay next to the scarecrow.

"How's it going?" he asked the woman he recognized as Kimmy, the waitress, who was now apparently some kind of sexy French maid. It was a wonder he recognized her at all behind the black feathered mask she wore. Her blue eyes were about all he could see of her face.

"I'm sorry about last Saturday night," she said, looking at him over the rim of her punch cup. "I went home and told that asshole to pack his stuff and get out of my life."

"That's good," Mick said.

"He was *so* immature." She took another sip of the rum concoction. "What a loser. He's here tonight. Someplace." She gestured toward the crowd. "If you see somebody wearing an asshole costume, that's him." Kimmy giggled and tossed back the rest of her punch.

Mick figured it probably wasn't her first cup. Her speech seemed to be getting a little slurred.

"You were so sweet to me the other night, helping with the cops and all. Did I tank you? I mean, did I *thank* you?"

"That's okay," he said.

Man. Speaking of tanked, poor ol' Kimmy was really on her way. Her blue eyes, peering out from the black mask, seemed to be dilating even as he watched.

"Well, thanks," she said. "I . . ." She rocked forward a bit. Then back. "Ooh, boy. I'm not feeling show great . . ."

Mick reached out to grasp her arm just as the woman's eyes completely dilated and a bit of orange foam leaked from a corner of her mouth.

He caught her limp body a second before she hit the floor, and he knew immediately what was wrong. Judging from the scent of almonds that wafted up from her open mouth, Kimmy wasn't just drunk. Jesus H. Christ. She'd just drunk cyanide.

CHAPTER TWENTY

~

The instant Shelby heard Mick cry out, she knew something was horribly wrong.

"Get a doctor," he yelled. "Somebody call an ambulance. Now!"

She rushed toward him to find Kimmy lying on the floor, her body twitching in convulsions as Mick knelt beside her. "Oh, my God, Mick. What happened? What can I do?"

"She's been poisoned," he said, glancing up. "And I don't want you to do anything except stick to me like glue. Do you hear me, Shelby?"

"Let me go find a doctor or something," she said. But when she started to turn, Mick's hand flashed out and grabbed her by the ankle.

"I said like glue, Shelby, and I mean it, dammit. I can't keep you safe if you're not right here with me."

"But . . ."

She looked down at poor Kimmy again, and suddenly the true horror of the situation hit her like a fist in the stomach. The poison had been meant for her. Whoever wanted to kill her was right here, in this room. Her knees were beginning to feel like Jell-O. Her mouth started to tremble, and she bit down hard on her bottom lip. It was no time to fall apart now.

Just then someone moved her aside, and she recognized one of their summertime neighbors at the lake, Dr. Richard Franz.

"I'm a doctor, young man. What've we got here?" he asked as he knelt beside Mick.

"Poison," he said. "I'm guessing cyanide from the odor."

"Judas Priest," Dr. Franz exclaimed. He shouted over his shoulder. "Kathy, run get my bag out of the car. Hurry. And somebody get an ambulance here ASAP."

Beth was beside Shelby now, looking stricken. She'd taken off her eye patch, and her bruise glistened purple with tears. "Poor Kimmy," she whispered. "Oh, my God, Shelby. This is terrible."

Mick stood up and reached for Shelby's hand. "Beth, tell the band to announce that nobody should drink the punch. Loud and clear. Then find some guys to stand at the front door. Tell them nobody leaves. Not anybody. For anything. Do it now." When Beth just stood there blinking at him, he gave her a little push toward the bandstand. "Go," he said. "Shelby, you come with me. We're looking for Little Bo Peep. Keep your eyes open."

He pushed his way through the crowd, pulling Shelby along in his wake. People were standing around looking shell-shocked, whispering and shaking their heads, most of them with their masks off now. But Shelby didn't see anyone who remotely resembled Little Bo Peep.

"Who am I looking for?" she called to Mick. "A

blonde? With curls? Is she carrying one of those sheep hooks?"

"Shelby!"

Even as she was being pulled forward, she turned toward the sound of her mother's voice. Suddenly both her parents were moving along beside her.

"Honey, are you all right?" Linda asked.

"What's going on, Mick?" her father asked. "What can I do?"

Over his shoulder, Mick said, "We need to lock this place down tight. Nobody gets in or out. Help me."

"You got it."

Then her father disappeared, but Shelby could hear him barking out orders. As Mick kept tugging her along, she thought she heard the wail of a siren in the distance. He came to an abrupt stop at the VFW Hall's back door.

"Stay here with your mother. I'm going to look around outside." He blasted out the door before Shelby could say a word.

"Who's he looking for?" her mother asked.

"Little Bo Peep."

"I saw somebody dressed like that going out the front door just as your father and I were coming in," Linda said.

"Are you sure, Mother?"

"Well, she looked like Little Bo Peep to me."

It didn't take Shelby more than a second to decide. She flew out the back door in Mick's wake.

Mick stood in the middle of Main Street. He could hear the wail of the ambulance as it neared Shelbyville, but he could hear something else, as well. The whine of tires as they spun in mud.

He started walking toward the wet field at the edge of town where he'd parked the Mustang earlier, slipping his gun out of its holster, just in case he got lucky. He didn't know who the hell Little Bo Peep was, but he guessed that her Marilyn Monroe simper was an act to disguise her true voice. Hell, for all Mick knew Bo was a guy.

He or she had to know that Mick was getting punch for Shelby and Beth, as well as himself, but since there was no way to tell who'd drink which, Bo must've slipped the cyanide into all three cups. Jesus. When he thought that he was the one who'd actually handed Kimmy the poisoned punch, he felt his stomach clench. And when he thought that it could have been Shelby instead, he nearly vomited.

The ambulance's siren was shrill now as it approached the town. He strained to hear the spinning tires ahead of him in the field. Had they stopped? He couldn't be sure, but he picked up his pace, running now instead of walking.

"Mick! Wait!"

Goddammit. He turned around. "I told you to stay the hell inside," he yelled.

Shelby kept striding toward him in that fucking blue suit. By God, when this was all over, he really was going to burn the thing. It was cursed.

His mind was racing now, trying to decide whether to keep her with him or to send her back.

"My mother said she saw Little Bo Peep going out the front door a few minutes ago," Shelby said. "I thought you ought to know."

"I'm glad you told me." She looked so pale and frightened that Mick decided that he needed to keep her close. Mostly there just wasn't time to see her safely back inside. "Stay close to me, Shelby. Do you hear me?" he shouted over the now nearly earsplitting scream of the siren.

The EMS vehicle, its blue and white lights flaring in windows all along Main Street, pulled up in front of the VFW Hall.

"Thank God," Shelby said.

"Stay close," he said again, taking her hand, listening once more for the spinning tires now that the siren had stopped.

"Where are we going?" Shelby asked.

Mick motioned for her to be quiet. He couldn't hear the tires. He couldn't hear the fucking tires. And just as that realization dawned on him, the headlights of a moving vehicle appeared ahead of them, just at the edge of the field. He and Shelby stood caught in their glare.

And then the tires squealed viciously, not because they were stuck in mud, but because the driver stepped hard on the accelerator, aiming the car right at them.

Shit. There were cars and pickups parked along both sides of the street. The ones on the right were a couple yards closer. They were going to need that smaller distance in order to make it.

Shelby stood like a doe, mesmerized by the oncoming lights, as if she couldn't believe this was happening, so Mick curved his arm around her waist and yanked hard, pulling her, pushing her with all his strength toward the curb.

At the same time, with his other hand, he was aiming

his Glock as best as he could at the speeding car. He got off four shots, two at each front tire, and hoped to hell he hit them before he shoved Shelby past the rear bumper of a pickup truck and onto the sidewalk.

The speeding car lurched left, caromed off a minivan, and then came careening across the street and crashed into a panel truck mere feet from Shelby and Mick. He could see its airbag deploy into Bo Peep's face, and then the car's alarm started shrieking.

Shelby wasn't even breathing anymore because her heart was pounding the hell out of her lungs.

"Stay here," Mick told her mere seconds after the car crashed. "I mean it."

"Okay," she answered, not bothering to add that she didn't think her legs were working all that well anyway.

It was all she could do to just maintain her upright stance while she watched Mick cautiously approach the driver's door with his gun drawn and an expression of grim determination on his face. He reached for the door handle, pulled it open, then stood with both hands on his weapon, taking dead aim at the driver.

"Step out of the car," he ordered.

From her vantage point on the sidewalk, Shelby could see a pantalooned leg emerge from the open door, followed by the ruffles of a skirt, a slender arm, and then—finally—a face.

"Kellie!"

Shelby couldn't even stand up anymore. Her legs just

buckled and she sagged down onto the sidewalk. She could hear Mick's voice then, but it seemed a mile away.

"Turn around and put your hands on the hood of the car. Spread your legs."

"I will not. Get your hands off me. I want a lawyer."

"You have the right to remain silent . . ."

With the alarm on Kellie's car still blasting, and people beginning to stream out of the VFW Hall and down the street, it was like some bizarre dream, some nightmare from which Shelby couldn't extract herself or shake herself awake.

There were clowns milling around. Abe Lincoln was checking out the damaged door of the minivan across the street. Little Bo Peep kept screaming that she wanted a lawyer.

"I'll get you a lawyer, young lady," Shelby heard her father say in his best courtroom voice. And then Shelby really did think she was trapped in a nightmare when her father punched a number into a cell phone and then calmly began a conversation.

"Maureen? Hello. This is Harry Simon. Is Franklin there by any chance?"

Her mother sat down beside her on the sidewalk, and then Beth the Pirate settled on her other side.

"Are you okay, baby?" her mother asked, putting an arm around her shoulders.

Shelby wasn't quite sure. "I think so. How's Kimmy?"

"They think they got her in time," Beth said. "They've taken her to the hospital in Mecklin."

"Thank God," Shelby said. She looked back at her mother. "Who's Dad calling? He's not really getting Kellie a lawyer, is he?"

"Yes, he is," Linda said. "He's calling Franklin Louche." She leaned closer to Shelby and lowered her voice to a whisper. "Franklin's new at your father's firm. And he's lost every single case he's tried so far."

She wanted to laugh, but she just couldn't. What she wanted, more than anything at the moment, was to know why.

Why had Kellie done this?

"I'll be right back," she told her mother and Beth. Then, with her legs still shaking, Shelby stood and walked toward the Mecklin County patrol car where Kellie sat in the backseat with her hands cuffed behind her back, looking less like an innocent Bo Peep than a deranged female in a blond, curly wig. Her lipstick and mascara were smeared. She looked awful. When their eyes met, Kellie regarded Shelby with utter contempt. The young intern who'd always curried her mentor's favor was looking at her now with hatred on her sweet-young-thing face. The expression nearly made Shelby's blood run cold.

"Why, Kellie?" Her throat was so constricted she could barely get the question out. "What did I ever do to . . . ?

"It's all your fault, Shelby." Kellie practically hissed her name. "God! Why didn't you just do the right thing? Then no one would've gotten hurt."

"My fault?" She couldn't believe she'd heard correctly.

"You stupid bitch. Why didn't you just quit right away after the letter bombs made it so clear that people hated your stupid column with all its self-righteous drivel and bogus good cheer."

Kellie shook her head to fling a hank of yellow curls

out of her eyes. "If you'd just resigned right then, the way you were supposed to, with no plan to come back, none of the rest would've ever happened. But, no. You were too selfish to give it up."

"I don't understand," Shelby said.

"That's because you're stupid." Kellie's eyes glittered almost feverishly, reflecting the lights of all the emergency vehicles nearby. "You wrote your dumb little column every day, year after year after year, and you never realized what an opportunity it was. It's a forum. A stage. A fucking grandstand."

"It's an advice column," Shelby said.

The young woman rolled her eyes. "That's all it was to you. And you were obviously content to just have your picture on a few crummy buses. I was going to make it something special. I was going to work a deal with Oprah for a regular weekly spot. And that was just the beginning, Shelby."

"Kellie. My God." Shelby still couldn't believe what she was hearing. "This was all because you wanted to write a column?"

"I told Uncle Hal before I started my internship at the paper. I was very clear about my ambitions. He knew. And he made a lot of vague promises about helping me, but the bastard never followed through, so I just had to help myself."

"With letter bombs? With poison?"

Kellie shrugged awkwardly with her hands fastened behind her. "Well, that was your fault."

"I didn't poison the student at Northwestern," Shelby said.

She shrugged again. "He screwed up. He wouldn't

have had to die if he'd just been smarter about those chemicals."

"And Derek?" Shelby asked, dreading the answer.

Unbelievable as it seemed, Kellie smiled at the mention of his name. "Poor Derek. He really loved me." There was a touch of wistfulness in her voice now. "He wanted me to turn myself in."

Shelby felt nauseous. "So you pushed him under a train?"

"He fell." There was no honey or mist in her tone now, and her smile flattened out to a thin, hard line. "Go away, Shelby. Leave me alone. I need time to think."

Without another word, Shelby turned away, determined to see to it that Kellie would have the next hundred years with nothing but time to think. She'd done it all for a column? For the dubious fame that came from writing advice to strangers in a newspaper every day? Whether that was insane or purely evil, Shelby wondered if she'd ever truly know.

And then, all of a sudden, it all seemed to hit her—the letter bombs, the poisonings, the fact that she and Mick had nearly been roadkill tonight—and just as her legs threatened to buckle again, Mick was there, wrapping his arms around her, telling her it was all over, everything was fine, telling her he loved her, over and over again.

～

After a week back in the city and a refill of her tranquilizer prescription, Shelby relaxed. Kellie Carter was in the slammer because Franklin Louche couldn't get her bail.

Ms. Simon Says was set to reappear the following Monday. Helm and Harris renewed her contract for an additional five years, and Hal Stabler moved her to a bigger office with a better view. Shelby and good old reliable, true blue Sandy had worked twelve and fourteen hours a day reconstructing all the files that Kellie Carter had deconstructed during her internship. The Chicago Transit Authority slapped her picture back on the buses.

Her mother called to say that Kimmy was home from the hospital, that Beth had moved out of Danny's apartment, and that Sam's surgery went okay.

Life was pretty good.

Except Shelby hadn't seen Mick since they drove back from Michigan and he dropped her off at her apartment. They played phone tag a lot. He was "wrapping things up on the street," whatever that meant. He'd see her soon.

But it had been a week, and Shelby was beginning to think she'd just hallucinated his feelings for her and the words "I love you" that terrible night. She had the sinking feeling that his job, such as it was, had ended. And so had they.

Which was really unfortunate since the day after she returned to Chicago, she'd bought him a dog, not just to express her gratitude for saving her life, but because he said he'd always wanted one and because she was just so damn in love with him. She sneaked the puppy past Dave the Doorman because the Canfield Towers prohibited pets of any kind, and she was now sleeping with a baby beagle in her bed instead of Michael Rainbow Callahan.

Mick parked where he always did, right in front of the Canfield Towers. Before he got out of the car, he speed-dialed Shelby's apartment.

"Can I come up?" he asked when she answered.

"Hey, stranger."

"Hey, yourself. Can I come up? I've got a question for you, but I don't want to ask over the phone."

"Right now?"

Jesus. He'd expected at least an iota of enthusiasm, but Shelby sounded as if she didn't want to see him at all. He could feel the sweat beginning to foam his Speed Stick deodorant.

"Right now," he said, punching through his fear. "How 'bout it? I'm parked out in front. I can be up there in two minutes."

"Well . . ."

He lost it. "Shelby, goddammit, I love you. What the hell's wrong? Are you telling me you don't want to see me?"

She was quiet a minute on the other end of the line. "I love you, too, Mick. See you in two." Then she hung up.

He sprinted through the lobby, yelling "I know. I know. I'll move it," to Dave the Doorman, who sat at his desk shaking his head. He almost leaped into the elevator and punched the button for the twelfth floor. He tried to keep the sweat to a minimum as he walked down the corridor.

After he knocked, Shelby opened the door just a couple inches. "I wasn't expecting you," she said.

"But you love me, right?" He tried to peek past her. What the hell was she trying to hide?

"I love you big time," she said. "Completely. From

here to the moon and back again. It's just that I have this surprise for you, and . . ."

He couldn't stand it a minute more, so he pushed the door and went through.

"What the hell is that?"

"It's a baby beagle. And she's yours. Surprise!"

Mick felt the most foolish grin work its way across his mouth as he bent to scoop up the puppy and nuzzle her under his chin. "What's her name?"

"Dunno," Shelby said. "I've been calling her Baby Beagle. You can name her anything you want."

"Baby. I like that."

"What were you in such a hurry to ask me, Mick?"

He'd completely forgotten. Then he remembered, and he started laughing so hard he could barely speak.

Shelby finally got exasperated. "What's so damned funny?" she asked, almost ripping Baby Beagle out of his arms.

"I came up here to ask you if you wanted to help me decorate my new apartment."

"You're kidding! You're moving? No more Hattie and Lena? No more Eau de Pine?"

"No more skid row. I've come up in the world, my love. Wanna see my new digs?"

"Sure. Let me put the puppy in her crate, and . . . "

"You don't have to. Bring her along. It's close."

"Well . . ."

"Trust me, Shelby."

She did. She trusted him implicitly. With her heart. With her life. So, with Baby Beagle in her arms, she followed him out the door and down the corridor.

But not that far down the corridor. He stopped at Mo Pachinski's apartment, pulled a key from his pocket, and inserted it into the lock.

"Wait a minute," Shelby said. "What is this?"

"My new place." He pushed open the door, revealing an empty living room.

"I don't believe this!" Shelby stepped across the threshold. "How is this possible?"

"Well, Mo needed a favor," he said. "Nothing illegal. Shady, maybe. But strictly within the law, I swear. I even checked with your father."

Shelby rolled her eyes.

"So, Mo needed this favor, and I needed an apartment."

She put Baby Beagle down on the thick gray carpet. "Don't piddle," she warned her. Then she looked at Mick. "Do I even want to know what you did for Mo?"

He shook his head. Then he draped his forearms over her shoulders, pressed his forehead to hers, and said, "I was hoping you'd decorate it for me. You know, in all those wild patterns and colors you always dreamed about."

Shelby smiled. "The way you always dreamed about a dog."

"Uh-huh."

"We're screwed, Callahan."

He blinked. "What do you mean?"

She could hardly keep from laughing. "You got an empty apartment so I could do the decorating I always wanted. I got you the dog you always wanted. But we can't keep the fricking dog in the fricking apartment."

"You're serious?"

"I'm serious. I've been in flagrant violation of the No Pets rule here for the past six days. You should probably arrest me."

"Well, shit. Let me think about this a minute." He pulled her closer and planted a score of warm kisses on her neck. "As I see it, we have two choices."

"Which are?"

"Getting rid of the puppy is not an option. So, we can move back with Hattie and Lena, where dogs are more than welcome, or we can look for a nice little house with a nice little fenced-in yard for Baby Beagle."

Shelby hugged him harder. She had to swallow the lump in her throat. "I love you so much."

"I love you, too. But you haven't answered my question. What'll it be, Ms. Simon? Skid row or the 'burbs?"

"I'd go anywhere with you, Callahan."

"But which? Hattie and Lena, or the white house with the picket fence?"

"Tough choice," she said.

"How about if I asked you to marry me? What would you say to that?"

She actually pretended to think about it for a second, before she said the words she'd been longing to say for such a long, long time.

"Ms. Simon says yes."

ABOUT THE AUTHOR

Mary McBride has been writing romance, both historical and contemporary, for a dozen years. She lives in St. Louis, Missouri, with her husband and two sons.

She loves to hear from readers, so please visit her Web site at MaryMcBride.net or write to her c/o P.O. Box 411202, St. Louis, MO 63141.

More

Mary McBride!

Please turn this page

for a preview of

SAY IT AGAIN, SAM

available in paperback

December 2004.

CHAPTER ONE

On a map, the township of Shelbyville, Michigan, resembled a startled face. Blue Lake and Pretty Lake, each very nearly round, formed a pair of staring eyes, set wide by the dense woods between them. The pinched lobes of Little Glory Lake sufficed for a nose, and just below it, Heart Lake was carved out like an open, astonished mouth.

Or, if you didn't have much imagination, Shelbyville township looked like five lakes and a hell of a lot of trees just above the 43rd parallel and a few miles east of Mecklin, the county seat.

The population of Shelbyville was 1,245 souls, give or take a soul or two. In June, July, and August, though, that figure swelled, almost doubling with the influx of tourists, or what the townspeople called "the summer folks." And the summer folks tended to get in a lot more trouble than the residents.

It was summer now, and Constable Sam Menden hall was responding to an early morning call about more trouble. He walked into the post office carrying the coffee he'd picked up at the Gas Mart.

"What's up, Thelma?" he asked the elderly post-mistress.

"Somebody stole my flag."

Sam took a thoughtful sip of the steaming brew, hiding his exasperation behind the paper cup. From her urgent tone on the telephone, he'd been expecting an actual burglary. He thought her cash drawer had been cleaned out, or that someone had made off with her stamps.

"It was a brand new one, too. I just got it a couple weeks ago." She slapped a liver spotted hand on the countertop. "Damn it all. In over fifty years, I haven't missed a single day—not one!—of running my flag up the flagpole out there. A lot longer than you've been alive, Sam Mendenhall, I'll have you know." She shook a crooked finger in his face.

Obviously Thelma didn't think he was taking this seriously enough. The last thing he wanted to do was to insult her. He'd known Thelma Watt his entire life. She been Shelbyville's postmistress for more than half a century, which meant she knew more about the local population than they knew about themselves.

Just by handling the mail, Thelma knew who was getting ahead, who was falling behind, who was simply holding on. She knew whose children wrote home once they'd left the nest, whose sweethearts abruptly quit their correspondence, whose hearts had been broken by lined paper and a ball point pen.

His, for instance.

Hell.

Sam didn't doubt for a second that the old gal had

read every post card that ever passed through this building and held every interesting envelope up to the light. He wondered how many of those cards and letters had been his.

"Any idea who might have taken the flag?" he asked her now.

She glared across her counter, looking down her nose at him—a pretty amazing feat since he was 6'2" to her diminutive 5'1".

"Of course I know who took it," she snapped. "The same criminal who's been taking all the other things around town. Who else would it be?"

She was probably right, Sam decided. There'd been a lot of weird stuff going on lately. Things just went missing. Weird things. The curtains in Carol Dunlap's sun porch. Every single jar of peanut butter at the grocery store. A Detroit Tigers coffee mug that Jim Bickford had been sipping from one minute, then the next minute—pfft—it was gone.

Last week, after graduation ceremonies at the high school, somebody noticed an empty space in the trophy case where the bronzed pigskin for the state football champs of 1968 should've been.

There was more. Sam had a list in the glove compartment of his Jeep.

Now he'd be adding Thelma's flag.

As crime waves went, this one seemed fairly innocuous. But still . . . Plenty of people were spooked, and Thelma was downright mad.

"How did it happen?" he asked her. "Somebody break in, or did they take it down from the pole?"

"I never had time to get it up there. I took it outside at seven-fifteen, just like always, hooked it onto the lanyard, but then the phone rang before I could run it up the pole. When I got back outside, the durn thing was gone."

"Who was on the phone?" Sam asked.

"Nobody." The elderly woman blinked. "Are you thinking that call was some sort of diversion?"

He shrugged. In fact, he was thinking it was probably just a wrong number, or that the octogenarian postmistress moved so slowly that the caller had hung up before Thelma reached the phone.

"I'll see what I can find out," he told her.

"You do that."

He was already on his way to the door when she called him back.

"Wait a minute, Sam. Mercy. I was so upset about my flag that I almost forgot to tell you. Beth Simon's coming back from California. Her mail's already being forwarded here."

"Oh."

It was all he could think of to say. His mind was suddenly a complete blank. His heart had given one hard kick and then seemed to quit beating entirely. He felt like an idiot, and probably looked like one, too.

Thelma's head was cocked to one side, and there was an expectant expression on her face. Sam couldn't decide if the slant of her mouth was sympathetic or snide. What was it she wanted him to say?

Oh, goodie. That's great. Glad to hear it. Good old

*Beth. I can't wait to see the woman who dumped me
sixteen years ago.*

He drained the rest of his coffee, crumpled the paper
cup in his fist, then lobbed it into the tall trash can
against the far wall.

"I'll let you know what I find out about the flag,
Thelma," he said, then turned and walked out the door
before the woman could say another word.

~

Poor Sam. Thelma had meant to warn him a bit
more gently, perhaps even accompany the warning
with some sage advice, but she'd been so discombob-
ulated by the stolen flag that she'd simply blurted out
the news about Beth, and the fellow had just stood
there, looking like she'd punched him in the gut.

Not that she would have expected any other reaction, considering the history of those two.

She reached beneath the counter for the rubber-
banded packet of mail that had arrived yesterday from
San Francisco, CA 94117. There was a Mastercard
statement as thick as a ham sandwich, a bill from San
Francisco General Hospital, and a subscription re-
newal to "Victorian Times". After more than half a
century in the post office, Thelma could tell an awful
lot from a few pieces of mail.

Obviously things hadn't worked out for little Beth
Simon in California.

She was broke, or at least heavily in debt. That no
good boyfriend of hers, the one she'd gone to Califor-

nia with, had undoubtedly hit her again, this time hard enough to send her to the emergency room.

She was headed back here, to her family's big old Victorian house on Heart Lake.

On second thought, it was probably good that Thelma hadn't fully apprised Sam. After all, the U.S. Mail was privileged information, not meant for passing on to third parties.

He'd find out for himself soon enough.

And for mercy's sake, she hoped he also found out who made off with her flag.

⁓

Sam sat in his Jeep, staring at the little spiral notebook and its growing list of oddities. There didn't seem to be a pattern. At least none that he could discern. The only thing that seemed to make any sense was that it was some kind of scavenger hunt. The culprits were likely to be some of the summer kids with too little supervision and too much time on their hands. Still, a bit of petty theft was preferable to drugs, booze, drag racing, or any other crazy stunts that kids could pull.

He wasn't going to lose any sleep over it. With any luck, he'd catch one of the young perps in the act, give him a stern talking to, then turn the little bastard over to Thelma for whatever punishment she deemed appropriate.

Thelma. He'd managed to block out what she'd told him for a full five minutes, but now her words hit him again like a slap across the face.

Beth Simon's coming back from California.

The woman might just as well have said a giant asteroid was going to hit Shelbyville, its date and time still to be determined. If she'd meant to inflict damage on him, the old crone could've just reached for the ancient revolver she kept illegally beneath her counter and put a bullet right between his eyes. Her words had had just about the same effect.

He didn't want to think about Beth. It seemed as if he'd spent the first half of his life thinking of nothing and no one else, and then spent the second half of his life trying to forget her. Not that he'd had much success.

Returning his attention to the list of missing objects, Sam tried to forget her again by concentrating on the mysterious thief. What sort of idiot would steal the curtains right off their rods in a person's house? They weren't even good ones, Carol Dunlap had said, but water-stained and bleached out by the sun. *Crappy* had been her exact description, and she was glad for an excuse to replace them, even as she was mystified by their disappearance.

The missing football trophy and the flag at least made sense. Especially the flag. Sam could understand a kid playing a prank on the postmistress who'd probably terrorized him at some point in his young life. Sam had been a pretty fearless kid, but Thelma Watt had made him stutter once or twice. He remembered one time when he and Beth…

No. He didn't want to remember.

"Hey, Sheriff."

Sam turned his head toward the sidewalk to meet the steady gaze of a little boy who was maybe seven or eight years old. "I'm not the sheriff," he said. "I'm the constable."

Actually he was more like a rent-a-cop. His salary, such as it was, was paid partly by the Heart Lake Residents' Association and partly by the Shelbyville Chamber of Commerce. He didn't wear a uniform. He didn't carry a weapon. His powers of arrest were comparable to those of any citizen. By and large his duties entailed patrolling vacant summer cottages, annoying teenagers, and making sure that all the drunks at The Penalty Box got safely home without killing themselves or anybody else. Now he was apparently in charge of errant curtains, coffee cups, and flags.

"My dad says you're not so tough," the kid said, his little freckled face twisting in belligerence.

"Oh, yeah? Who's your dad?"

"Joe Dolan."

Well, that explained it. Sam pictured the freckle-faced boy he'd gone to school with. Joe Dolan was built like a fireplug and had even less personality, if that was possible. He was a lazy, flat-footed wrestler, a face mask grabbing defensive end, and an avid bully. Like all those of that ilk, he picked on the kids who were smaller, lighter, less apt to defend themselves. From kindergarten through their senior year, Joe had steered clear of Sam. Apparently he was still steering clear of him because in the year or so that Sam had been back here, he hadn't seen Joe Dolan once.

"What's your dad up to these days?" he asked as if he truly cared.

"Nothin'," the boy said. "He's got a bad back."

It probably matched his bad attitude, Sam thought.

"My dad says you were a Green Beret."

"Something like that," Sam replied.

"He says that's no big deal."

Sam shrugged. He wasn't going to argue with an elf in a striped T-shirt and red canvas Keds.

The elf sneered. "I bet you don't even wear a gun."

"Don't need one," Sam said in a voice faintly reminiscent of Gary Cooper in "High Noon."

"How tall are you?" Joe's offspring demanded.

"Six two. How tall are you?"

The boy lifted his shoulders, then let them drop. He probably didn't even know how tall he was, or maybe he figured it wasn't cool to proclaim he was all of four foot two or three. "What do you weigh?"

"Depends," Sam said.

"Oh, yeah? On what?"

"On whether or not I've eaten a little boy for breakfast."

The kid's eyes bulged like little green crabapples, and it was all Sam could do not to laugh.

Just then a fire engine red Miata sped past him, doing at least sixty down Shelbyville's main drag, where the posted speed limit was a stodgy twenty-five. Sam turned the key in the ignition, reached under the seat for his red light, slapped it on the hood of the Jeep.

"See ya, kid," he said, and then took off in pursuit.

It took about two minutes—and two miles down the road—for Sam to feel less like Gary Cooper and more like one of the Keystone Kops.

His ancient, Army surplus Jeep could barely keep up with the speeding Miata. The red light he'd slapped on the hood broke loose when he hit a pothole in the road. Little wonder since the rinky-dink, battery powered implement was only attached by a flimsy rubber suction cup. And for lack of a siren, Constable Sam Mendenhall was forced to honk his horn like some maniac.

Meanwhile the guy behind the wheel of the Miata wasn't slowing down a bit. When Sam was able to pull up close enough, he could see the baseball cap on the guy's head, and he was pretty sure that the son of a bitch gave him the finger just before turning off onto Eighteen Mile Road. Man, he couldn't wait to run this asshole to ground.

That happened thirty seconds later when the little red sports car's right rear tire blew, sending the car veering into the oncoming lane for a couple hundred feet before the driver was able to get control and maneuver off the blacktop onto the weedy shoulder of the road.

Sam pulled over and killed his engine. He hoped it was Joe Dolan in the Miata. He was going to pull him through the driver's window by his earlobes and then drop kick him all the way back to town.

"You could've killed somebody, asshole," he

shouted, striding toward the red car, slapping its rear fender before he reached the driver's door.

"I know. Oh, God."

The female voice floated through the open window. Well, it wasn't Joe Dolan unless he'd had a sex change operation. Sam's anger ratcheted down a notch. Maybe he was a sexist pig, but he didn't treat women the way he treated men. Never had. Never would. Not in this life.

"Are you okay?" he asked.

"Just a little shaky," she said. "That was really stupid of me. I'm sorry."

As she spoke, she took one hand off the wheel and reached up to pull the baseball cap from her head. Blond curls—a torrent of them—cascaded onto her shoulders. And then she turned and blinked up at him with those perfect-day-in-June blue eyes.

Jesus. He couldn't breathe.

"Sam?"

"Hello, Beth."

THE EDITOR'S DIARY

Dear Reader,

No matter how hard you kick and scream, you may find that fate has a funny way of telling you who is the boss. For Cupid's arrow always lands in exactly the right place—just ask Shelby Simon and Maggie O'Mulligan in our two Warner Forever titles this March.

Susan Andersen says that she's "hooked on **Mary McBride!**" and it's easy to see why in Mary McBride's latest book, **MS. SIMON SAYS.** Shelby Simon is too busy giving people advice to get a love life of her own. As the author of "Ms. Simon Says," her weekly advice column, Shelby reaches thousands of readers each week . . . until a series of letter bombs blow widowed cop Mick Callahan into her carefully constructed single life. Sent in to protect Shelby from these dangerous threats, Mick takes her away to her family's country home. Here, in a secluded paradise called Heart Lake, the rugged but tantalizingly secretive cop must protect the enticing but ever-meddling journalist. But resisting her is another matter. As danger comes to Heart Lake, putting them both at risk, Shelby keeps telling herself she can't fall for the one man sent to watch over her . . . or can she?

Moving from the intrigue of undercover cops to the excitement of Internet dating, we are pleased to offer **ONCE UPON A BLIND DATE** by Wendy Markham.

Romantic Times raves that Ms. Markham's previous book is a "wonderfully touching romance with a good sense of humor," but they haven't seen anything yet. Maggie is the best friend of Dominic. Charlie is the best friend of Julie. Through the magic of an on-line dating site, Maggie and Charlie will do anything it takes to set their buddies up on the most romantic blind date ever . . . even if it means tagging along. But from the moment they meet, Dom and Julie fizzle while Charlie and Maggie sizzle. She's involved with someone else. And he's Manhattan's most committed bachelor. So what will it take for these two matchmakers to give into Cupid and accept that love doesn't always go according to plan?

To find out more about Warner Forever, these March titles, and the authors, visit us at www.warnerforever.com.

With warmest wishes,

Karen Kosztolnyik

Karen Kosztolnyik, Senior Editor

P.S. Forget that spring cleaning! We've got two wonderful reasons to put your mop down and relax with these two Warner Forever titles. **Annie Solomon** pens an edge-of-your-seat suspense about a woman who's determined to bring her father's killer to justice and the detective who's out to unravel her secrets in **TELL ME NO LIES**; and **Shari Anton** delivers a spellbinding tale of a fiery woman determined to protect her family's holdings and the roguish knight who stands in her way in **ONCE A BRIDE**.